Waiting For Mr. WRIGHT

Marcia Williams

The X Press

Published in United Kingdom by
The X Press
6 Hoxton Square, London N1 6NU
Tel: 0171 729 1199
Fax: 0171 729 1771

Printed by Caledonian International Book Manufacturing Ltd, Glasgow, UK.

Distributed in UK by Turnaround Distribution, Unit 3, Olympia Trading Estate, Coburg Road, London N22 6TZ
Tel: 0181 829 3000
Fax: 0181 881 5088

ISBN 1-874509-49-2

Third book and still going strong...
Thanks to:
YOU
my family
friends
The X Press crew — Steve, Dotun and Sue.

This book is dedicated to my sisters:
Charlene, a promising young horror writer. Keep going Sis.
Den, the brains of the family. Proud of you.

waiting for
Mr Wright

ONE

"Yo, dude, wake up and get outta bed! Yo, dude, wake up and get outta bed…"

Errol Wright pulled the duvet over his head and attempted to sink himself back into his dream, where Jada Pinkett was trying to persuade him to give everything up and live with her in America.

"… Yo, dude, wake up and get outta bed!"

Groaning, Errol threw one arm out from under the cover. "That's it, man," he grunted. "Cho', me an' yuh nuh spar no more."

The alarm clock fell to the floor with a thud, but Bart Simpson had not yet got the message.

"Yo dude…"

"Damn!" Errol fumbled blindly for the clock once more, grabbing the damn thing by its plastic head and hitting the shut-off button. A Christmas present from his son, Bart Simpson was the only childish thing in Errol's bedroom.

He sat up in bed and waited for the walls to stop spinning. Last night had been the final time he would ever listen to his bone-headed mate, Colin. "I've only got a few more hours of being a single man," Colin had said. "You can't turn down a bachelor's last request. Let's invite some ah the lads round…" Well, a few of the lads had brought a few ladies, the drink-up had turned into a wild party, and Errol now felt like a fifty year old. The brandy and champagne had poured until five o'clock in the morning, and mixed with the fried chicken, rice and peas and hard dough bread that Colin's mum had brought round, Errol's stomach was now planning a walk-out.

This was not good. He had to get Colin to church in four

1

hours' time, and Errol knew that cameras don't look too favourably on TV presenters with hangovers, whether they were the best man or not.

Media success had made Errol more 'friends' than he could handle. Everybody expected him to have ready money and to be willing to party at the drop of a hat. None of them seemed to realise what hard work it was, how his life didn't belong to him any more.

Errol flopped onto his back and became aware of a warm body in bed beside him. He shot upright again and regretted it instantly: his brain spun and his stomach churned. He fell back onto the pillows and held his aching head, shaved smooth only yesterday.

The body beside him turned over and moved closer. "Col?" she murmured, throwing an arm over his chest.

Errol held his breath.

"What's up?" she snuggled closer.

It was Melanie, one of Colin's ex-girlfriends. How in hell had she got in here?

Before she could come to completely, Errol swung his usually strong legs off the bed and gave a sigh of relief when he realised he was still wearing his boxer shorts. He moved as fast as he could in his condition, and grabbed a shirt from the heap of clothes on the floor, then gingerly tiptoed from the room.

The door to the spare bedroom was open as he made his way to the stairs. Errol's temporary lodger was sprawled across his bed, fully dressed. No wonder his ex had found her way into the wrong room last night. Lucky for Mr Baker... but it could have been very unlucky for Errol if Yvette had decided to pay a surprise visit.

The house was almost deadly quiet. Almost. Somewhere downstairs a radio had been left on. The small modern house in Mitcham was Errol's pride and joy, his treat to himself for getting where he was today. He'd bought it six months ago, after landing the job that had since made him a TV personality. Now he had money, an instantly recognisable face, his own home and a brand new car — a far cry from the bedsits he had stayed in during his student days.

He relieved himself in the bathroom, avoiding his reflection in the mirror until he'd woken properly. Coffee — that's what he needed. Hot, black and strong, like himself...

Damn! It hurt to smile.

He reached the top of the stairs and very nearly fell headlong down them, blinded by the sun's rays pouring in through the skylight. Raising a heavy arm, he blocked the glare from his eyes, gripped the banister, and slowly descended on shaky legs.

The hall still held mementos of the night before. Although smoking was banned from his home — the guests had had to smoke in the garden — bottles, cans and dirty plates littered the furniture, and the faint scent of aftershave hung in the air. He'd have to call his housekeeper in to deal with it.

The party had been Colin's idea and, now Errol came to think of it, the guests had been mostly Colin's friends.

Errol pushed open the swing door to his kitchen and stopped in his tracks. A woman stood at the sink, in front of the window overlooking the garden. She was singing along to Smooth's "Undercover Lover" oozing out of the portable radio, while rinsing mugs under the tap. The woman's hair was natural and pulled back into a ponytail. Her skin was fair, and smooth as caramel. Very slim, and with a neck that begged to be kissed, she was dressed in a long-sleeved black satin dress, the sleeves made of chiffon. She made an unforgettable first impression.

Errol stood in the doorway, a hand on the door, his head tilted to one side, and one eyebrow raised. Women were turning up in the most unexpected places this morning!

Her singing voice was rich and confident and, for some reason, Errol didn't want to disturb her. For a moment it felt as though his headache had disappeared completely.

He let go of the door and it swung back behind him, making a whooshing sound. He saw her jump as she spun to face him.

3

"Errol!" she said with mild surprise. "Good morning."

So, she had the advantage — she knew who he was. Which wasn't really surprising as he was on television every week, and she was in his house, where he'd just thrown a party. But for the life of him he couldn't place her.

"Morning…" He hurriedly began to button his shirt to cover his semi-naked torso. Her eyes sparkled with amusement as she watched him. Ambling over to the dining table, he scratched his head and asked, "Have we met?"

She turned off the running tap. "Sort of." She was giggling as she reached for a hand towel. "I fell into your lap last night — well, actually it was the early hours of this morning. I lost my ride home and camped on your sofa."

A vague memory crept back into his consciousness like a traveller in the fog. "Your name begins with 'A'?"

"Yeah." She smiled, an enticing smile that was so friendly he had to grin back. Her voice was sophisticated, cultured, the enunciation exquisite. "Anne-Marie Simms." She held out her right hand.

Errol shook it. Her skin was soft — as if she hadn't done a day's manual work in her life — and moist from washing up. His head still ached, but now he remembered her. Anne-Marie had spilt white wine on his silk shirt and he'd had to go upstairs and change.

"Coffee?"

"Yes, please." She lowered her eyes shyly. "Sorry, I was going to help myself…"

"Don't worry about it."

Errol watched her move back to the sink and retrieve two mugs that she had rinsed and dried. She placed them on the table as Errol flicked on the kettle. He found himself wishing she had found her way into his bed last night instead of Melanie, but he quickly abandoned the idea. After all, he was almost spoken for.

Errol had been ready to make instant coffee, but because he had a guest he filled the percolator with water and produced fresh coffee and filters from the cupboard.

"What a night, eh?"

4

He shook his bald head. "Yeah, what a night!" He tried to laugh but received a bolt of lightning to his temples for his trouble.

Anne-Marie must have noticed his wince. "Feeling a bit fragile?"

He touched his temple gingerly. "Just a bit." His voice was hoarse and deeper than usual. Hopefully that would clear before he had to make the speeches later on.

Crossing the kitchen floor, he pulled a drawer open and searched for some pills to cure his headache. "Care for a painkiller?" he offered.

Anne-Marie laughed, and there it was again: that very open, welcoming smile. "No thanks. Coffee will be fine."

Errol spooned fresh coffee into the filter.

"So, where's the groom?" Anne-Marie asked.

Errol slapped his forehead and felt himself sway. "Shit! I knew there was something I was supposed to do before I came down."

Anne-Marie shook her head, laughing. "I think you'd better go and see to him. I'll make the coffee."

Groggily, Errol passed a hand over his smooth head, a gesture he often made when he was thinking. He left the kitchen feeling Anne-Marie's eyes on his back.

Colin was in the same position he'd been in when Errol had gone down to the kitchen. Errol crossed the threshold and yelled, "Colin, man, get up!"

There was no movement from his friend, so he went over and shoved him. "Yo, homie! It's your wedding day!"

That got a reaction. Colin rolled over onto his back. "Wha... ?"

"You're expected in church in less than four hours. Now get your arse up and into the shower!"

"What time you call this to wake me up? You're supposed to be my best man!"

"Stop complainin'. Four hours is plenty of time to get ready."

"It might be plenty of time to dress, but what about my contemplation time, man?"

"You had that last night." Errol crossed to the airing cupboard in the hall and slung a towel over Colin's prone body. "I'm cooking breakfast. Be down in fifteen."

Colin groaned and struggled to sit up straight.

Back downstairs, Anne-Marie was sitting at the pine dining table, resting her chin on her hands. "Is he okay?"

Errol found himself feeling glad she was still here. They had only just met, but it felt good to have someone about to ease his best man's nerves. He reached for the coffee pot and brought it to the table. "Fine. I just hope he stays awake."

"You've got a beautiful house. Do you live here alone?"

"Thank you. Yes, I do."

Anne-Marie turned in the chair, rested one arm across the back of it and crossed her legs. She took a closer look at Errol Wright and couldn't help feeling that, under the two pieces of clothing he had on, there was a lethal weapon. "I'm a big fan of yours, you know. I wouldn't watch *Do the Wright Thing* if it wasn't for you."

"Thank you again." Errol was used to people sucking up to him, but Anne-Marie seemed genuine.

Still studying him as though he were a rare artefact, she asked, "Do you know Marion Stewart?"

"Yes. In fact she's interviewing me on Monday for *Mantalk.*"

"Really?" Anne-Marie's brown eyes glittered. "I went to school with her. We're having lunch together on Monday."

Errol raised an eyebrow. "Small world!" Marion was also a close friend of his — she and her boyfriend Paul. He was an honorary godfather to her son.

"Isn't it, though? I'm an author — *Internal Bleeding*..." She said it as though he should know it.

He didn't. "So what's the book about?"

She lowered her eyes modestly. "I hate telling men what I write about. They get very... sceptical."

Errol smiled reassuringly, automatically slipping into talk-show-host mode. "Trust me," he said.

She smiled and shrugged. "It's about the pain we go through when our loved one walks out on the relationship."

"Oh?" he said. "From experience?"

"Mine — and others'."

"I see… Well, good on ya. I might read it myself."

The smile lit up every feature of Anne-Marie's face. Like every writer Errol had ever met, for her, praise was as necessary as food or sex.

She watched him through the haze of steam rising from the large mug she held to her lips, her eyes travelling down the smooth outline of his chest. He was gorgeous. Last night she had tried to talk to him and it had been virtually impossible; he'd been most certainly in demand. Now, here, she had him all to herself.

"You know, no one's gonna believe me when I tell them I was with Errol Wright for breakfast."

He ran a hand over his chin, hearing the unusual rasp of bristles on his usually clean shaven face. "Is that your way of asking for my autograph?"

She ran a finger round the rim of the mug. "Does that seem childish?"

Was she flirting? It was hard to tell. Since becoming a celebrity women had practically thrown themselves at him. If Anne-Marie was flirting she was doing it with subtlety. "Course not." He gulped down some warm coffee. "I'll sign a photo for you if I can get a discount on your book."

She giggled, her eyes shining. "It's a done deal."

They shook on it.

"So, did you enjoy your party?"

"It was Colin's party really — a second stag night. Colin must be the only groom I know that isn't satisfied with one going-out party. But what I can remember of it — yes." He met her eyes across the table, suddenly curious who invited her. "Are you one of Colin's friends?"

"Kind of." She went shy again. "Actually, Colin and I were lovers a while back. We still keep in touch."

Errol's spirits dropped as soon as the word "lovers" came from her lips. He avoided her eyes by staring into his coffee. That was it, then. He made it a rule never to go out with anyone within his circle of friends — he'd found that his personal life stopped being personal whenever he let that happen. Anne-Marie was one of Colin's ex-girlfriends, she knew Marion as well... and that made her a no-go zone.

She must have noticed the change in his demeanour, because she quickly changed the subject. "You should eat, y'know. You're going to be much too busy later."

He realised he was a little hungry, and he certainly needed something to soak up last night's alcohol. The coffee had settled his stomach, but now it felt empty. "Toast!" He scraped back the chair on the stone-tiled floor and headed for the wooden bread bin.

Anne-Marie stood up too. "Why don't I make it for you? Then you can check on Colin and start getting ready."

"I couldn't let you do—"

"I'm offering." She held up a hand.

He paused for a few seconds. Here he was, standing half-naked in his kitchen with an extremely attractive woman, the first intelligent woman in his life since God knows when, and he couldn't touch her. He'd be making a big mistake. Where was the justice in this world?

She was right, though. He did need a shave, and the traffic heading into town wasn't going to be easy. "Thanks, Anne..."

"Anne-Marie, please."

"Sorry..."

"Don't apologise. My mum just never liked it shortened; I guess it rubbed off."

They stood there, neither of them moving, a slight smile playing across Anne-Marie's eyes and lips. Then the door was thrown open aggressively, and Colin entered as only Colin could: newly cut hairdo so neat he'd have to do nothing to it, bleary red eyes trying to stay open, string vest and baggy trousers crushed and musty. "I smelt coffee. Make us a cup nuh, man — you know dat's your job today." He slumped down on a pine dining chair.

"Cho, what d'you think this is, a café?" Errol scolded, apologising with his eyes to Anne-Marie.

Colin forced his eyes open and they came to rest on

Anne-Marie, who was leaning against the counter. His expression was a dreary parody of surprise. "You still here?" he asked, looking suspiciously from her to Errol and back again. Then he smiled. "Oh, yeah…"

Errol knew exactly what was going through what passed for Colin's mind. "It's not what you think. Anne-Marie slept on the sofa."

Colin got up, smacking his lips thirstily. "It's not my business." He pulled a carton of orange juice from the fridge and raised it to his lips, gulping noisily. Nodding towards the bread in Anne-Marie's hand he asked, "You mekking breakfast? I'll 'ave some ah dat too." Then he was gone, the door swinging behind him.

"I suppose I don't need to apologise for my friend. You know him already."

Anne-Marie laughed and brushed breadcrumbs from her fingers. "Yeah, I suppose I do."

Their eyes met again, and Errol felt as if he couldn't bring himself to leave her. He could walk out of the kitchen and never set eyes on her again. A self-confessed bachelor, he was already involved in a sexual relationship that had satisfied him for the past year or so. Now he was confused about why a woman he'd just met was making him consider cheating on his girlfriend.

"Hadn't you better get ready?" she reminded him.

"Sure… yeah. You all right down here?"

"Fine," she assured him with that knee-trembling smile.

She wasn't Colin's type at all — she had brains and beauty. Just what had she seen in him? A bit of rough? "Right then, catch you later." Errol edged towards the door.

Anne-Marie was fully aware of the effect she was having on him, and it warmed her inside. "Yeah."

Pushing the door, he couldn't stop himself taking one last look at her backside… And the rest of her was exactly the same.

Damn!

On the upstairs landing, Errol passed Melanie coming out of the spare room. The girl was cool to hang out with —

a little brainless, but that was what Colin had gone for before Joan.

Melanie had a bad case of 'bedhead' and redeye. She ran an embarrassed hand through her hair, not that it made much difference. "Hi, Errol! Sorry about last night... I was well gone, man."

He stroked her arm playfully. "It's all right, Mel. Hoping to give Colin a send-off were you?"

She giggled. "Sump'n like that."

Yeah — she had probably walked into the wrong room on purpose, and instead of the seduction she'd planned had most probably passed out.

Errol's bath took him approximately thirty minutes, during which time he soaped himself with Lynx shower gel, scrubbed his fingernails, and shampooed his head. Washed, shaved and back in his bedroom, he began to feel a little like his old self again.

He liked the pattern of days he had to himself, enjoyed the routinelessness of it all, hated to be jarred or hurried into the day. But this morning was an exception. Today, he was to be a best man for the second time.

Thirty-four and still single, though he had a son. He looked good, though. Didn't he? As if to prove it to himself, he turned to his full-length mirror and studied his face and naked torso, turning this way and that, flexing and stretching. What he saw was an inviting smile, long-lashed brown eyes, silky, arched eyebrows, not one wrinkle... juicy lips, and a male model's jawline. His dark skin was supple, smooth and free of scars. He stood a solid six foot two, with broad shoulders, hard pecs and pumped biceps. No way did he look thirty-four... Twenty-seven at the most...

"Here's a 'deddi' going out to bridegroom, Colin Baker, gettin' married at St Mark's in Peckham today. Your bride, Joan Ross, soon to be Baker, wants us to play 'Tonight I Celebrate my Love for You'. She loves you, man — mek sure you treat her right..."

Daddy Ernie spun the track, and as the first bars rang out

the groom stepped out of the shower.

Dressed in a towel, Errol smiled to himself and crossed the room to rummage around in his underwear drawer for the g-string he wanted to wear today: Yvette's favourite. He half-turned and directed his voice towards the en suite bathroom. "Colin, you hear dat? Your bride just sent you a dedication over the airwaves."

Colin was mopping himself down with a towel. "Yeah, I heard," he replied proudly. "Ah my girl, dat!"

Errol laughed and padded barefoot across the bedroom to dust down their hired suits with a clothes brush. Always the best man, never the groom... He hoped Colin knew what he was letting himself in for.

Errol was a very confident man, sure of himself and his future, although he'd never seen himself as the marrying kind. His parents were strong, independent, professional people, who'd instilled in their only child a firm sense of confidence and self-worth. "Believe in yourself and you can do anything," his father had told him. "Never be frightened in life," his mother had said. "Face whatever comes your way with dignity and strength."

It was all right for them — they had each other. Errol often felt like an intruder in their presence... especially when they didn't wait until he was asleep to perform sex.

So when they'd decided to move to the States he had known that this was his chance to practice what they preached. He was eighteen at the time — an adult, with nothing but the thousand pounds they had left him. But he had found himself filled with the energy and enthusiasm of an independent youth with something to prove.

While he studied he'd moved from one friend's couch to the next, struggling to survive on a measly student's grant. After college he'd held down several jobs to repay his overdraft — shelf-stacker, hired hand, mechanic — before finally landing a job with a local paper as a journalist. From there he had made contacts in television, gone back to college to get the right qualifications, signed on with an agent — and his life had changed dramatically.

"You got two more hours of freedom before she slap dat chastity belt 'pon you an t'row away de key."

"There ain't no chastity in my relationship, believe."

"Marriage changes people. You wait — give it six months and you're gonna be making appointments to have sex with your wife," Errol joked.

"Leave it out! If that was gonna happen it would have happened already. At least I know where my next lay is coming from, unlike some people I could mention."

"Leave my sex life out of this."

"But when are you gonna settle down, Errol?" Colin quizzed. "You gonna be left on the shelf if you don't find someone soon."

What was this man on? How could anyone answer that question? Errol stepped to the bathroom door and watched Colin lather his face for a shave. "I chose to have one specific woman because she pleases me sexually; I go out with other women because I also need mental stimulation. Why not share what I've got to offer?"

Colin turned to him, razor in hand. "You see! Did you just hear yourself? You got more ego than sense."

"Don't you worry about it, Col. In my own time I'll decide which woman I end up with. You should know how hard a decision that is anyway. Look how long it took you an' Joan to decide you were meant for each other."

"Mmm." Colin twisted his face to one side to get a clean shave. "Joan wasn't easy though, man. I had to fight to hold on to that one." He rinsed his razor in the sink. "You know there's always women on the lookout for eligible bachelors at weddings. You'd best watch your back."

"Easy, star! I'm picking Yvette up for the reception. She should finish work by about seven."

"Oh, she's the one you're sporting tonight?"

"She's not a suit, man. An' jus' watch what you say in front of her."

"Hey, rude bwoy. Is me you ah talk to." Colin wiped his face with a flannel and threw it across the room. It hit Errol in the chest. "I ain't gonna drop you in it. Stress getting to you?"

"I'm not the one getting married." Errol threw the flannel back. Colin caught it in his fist. He now looked fresh and alert, belying the fact that they had been up until five.

"You jealous?"

Errol raised an eyebrow. "Yeah, right! Listen, you got another hour to make yourself look like a bridegroom."

Errol could have been in Colin's present situation many times over. Instead he was the ultimate bachelor: eligible, with charm, charisma and looks. That wasn't all he had going for him. He could also communicate with women on their level. All he had to do was go into talk-show-host mode and say, "Talk to me." A few sympathetic words, and women couldn't resist confiding in him. The only problem with his talent was that it had no limits. Once he was on a roll, once he'd got the woman on his side, it snowballed until he suddenly realised he was in a relationship.

It also drew a certain type of woman. They would be sophisticated, interesting, independent, intelligent and attractive — but unfortunately they would be searching for Mr Right. They were usually hard to spot, because everything they said and did seemed so confident and self-sufficient, and it was this I-don't-need-a-man attitude that was deceiving. Errol had learnt one tell-tale sign: they always made the first move. They would be so intent on getting their man that they would soon start to worm their way into his life. Often carrying the scars of being treated unfairly by the opposite sex, these women were on the lookout for a healer, a man who wasn't going to hurt them, one who actually liked women, and not just for the obvious.

In other words, someone like Errol Wright. After four of these close calls, he'd simply given up. He'd met Yvette, and they had hit it off straight away. She'd made it clear that she wasn't into changing herself for any man, that a prospective partner would have to take her as she was. So they had gone out for a drink and ended up in bed — and that's the way it remained between them. They were both happy with the situation, and more than anything they were friends. She was his homie/lover/friend.

Errol slid open the door of his walk-in closet and paused in front of the long row of suits. There was thousands of pounds worth of clothing here: royal blue, midnight blue, bottle green, khaki green, greys and black... these were his serious suits. Then there were the checks and flamboyant materials for the occasional "special appearances". On the other side of the closet were several rows of shoes, sorted into categories of dress, casual, sport and evening. He selected a highly polished Italian leather pair, to match his suit, then, feeling like Errol Wright, Voice of the People, he left Colin to dress and skipped down the stairs.

He entered the kitchen with a flourish, immediately disappointed to find it empty.

His eyes fell on the note propped up on the marmalade jar. It was from Anne-Marie:

We'll swap autographs at your earliest convenience.

Underneath was her phone number. Errol smiled and slipped the paper into his jacket pocket. Then, grabbing two pieces of cold toast, he switched on the kettle to make some fresh coffee. It was going to be a long day.

The Saab pulled up across the road from the small church, and two young men — dapper, handsome, and groomed to perfection — stepped into the brilliant sunshine of the day.

Martin, Colin's brother, accompanied the groom shoulder to shoulder up the steps of the church, while the best man locked the vehicle and checked out the scene.

Inside, the church was lit from high windows in the roof and along the tops of the walls. A bulky man dressed in black with a white waistcoat was bustling up the aisle towards them, a camera bouncing on his chest. "Where've you been? We need to get some pictures of you and your escorts before the bride's party arrives."

Errol whispered to Colin, "I guess that's the

photographer."

"Don't look at me, I didn't find him," Colin hissed back.

Behind the three of them another four men in identical suits entered.

"Oh good, you're all here!" The photographer bustled the group back towards the entrance of the church. "Okay. Outside now, gentlemen. If we could get a move on here…"

"Yo, D!" Colin called out to the youngest of the ushers. "You look criss in that suit. Ah your turn next!"

Duane, fifteen years old, waved him away with a shy grin.

Like an army sergeant the photographer lined them all up and started to order them around, telling them to stand up, kneel down, smile, hug, shake hands, even lift the groom up for the bumps.

The groom's mother arrived fifteen minutes later and fussed over him until she had to be pulled away: "Colin, you have you 'kerchief? Put it in de pocket. Straighten yuh tie! You don't see you 'ave de pin *h*upside down?" "Colin! Who iron yuh trousers? De crease nuh straight…"

Errol kept Colin's mind occupied with jokes about the bride not turning up, and started a mental countdown to the ceremony that would end Colin's single life. The church was filling up quickly, and they turned and waved to family and friends as they were ushered in behind them.

After a few minutes, the whisper reached them like a wave from the back of the church that the bride had arrived. Colin grabbed Errol's arm and swallowed hard.

His best man grinned. "You feeling it now?"

They stood up together, moving to the altar as the organist struck up the wedding march. The congregation stood as Joan, her daughter and her father, followed by six bridesmaids, stepped in time down the aisle. There was an audible sigh from the females admiring Joan's dress as her five year old daughter dropped rose petals up the aisle as she stepped ahead of her mother and grandfather.

Errol did his duty as ring bearer and then bowed out, grateful to be able to take a seat.

TWO

"Mm-hmm. Michael, your buns get tighter every time I see 'em." Yvette slapped the fit black man's buttocks, giving him a flirtatious smile before moving on to the next piece of fitness equipment. Michael watched her sheepishly, his eyes flitting to her Lycra-covered bottom, before he stepped up his pace on the treadmill. At thirty-seven years old, he was one of her regulars at the gym. He was also one of the few gentlemen.

The men who frequented The Body Beautiful knew what Yvette was like, which in most cases was why they came. The ones who found her too familiar never returned. This was *her* gym, and she loved it more than her own home. The Body Beautiful was a beauty parlour, offering the services of masseurs and toning tables, as well as a fully equipped gym. And Yvette occasionally led aerobics classes. One day she planned to expand to include saunas. She was still a youthful-looking thirty-two — she knew she could eventually achieve everything she wanted.

She had an eleven year old son — My Man, she called him. Tyrone used to have this thing about vetting her appearance before she went out for a date. He would tell her if her dress was too short or cut too low, if her hair looked good, or if she had on too much make-up. Tyrone used to also be her protector, the man of the house. Any man who tried to muscle in on his territory was soon put in his place — and if he didn't like it, then he was out. Tyrone was definitely his mother's son.

That is, before she'd started seeing Errol, who had had the boy eating out of his hand from day one.

Errol had walked into their home one evening and shaken Tyrone's hand, then had taken an immediate interest in what the boy was doing. Tyrone hadn't recognised him from the TV; they had talked and played with the computer until the early hours of the morning before Errol told him he was a celebrity.

"Never mind me," Yvette had said as she'd pouted in front of the television. This male bonding shit stinks, she'd thought. Tyrone didn't see Errol as a threat because Errol had shown him respect, that he was friend, not foe, before the boy had even had a chance to consider it.

That had been almost a year ago, and already Tyrone had asked if he could call Errol "Daddy". Needless to say, Yvette had refused, feeling the jealousy boiling up inside her. "He's *not* your daddy," she'd said angrily. But she had been secretly glad that her son had accepted Errol, that he obviously felt the same way she did for the man. Later, when she'd asked Errol how he would have felt if she'd said yes, he'd replied, "I would've been honoured, but I'm not in the position to be a father to him at the moment."

The only thing stopping them being a family, Yvette felt, was their need for independence.

"Yvette, man, what's wrong wid dis machine?"

"You having a problem there, Kyle?" Another black hunk — God, she loved this job.

"Nothing's happening." The man tapped the side of the console twice.

"Don't you go hitting my equipment wid dem hammer-fists a yours!" Yvette strode lithely to the rowing machine, where the featherweight boxer was getting frustrated. She adjusted her cut-off top so she wouldn't reveal anything as she bent over.

"It ain't lightin' up."

"You tried turning it on?" Yvette flipped a switch on the side of the console and it beeped into life.

Kyle shrugged. "New technology — I still ain't got the hang of it."

"You just a big baby, ain't ya?" She squeezed his cheeks playfully. Observers chuckled as Yvette teased the big man. "Don't worry, babe — when you're ready for lessons you know where to find me…"

The innuendo was not lost on her audience. Yvette always caught nuff jokes in the fitness room. She would

17

stride around in her work-out gear, catching up with her patrons' lives and praising them on their efforts to keep fit. She made friends easily — that was how she had met Errol.

Speaking of which, it was time to get showered and get out of here. He was due to pick her up in half an hour for a wedding reception.

"Fellas, I'm gone. I'll catch you later."

She was answered by grunts, growls and wolf-whistles.

Yvette was making her way through the mirrored corridor of her domain when Babs, the receptionist, met her. She was tugging at the cord of her track-suit bottoms, tightening the twenty-four-inch waist. "I was just coming to get you…"

Yvette was already walking away. "Yeah, well whatever it is can wait until tomorrow. I'm on my way out."

"But you can't—"

"Sorry?" Yvette placed a hand on her hip and cocked her head to one side.

Babs quickly started to apologise. "I'm sorry… It's just that Elaine called. She's twisted her ankle and there's no way she can take the class tonight…"

"What! You're kidding."

"I know you were planning to get off, but the women are already arriving…"

"Shit, shit, *shit*! Why now? I just don't believe this…" It was too late to get anyone else to cover — the class started in ten minutes.

Cussing and stamping her feet, Yvette turned and headed towards her personal changing room to get ready. She wouldn't cancel a class; cancelled classes meant lost money and a damaged reputation.

Errol knew he must have looked like a fish out of water as he strolled up Woolwich High Street in his three-piece suit. He had taken his time sauntering up the road from the car park, because he knew that there was no way Yvette would be ready on time. She would still be doing her hair or make-up. He had learnt that the woman didn't know the meaning of time. You had to give her an hour in advance to be anywhere. Although if you kept her waiting you'd soon know about it. He wasn't obsessive about punctuality; it was just that he endeavoured to turn up for people on time, even if it meant getting to places early and having to wait around. That's just the way he was.

The electronic buzzer on the door alerted Babs to Errol's presence. She looked up and smiled. "Hi, Errol! You're looking good. No gym bag today?"

"Not today, Babs. I'm escorting my lady to a wedding reception." He had a twinkle in his eyes, and his smile brought out his charming, boyish dimples.

Babs was always glowing. She was mixed-race, with lots of wild ringlets that always did the opposite to what she wanted. Today she had attempted a ponytail, but her hair wasn't having it and only half of it had stayed in the band. She smirked, giving him a wink. "But you still getting a work-out though, innit?"

Errol winced. The way women just came out with things these days… they didn't leave anything to the imagination. It wasn't as if he didn't occasionally make quips like that himself, but there was a time and a place for everything. "Is it all right to go through?" he asked, eager to be away from Babs's appraising eyes.

"Yeah, but she's still working. She had to take an extra class."

Errol nodded and raised a hand in thanks as he went through the entrance to the staff quarters. Along one side of the corridor was a mirrored wall; flick off the lights and it became a two-way mirror through which the staff could watch the goings-on in both the gym and the aerobics hall, where Yvette was presently taking her class. On the other side were doors that led to the staff room, Yvette's office, and the private changing rooms. At the end of the corridor was another door that led to the patrons' changing rooms, the showers and the treatment rooms. From the outside, no one would ever guess that there were so many rooms in here, and yet Yvette wanted more.

Errol stood alone in the corridor, contemplating whether to wait in her office or take a seat in the staff room, watch a bit of telly. Absently he flipped the light switch, and was suddenly given a view of rows of women doing their step aerobics. Dressed in leotards or leggings and T-shirts, they moved in unison to the beat of "This Is How We Do It" by Montell Jordan. Yvette was at the front of the class, her back to the mirror, shouting instructions and encouragement. Her extensions were tied high on her head with a band, and a layer of perspiration gave her skin a sheen.

She was good — in more ways than one — and Errol felt a surge of pride just watching her. People loved her. She was sometimes too loud, too flirtatious, too outspoken, too tactless and pushy, but underneath all of that was a good woman, an ambitious woman, with pride and much love for her son. She could be just as affectionate as she was brash; it just took the right person to bring it out. It suited them both to be permanent lovers. She knew how to be discreet, and didn't demand to be taken out to the expensive places Errol frequented in business.

And from his vantage point she had a great body. What was it his American cousin always said about black women? "Baby got back," he mouthed to himself, cocking his head to one side and running his tongue across his lips. Mm-hmm, Miss Barker definitely had back, as well as front. Tina Turner in her youth — that was Yvette. She even had those lips... snogging lips, legs that went on for ever, and muscles screaming out to be touched, caressed, massaged...

All it took was watching her. He could go to see her at her home thinking, Tonight I'm not going to touch her; tonight we're just going to sit down and talk, have a drink and cuddle up and talk. But what actually happened to him after a few minutes in her company was completely different. His hormones would take over, his dick would start bobbing and throbbing, and before his very eyes she would be a naked Goddess — ripe, juicy, hips pumping...

At first, that was all they had done. They had tried doing

the dating thing once — their first date — but by the end of the evening they'd damned near torn the clothes from each other's bodies on her doorstep.

They had it going on, uncontrollably, and it just kept getting better.

The class was winding up. The women were now lying flat on their backs doing cool-down exercises. They lifted their pelvises off the floor, holding, then down, then up again...

Errol turned away. Enough was enough. Just watching her do dem t'ings made him not only horny but thirsty too. He headed for the drinks machine and bought himself a lemon Tango.

By the time he'd strolled back up towards the hall the ladies were emerging, hot, perspiring, giggling and chatting, some were mopping perspiration from their face and shoulders with towels, others were taking swigs from bottles of mineral water. Errol waited for them to exit before making his presence known.

He cleared his throat, as Yvette's back was to him.

"Hi, baby." She sat on a bench and bent to untie her trainers. "Boy, what a day I've had! My brother this morning, going over the books and giving me headache, a self-defence class at the Waterfront this afternoon, then I get back here and have to supervise the inductions for the fitness room — I swear, some of the people we get in here should stick to a skipping rope... Oh, and then Elaine couldn't make it in to do this evening's class so I'm stuck here for another hour... So, obviously, I'm not ready..."

She stopped and looked at him. Standing up, she put her hands on her hips. "You listening to me?"

He was leaning against the door, arms folded, one leg overlapping the other, the toe of one shoe on its tip. He had that you-know-what-I-want-to-do-to-you look in his eyes and was pulling his top teeth over his bottom lip seductively. "Of course I'm listening to you," he answered.

Yvette kissed her teeth. Shaking her head, she turned her back to him, but he could see in the mirror that she'd allowed a sneaky little smile to play on her lips. Yes, she loved it when he watched her like that. He knew he turned her on in the worst way. And she did have a body worth watching — she wasn't a fitness instructor for nothing.

Yvette liked the fact that Errol went in for style in an understated way. Stylish hair, sharp suits and a penchant for hand-painted silk ties. He had been known to pay out a hundred pounds for one. She had often told him that he must have come out of charm school with a diploma. But of course she wasn't falling for any of that sweet-boy crap. She was one woman you either gave it to straight or not at all.

When they'd first met she'd taken time to impress, which made a difference to Errol. She'd known who he was, and yet she hadn't fallen into his arms or gone all gooey. Still, four months later she'd been hooked. Although she hadn't said anything — Errol had simply exercised his male intuition.

"Well, as I was saying…" she started again.

"I know what you were saying." He approached her slowly, purposefully, his hands in his pockets. "And I'm here to make it all better." Placing his hands on her waist, he drew her to him, the bulge of his erection pressing against her bottom. He was just a couple of inches taller than her. Perfect.

She grinned. "You want some play, bad bwoy?"

"You offering?" He turned her to face him and slid his hands down her back to cup her taut buttocks, the smooth fabric of the leotard she wore arousing him more.

"Looks like you don't wait to be offered."

He took a step backwards, his arms still around her, and looked her in the eyes. He played into her little game. "Is that a complaint?"

Yvette looked around exaggeratedly. "I don't see anyone else in here. Did you hear a complaint? 'Cause it sure didn't come from me." She snaked one arm between their bodies, reaching for his hard-on. Her fingertips ran over the head and her palm cupped the shaft.

Errol groaned.

"Aren't you supposed to be at a wedding?" she whispered.

"A reception." He nibbled her ear. "Not the same. We have time."

"Come," she said, taking his hand. "Lets' go somewhere a little more private."

Following her out of the gym, Errol smiled to himself. And there he had been, thinking she loved to do it in public. But he had no objections. Secure in his manhood, he had no problem with women who liked to lead in the bedroom — and Yvette certainly knew what she wanted.

If there were a female version of himself, he knew he'd found it in Yvette. Impulsive and unashamedly highly sexed, she knew he was always ready for her.

The corridor was still empty as they crossed it and entered her private changing room. As soon as the door was closed he spun her round and captured her lips with his own. The kiss was full of heat, passion and longing. Its urgency didn't surprise Yvette, and she grabbed the back of his head in both hands, making their embrace as deep as it could possibly get.

Errol inhaled the scent of her flesh — a mixture of perspiration and cocoa butter body lotion. He sucked the skin on her neck, revelling in the way he made her feel — so totally on remote control. His hands were under the straps of her leotard now, pulling them away from her shoulders and down her arms. Her breasts sprung over the top of the material, the nipples erect and pointing at him. His mouth travelled down her neck, kissing, sucking and biting.

Just as eagerly, Yvette was fumbling with the buckle of his belt, her fingers working to undo the zipper and release his erection. Then her hands found their way under his jacket. The jacket fell to the floor and she began to step backwards, towards her desk in the centre of the office. Her hands never stopped moving as she worked his trousers over his hips, simultaneously releasing herself from her leggings. He helped her drag his waistcoat and shirt over his head; they spun in the air before being fired across the

23

room to land over the back of her swivel chair.

Errol knew how much g-strings turned Yvette on. They left his buttocks bare and his balls encased in thin fabric, leaving little to the imagination. She eased herself onto the corner of her desk, pulling him against her, cupping his buttocks in her hands and wrapping one leg around his thigh.

There were no words spoken, just heavy breathing and whispers of encouragement, each of them completely immersed in giving pleasure. First he teased her with his erection, giving her a taste of what was to come, rubbing his length against her groin, making her arch her back towards him, almost begging. Then he used his fingers, finding her clitoris and massaging the tiny, erect bud until she bit into his shoulder with pleasure. Then both of them simultaneously gasped as he entered her, tentatively at first, then letting himself go and taking as well as giving what they both wanted.

Suddenly Yvette was pushing him away and she stood, grabbing his hand. They were travelling again. She made him wrap his arms around her as they crossed the room, joined belly to back, heading for her private bathroom. She unlatched the door and they tumbled against it as it swung inwards. Yvette pressed her palms against the cold, tiled wall to brace herself, and Errol kept the pace going and entered her from behind.

Again Yvette changed the position after a minute. She whirled round, leant her back against the wall, and placing her hands on Errol's shoulders she pulled herself up on to his hips, wrapping both legs round his waist.

He entered her with lubricated ease, and she cried out as she took the full length of him. He let her take control, riding his cock as he carried her towards the shower. She cried out, as if the water hitting her were as sharp as a knife's blade. Errol felt the cool stream wash the perspiration from their hot bodies. Yvette's legs began to slip on his wet skin, so she lowered her feet to the floor. Again, he concentrated on her body. She gripped the towel rail to keep her balance as he went to work with his mouth. First he circled her nipples with his tongue, then he took each one in turn into his mouth, flicking their already hard tips.

Then Errol went downtown, giving her pleasure she had never thought possible before he had initiated her to it. Nipping his way back up to her neck he turned her around, all the while massaging her clitoris with his middle finger. He entered her from behind. Taking it slowly at first, then speeding up his thrusts, matching her own movements.

The sex was as good as always, maybe even marginally better. The explosive climax at the end of it left Yvette breathless and weak, but Errol's manhood still stood to attention, glistening and dripping wet, so she made sure it wasn't going to waste.

Marion spotted Anne-Marie standing alone, and stepped carefully over to her in her bridesmaid's dress. Her friend appeared to be looking for someone and, seeing as she knew only the groom and herself, Marion assumed it must be her.

"Anne-Marie!" She kissed her cheek and gave her a brief hug. "You look great! Heard you were partying last night..."

"The bachelor party, yeah. I went home and had a few hours' sleep." Anne-Marie's eyes were still scouting the room.

Marion followed her gaze. "Are you looking for someone?"

"Errol, the best man. I met him yesterday. Thought I'd say hi."

"Oh, Errol's gone to pick up a friend. He'll be back later. Listen, are you okay on your own? I've just seen someone..."

"Yes, fine, you go on."

The tables and chairs had been pushed back against the walls by now, and the sound system was playing warm-up music. A few people were still dressed as they had been at the service, but others had gone home and changed or brought outfits to change into. A group of kids were chasing

25

each other in and out of the milling adults' legs. One child went skidding past Anne-Marie on his backside, probably ruining a perfectly good pair of dress trousers. She helped him to his feet and, without saying thank you, he dashed off again after the others.

Anne-Marie browsed, walking round the hall and pretending to smile or nod at acquaintances, and all the while her eyes kept drifting back to the door. There had been a sense of fate about her encounter with Errol that morning, a sense of inevitability. A sense of unchangeable purpose. She was sure he had felt it too — and that was why she had changed her mind and decided to come to her ex-boyfriend's wedding reception.

Errol arrived an hour later, dressed in a blue suit. His back view alone was the most beautiful thing Anne-Marie had ever seen. Starting with his shaved head, her eyes worked their way down his long, strong neck and over his shoulders, wide and confidently squared. The length of his spine was impressive, making her fingers itch to trace his vertebrae. The narrowness of his waist was evident even under the made-to-measure blue jacket, and his long legs ended in elegant blue leather shoes.

Anne-Marie's heart started to thump as he turned almost fully round, but his arm was grabbed possessively by a striking woman with long, braided hair plaited into a rope that hung down her back. She had a perfect figure, if a little muscular. She was dressed in a sapphire and black dress that passed her calves, and silver adorned her ears, neck and wrists. They crossed the room arm in arm; she walked as though she had a right to be where she was. There was no coy dropping of the hands as some couples do; he was proud of her.

She said something to him, and he whispered a reply which brought about a tinkling laugh that hurt Anne-Marie like a slap in the face. She froze on the spot, immediately trying to think of a way she could get out of here without drawing attention to herself. She looked around for Marion, but she was standing at the head table, chatting and laughing with the bride, who was actually sitting on the table-top and smoking. Very unbridelike.

Anne-Marie shuffled towards the door, trying to make herself as invisible as possible. She was almost there when someone grabbed her arm and whirled her round.

"Hey, no dance for me?" Colin was grinning like a gremlin and had obviously had a skinful to top up what he had consumed last night.

"I was just about to leave, Col."

"What? You cyan't do that. The party just start, and all my exes have to dance with me before they leave." He drew her into his arms, breathing beer fumes in her face.

"Are you drunk, Colin?"

He pulled her away for a second and frowned at her. "What you take me for? I wouldn't get drunk at my own wedding. Naw, man — I'm just mellow..." And he drew her to him again, cheek to cheek. As he danced her slowly round she caught sight of Errol watching them, and desperately wanted to let go of this immature, drunk, married man and run into his arms.

He lifted his hand in acknowledgement and she smiled back. But his attention was soon taken away by another woman.

"Colin, who's the woman Errol came with?'

"Woman? What woman?"

"Errol brought a woman to the reception with him..."

"Oh, her." He shrugged. "I don't know. Errol has the agency set him up with models for functions — you know, keep his private life private," Colin lied.

Anne-Marie nodded, but her heart rose again. So, there was no competition.

As soon as the record was over, she rushed to the ladies' to freshen up.

Errol had seen Anne-Marie dancing with Colin, and was mildly surprised that Joan hadn't got up and slapped him silly for behaving like a fool on her (and his) wedding day.

27

It seemed that they were both out to enjoy the day thoroughly, however, when Joan accepted a dance from another man.

Errol saw Anne-Marie dashing out of the room after her dance with Colin, and decided to follow her. It was a totally impulsive thing — he didn't even know what he intended to say to her. He waited outside the ladies' room, occasionally signing a napkin for a fan or chatting to an old friend.

When Anne-Marie emerged she looked a little stunned to see him leaning against the wall, obviously waiting.

"Hi," he said.

Up close, Errol looked almost regal in his suit. His aftershave tempted her to reach out and touch him. She looked down at her shoes before saying, "Hi yourself."

"I didn't know you'd be here. I would have brought that signed photo."

Anne-Marie smiled charmingly. "I only decided to come this afternoon. I wasn't sure how the bride would take an ex-girlfriend turning up, and then I decided she wouldn't know who I was anyway. And how often do I get invited to a wedding?"

Errol smiled too, glad that she had decided to come. "Enjoying yourself so far?"

"As a matter of fact, no," she said, almost apologetically. "I was getting ready to leave."

"Not on my account, I hope. I mean, I just got here and you're leaving."

"I wish I'd brought a date. I see you did."

"Yeah, well it stops all the bridesmaids coming on to me."

She looked up at him, a brand new interest in her eyes. Errol Wright was a man who didn't have an interest in being caught, a man who covered all possibilities.

He looked at her carefully; he could tell what she was thinking. She was cool, though, with skin that looked as if she used only the best cosmetics. She had smiling eyes that always seemed to be thinking, digging deeper than she could actually express. Her hair was quite long but she wore it naturally, probably pressed or blow-dried for the occasion and wrapped into a bun. She wore no make up except for the functional lipstick. She stood straight, like one who has been taught the value of standing up for oneself, and she wore a long cream dress and a matching bolero jacket with a pink stone and diamante brooch on one lapel.

"So, are you a little jealous of the bride?" Errol asked.

"Me? No — not for marrying Colin."

"You didn't want him then?"

"No. If I'd wanted him I'd still have him."

"A woman who gets what she wants."

"Always."

"Not a person who gives up?"

"Never."

"Do you always get *who* you want too?"

"I've never really wanted anyone." She caught his eyes and they held their gaze, each trying to read the other's expression.

Errol held up his glass. "A toast," he said, "to the day you get who you want."

Anne-Marie smiled coyly as he handed her his glass to sip from.

"I'd better get back. They'll be sending out a search party for the best man. I'll catch you later..." He ran a hand down her arm, like a caress. He knew women went weak for it, but he'd done it anyway.

Errol knew she was watching him as he walked away from her.

THREE

Monday came sooner than expected. Another timetabled day. Errol opened the glass doors that led onto his roof balcony from the bedroom. It was six o'clock on a chilly morning. The sun was not quite in the sky, but he could tell it was going to be a lovely day.

He shivered in his thick white towelling robe, stretched his arms above his head and breathed in, looking down at the tidy gardens beneath him. He remembered the doubts he'd had about buying this place. There weren't too many black people in the area, and although he hadn't been worried about being accepted he'd wanted to feel comfortable with his neighbours, had wanted them to come round for barbecues, at which he could play his own music and the music his friends wanted to hear.

He had a regular housekeeper — a luxury, his friends thought, but when you worked the hours he did it was most certainly a necessity. His suits were always dry-cleaned and hanging ready in his walk-in closet; his bed sheets, pressed and sweet smelling, were changed every other day; he had cooked meals to order, and there was not a speck of dust anywhere. Errol was still living in the style his parents had accustomed him to, and he'd done it without their help.

It seemed to him that all his spare time was spent networking. He partied with interesting people — established celebrities and the up-and-coming — with ease. The only problem was that sometimes he did not know what was pleasure and what was business.

He still occasionally found his situation unbelievable, incredible. He'd be watching television, and would flick channels to see himself on the screen. Or he'd be walking the streets and spot someone reading a magazine with his face on the cover. So he didn't mind being alone. Loneliness was a welcome rarity in an otherwise crowded life.

Errol began to dress. He couldn't afford to look anything

but totally presentable at all times. He put his clothes on slowly, noticing every detail. The light beige Donna Karan wool jacket looked as though it had never been worn; the trousers, clasped at the waist by a Hugo Boss belt, were creased just so, and hung to show off his finely toned figure. Under the jacket he wore a chocolate-coloured short-sleeved V-neck sweater that co-ordinated perfectly with the suit. Mr GQ he most certainly was.

He glanced at his watch. It was about that time again, so he reached for his mobile to make his wake-up call.

"Good morning, my queen."

The greeting made Yvette grin with pleasure. "Good morning, Errol."

Every morning Errol would call her at around seven thirty. He'd wish her a good morning, would let her know that he was thinking about her, giving her a positive vibe for the day. Yvette slid into the armchair by the telephone and curled up her legs. Errol's voice sounded real good, she could almost see him in front of her, wrapped in nothing but a bath towel.

"How are you this morning?"

"I'm fine." She would have gone on to say, "and all the better for hearing your voice," but she didn't want to sound too eager.

"So, my black butterfly, you miss me?" he asked.

"Get real!" She grinned. "You know there's only one thing I miss about you."

He laughed. "My smile, right?"

"What — you have one down there too?"

Errol laughed again. That's what he liked about Yvette. The bullshit didn't work, but he had a laugh trying.

Yvette pulled her long, braided hair back with one hand. "What you up to today?"

"The only thing I got on my schedule is an interview with that paper, *New Nation*."

"So, you're basically free today…"

"Yeah. Why?"

"Well I thought you could cook us dinner. You know how Ty loves your roast potatoes, and the way you cooked that chicken… Boy, it didn't even taste like chicken by the time you'd done with it."

Errol took the compliment in his stride. Yvette couldn't prepare anything more than whatever she could simply heat up in the oven, chop up and boil, or eat raw. "How is Ty?"

"Keeps asking me when you're going to take him to Planet Hollywood."

"Damn. I didn't forget, honestly. It's just time. Why don't we eat there tonight?"

"You serious?"

"Sure. Tell him I'll pick you both up around five."

"You know, Errol…" She stopped as though she had been interrupted.

"What?"

"It's okay. I'll see you later."

"Looking forward to it."

"Me too."

Yvette replaced the receiver and pinched her arm. God, was she getting soft? She'd almost told him she loved him. Would that have been a mistake or what?

Later that afternoon, Errol ran a finger round the inside of his collar. He was cool, but he didn't feel it. It was swelteringly hot even off the set — or was it just him? The air conditioning was definitely on. He stood in the wings, breathing deeply. Why was he always so nervous before going in front of the cameras? Once they were rolling he was fine; he was Errol Wright, TV personality.

Marion Stewart was coming to the end of her introduction. This was his cue. "… so please welcome presenter of *Do the Wright Thing*, Errol Wright!"

The studio was filled with the sound of his signature tune and rapturous applause. He could see his image on a monitor as he took the stairs down the centre aisle of the auditorium: a tall, dark man, casually smart in a blue suit and white T-shirt, the beam of a follow-spot bouncing off his shaved head, his grin wide, confident, natural.

His hostess stood before him, joining the mainly black audience in their applause. Marion and Errol had jumped on the Channel 6 bandwagon at the same time. Errol Wright and Marion Stewart: young, black, active in their communities, with views and attitudes they wanted to share with the world. As newcomers together they had formed an instant bond. Now they were good friends, comrades against the critics.

"Thank you, thank you..." Errol turned to the audience and bowed deeply, dramatically. "Boy, you guys flatter me. I get more applause doing guest appearances than I do on my own show!"

The audience rewarded him with a burst of laughter.

Laughing with them, Marion invited him with a gesture of her hand to take a seat on the comfortable pink sofa opposite her.

Errol shook her hand as though they'd just met, belying the fact that they had spent the last two hours rehearsing the interview and chatting over coffee. He smiled, sat down and crossed one leg over the other. The applause and laughter subsided, and he turned to the audience and delivered a passable impersonation of Eddie Murphy: "Couldn't you just eat this woman up? She's like one a dem Barbie dolls — y'know, good to look at, but you play a little rough and the legs fall off!"

Laughter burst out again. Marion crossed her legs demurely and leaned towards him, her eyes flashing a warning. She knew Errol very well; he was always ribbing her about her size.

She waited for the audience to settle. "So, Errol, how does it feel to be on your rival show?"

"Rival?" He raised an eyebrow, a trademark he had made his own. "I wouldn't say we were rivals, Marion. We're like brother and sister shows — you're my female equivalent." He uncrossed his legs and placed both feet on the floor, clasping his hands and resting his elbows on his knees.

"So, you don't see us as being in competition for the ratings?"

Errol turned to the cameras and a mischievous look came into his eyes. Let's be spontaneous here, he thought. "Okay. All you fellows out there — which programme do you watch regularly? *Mantalk* or *Do the Wright Thing*?"

The men in the audience were unanimous. "*Mantalk*!" came the chant.

"Now the ladies…" He stood up. "Which do *you* prefer?"

No less fervently the female cry came up: "Errol, Errol, Errol," followed by screams, just to confirm his point.

Marion smiled. It was a good thing she knew this man; she hated people deviating from the script. "That doesn't surprise me, Errol. My show's studio audience is largely made up of men who come to hear what women are all about. And how often do we get to see a young, good-looking black presenter on our screens?"

The audience agreed with applause and wolf-whistles.

Marion chose her next question from the tele-prompter. "Errol, I always thought your over-confidence was put on for the television. Tell me, are you always like this?"

"Like what?" He shrugged, keeping that cheeky grin. "No, of course not. Believe me, Marion, really I'm kinda shy." He fluttered his eyelashes at the camera and the audience laughed again. They were most definitely on his side today. Women were practically sliding off their seats at being in the same room as him. It gave him a buzz better than an aphrodisiac. "No, seriously…" He held up his hands. "I do have two personas, if you like. What you are seeing is the showman; at home I try to lead a quiet life. I read, work out in my purpose-built gym…" He secretly crossed his fingers. "… have quiet drinks at home with just a few close friends. If I was like this all the time I probably wouldn't *have* any close friends."

Marion smiled knowingly. "What is it like to be the first black British male talk-show host?"

Errol leaned back on the sofa and spread his arms along the back. "I'd like to say it's been great, but it is a really challenging job — and I don't mean that in the aspiring way."

"What exactly *do* you mean?" Marion clasped one knee with her fingers.

"Well..." Errol paused, appearing to be considering his answer. "People like yourself, Oprah, Esther, Ricky, Vanessa... you all have the advantage of being female. People respond to you females so much better. With me they feel I'm being pushy, nosey, sometimes even aggressive." He shrugged, and the audience chuckled. Errol did occasionally get tough with his guests, usually when he had to get them to admit to something.

Marion laughed modestly. "For all those aspiring TV personalities out there, what advice would you give them?"

He glanced upwards, then, as a camera zoomed in, looked straight into it. "Opportunity knocks when you least expect it. I started out as a journalist. When I realised what I really wanted to do I got myself a good agent, made them work for me and, after much hard graft and with a firm belief in myself, here I am today. So I suppose my advice is, if you've got talent, find yourself a reputable agent, show them how enthusiastic you are, sell yourself, dedicate yourself to a sole purpose — or two — and go for it. You can't sit around expecting your dreams to land in your lap; you gotta go out and search for them."

"We've seen several of your shows aired now. What else does *Do the Wright Thing* have in store for us?"

"Now, that would be telling..." Errol threw another heap of charm at the audience and grinned. "No, seriously, next week I believe we're showing the programme on teenage parents and single-parent families." His tone became more grave. "And we'll have a special programme for national AIDS week, giving a chance for the victims of this terrible disease to express their feelings about the prejudice shown to them... But on the up side, we do like to break the seriousness of the show with a little occasional fun, so we'll be doing a programme on what the nineties ladies are looking for in a man. We'll have twenty bachelors in the studio for you to put to the test."

This statement was met with more wolf-whistles, howls and screams from the ladies.

Marion asked what all the women in the audience wanted to know. "Will you be one of them?"

Errol smiled sweetly and shook his head. "It's a shame, but no."

A communal sigh rose from the studio.

"Errol, why did you choose to accept a position in a form of TV that is so densely populated at the moment by women?"

Without hesitation he answered, "I love the idea of being unique as well as popular. Of course, it's only a matter of time before it catches on. Men were talk-show hosts as far back as black and white TV, black males only more recently — but I hope to be the first of many in England. We have several ideas lined up for a future series. Who knows — you might get a chance to be my guest sometime, Marion."

"Well, thank you... Although I'll know you're only inviting me to boost your ratings!"

Now the audience laughed with Marion. Errol wagged a finger and shook his head in jest.

Marion introduced a clip from one of Errol's shows, where he was soothing a weeping teenage adoptee whose natural mother, after being tracked down, still wanted nothing to do with her. His arms were around her trembling body, her head rested on his shoulder. He spoke with the docile, trained tone of a professional counsellor, instilling a pride and strength in the youngster, encouraging her to think beyond this one person to the family she already had.

As the clip ended Errol replaced his glass of water on the table. The audience was full of unrehearsed admiration, and the applause took a little longer to subside this time. "Ladies and Gentleman, Errol Wright!" Marion clapped along with the upstanding audience.

Marion concluded the interview professionally, made

her thank yous, and the recording stopped. A stills photographer rushed onto the set for shots of Marion and guests, then, once the tape had been checked and the audience departed, they were allowed to relax.

"How'd I do?" Errol asked Marion as they left the set.

She stretched her arms in the air, relieving her shoulders of tension. "You're so vain you have to ask?"

"No, I just want your opinion. As a colleague and friend, your view is important to me."

Marion blushed. "Okay. You were good as ever. But do you always have to try and steal the show?"

Errol put an arm across her shoulders. "I guess I'm just not used to being in the firing line of the interview."

They walked behind the wings, where the studio hands were going about their duties. "Paul wants to know why you missed training again this week," Marion said coyly.

"Yeah?" Paul had taken Errol to a judo session a few weeks previously. It wasn't Errol's sport, but he didn't want to hurt Paul's feelings — after all, judo was Paul's life.

"Yeah."

"Yvette, you know — she's been putting me through my paces. I'll give him a ring later. Will he be in?"

"Yeah, he's baby-sitting. I'm going out for a change. So, you and Yvette getting serious?" she asked in that casual way women have.

"Who — me? Naw. We see a lot of each other, but I wouldn't be hearing any wedding bells."

"One day someone's going to get you to settle down." She smiled, but there was a seriousness in her voice.

"Been there, done that."

She laughed.

From the shy little woman Errol had met a year ago, Marion was turning into a very shrewd, confident businesswoman. She exuded cunning know-how, and could soak up information like a sponge.

Marion half-turned as a tall, gangly woman came running up to them, long, curly brown hair flapping about her head. "Marion, thank goodness I caught you," the set manager said, out of breath. "Hi, Errol…"

He nodded a reply.

"What is it, Jayne?"

"Derek wants to see you in his office — now, please."

Marion sighed deeply. Derek was always keeping an eye on her. She felt as though he still considered her his special project. He always introduced her as "my presenter". But, being the producer, it was important to keep him sweet. "Errol, I'm sorry. Look, why don't you meet us later for lunch? I'll be bringing someone with me. Our usual restaurant?"

"Yeah, sure. Two o'clock?"

"Fine." She kissed him lightly on the cheek. "See you later."

He watched her hurry away, chatting to Jayne about the show, before heading to the dressing room to remove the special matt foundation used solely for TV and film work. (After recording his first show he had been glad to rush out into the fresh air. He'd been so full of nervous tension that he'd felt he was going to explode. It wasn't until he'd got back to the studio and taken a look at his face in the mirrored lift that he'd realised his face was still covered in the heavy make-up they used to stop the glare of the lights bouncing off his skin.)

With an hour to kill, Errol went window shopping. In Marks & Spencer he bought himself a cold drink, then walked the streets, stopping occasionally in a clothes shop or furniture shop He was always looking at ways to improve his already perfect home; now he could afford to change whatever he liked he did it just for the shopping buzz.

He was gazing into an antique shop window when someone tapped him on his shoulder. Thinking he had been recognised by a fan, he was already reaching inside his jacket for a pen as he turned round.

"Are you sure you can afford anything in there, sir?" Anne-Marie was grinning at him in that open, friendly way of hers.

"Anne-Marie! How are you?" Errol shook her hand. She was in a long, navy-blue suit. The blouse underneath was a pale green, and she wore another of those brooches which always caught Errol's eye. Her wavy hair was pulled back from her face and fastened at the nape of her neck with a clip.

"Fine. I heard you might be walking the streets on your own."

"You saw Marion?"

"I did. Remember? I told you I was having lunch with her today."

He nodded.

"She's still working, so I thought I'd come and find you."

They fell into step, and walked together to the restaurant.

The place where they were to meet Marion was very modern and bright, its open-plan dining area tastefully decorated with contemporary paintings on the wall and a mosaic floor. They sat at a table surrounded by windows, but were not worried about gawking passers-by because the building was surrounded by shrubs. Errol was pleased for Anne-Marie's company, and she was just as pleased to be with him again. She'd done nothing all weekend except sit at home alone, and hope that the phone would ring and it would be him.

"Where are your family from?" she asked him.

Errol sipped at his sherry and placed the glass back on the table before answering. "My mother's Jamaican and my father's from Chicago. They met in England."

"Really! So you're 'mixed blood'." She smiled.

"I hadn't really thought about it like that. Although I do consider myself to be of mixed culture, like most black folk."

"*Touché.*"

Errol leant forward, his elbows on the table, and turned on his talk-show-host voice. "What about you? Where are your folks from?"

"My parents were both Jamaican. Mother died just three months ago, and Dad… well, Dad went back to Jamaica."

Errol felt gutted that he'd asked. His eyes filled with

remorse. "I'm sorry to hear about your mother."

She waved his sympathy away. "It's fine. *I'm* fine. It's more of a relief really: she was suffering for two years before she went... and she did leave me quite well off."

Errol let a reasonable silence follow before he picked up the conversation again. The lunchtime crowd was evaporating as it neared two o'clock.

"My parents abandoned me too."

"Oh?"

"Well, I was eighteen at the time. They decided to go back to the States. I try to visit once a year, but you know... work..."

"Yes, it must be difficult." Anne-Marie nodded. "But at least you have them."

"You don't keep in touch with your father?"

Anne-Marie fiddled with a ring on her finger. "No. He left under a cloud, so to speak. Maybe I'll pay him a visit one day, who knows?"

Errol felt that there was some element to the story she wasn't telling. Something dark, that skeleton in the cupboard. He changed the subject. "I'll bet there are stories you could tell about Marion."

"Well, some... but at school we didn't actually go around together. We knew each other, but just to say hello to. I sometimes sat with her at lunch or when her other friends weren't around. I think we're better friends now than we were then."

"I see."

Perhaps Anne-Marie was a bit of a loner, he thought. She had come to his party alone, had turned up at the wedding reception alone, and was now hanging around with an old school acquaintance to whom she was never really that close. But he couldn't see why. She was attractive, intelligent, and a good conversationalist; she should have no trouble making friends.

"Any brothers or sisters?" he asked.

"No. I guess my parents tried it once and didn't like it."

Errol laughed. "I'm an only child too. I believe my

parents thought of me as a status symbol. They're both very professional people; they actually had to make time to have a child. I was brought up by a nanny who taught me at nursery age before I went to school."

"A sheltered childhood."

"Quite. I was lucky, I guess, that I didn't end up rebelling. It happens that way sometimes."

"So you had to look after yourself from an early age. I mean, when your parents left."

"Yes — cook, clean, wash, iron for myself…"

"And what do you eat — beans on toast?" Her eyes danced with humour.

"No." He laughed modestly. "I can cook. I taught myself from books. Italian, Chinese, gourmet… I can turn my hand to anything."

"Can I put you to the test?"

Errol raised an eyebrow curiously.

"How would you like to cook dinner for me sometime this week?"

Was she asking him out? Errol remembered his motto: never date mates or your friends exes. He also knew about women who made the first move. But…

"Well, I'd have to check my schedule…"

"Okay. I'll call you tomorrow and we can arrange a date. Give me a chance to see if you're just boasting."

Just then Marion rushed in, flustered but still smiling.

"I'm so sorry I'm late. Got held up about half a dozen times. You two getting on okay?"

Errol and Anne-Marie looked at each other and said in unison, "Fine."

After lunch they chatted over coffee. They had the whole afternoon, and no one wanted to hurry away.

"I like being in control of my life again," Anne-Marie was saying. "Any man who wants to share it with me now will have to learn to compromise, if he doesn't know how to already." She'd had a fair amount to drink while they had waited, more over lunch, and her voice had risen a little above normal conversational level.

Errol leant back in his chair, studying her oval face. "So how do you stay in control? I mean, you can't change people…"

"I don't rely on others. I make my own plans, have good back-up systems. In a relationship I call the shots; if the man can't handle it then he's not the man for me."

"Hmm." Errol was a little worried. This attitude wasn't gelling with what he already knew about Anne-Marie. She hadn't come across as one of these hard, career-minded women of the nineties before.

"And I don't let others pressure me to conform. Some of my acquaintances seem all geared to becoming like everyone else thinks they should be at thirty. You know — find a man, settle down and have babies. There are more important things in my life."

She was certainly trying to sound convincing. Errol leaned forward. "Such as… ?"

"Well, my career as a counsellor. My writing. I studied hard to get where I am today, came out of a rough relationship to live a fresh new life. No man could give me greater satisfaction than I get seeing my creations on bookshelves all over the country, knowing that others are reading my thoughts and views and living by them."

Marion had listened to Anne-Marie's words quietly. She didn't understand it. Both these young, attractive professionals giving up on love for their careers? It didn't make sense. What could possibly be more important than love and family? Who did they come home to at nights? Who was around to listen, give encouragement, motivation?

Errol voiced the question for her. "I can see your point, Anne-Marie. But, although I'm… a bachelor," he lowered his voice and flicked his eyes around the room, "I'm not planning to be that way for ever. My career is only going to take me so far, and then I'm going to want someone to share my success with me."

Anne-Marie couldn't hide her smile. "You see, it's different for men. A single man can have casual sex to satisfy his needs. He can date as many women as he wants without commitment, and that is considered normal in our age-group. But a woman could only carry on like that in secret.

"Did you see that documentary on the single mother who goes to clubs specifically to pick up men? You should have seen the papers. The outcry! 'It should have been banned.' 'This woman has no self-esteem — what kind of role model is she for her child?' I actually sat through that programme feeling sympathy for her, even though I knew I wouldn't do something like that myself."

"Sympathy!" Marion turned down her mouth in disgust. "Sympathy for a woman with a baby, who sleeps around?"

Anne-Marie tried to defend her position. "She said she does it because there are no emotional ties. The last thing she wants is a man telling her he loves her. She doesn't see why, as a single mother, she should have to give up her independence to be happy. And she *is* happy…"

Marion still couldn't believe what she was hearing. "How can you say that? As a counsellor you meet plenty of women like that — how can you seriously believe she's really happy?"

"In her conscious mind she is. She's a good mother throughout the week, she loves her daughter, and she goes to bed most nights on her own. One night a week, or once a fortnight, she goes out to find a sexual partner…"

Errol rejoined the conversation. "But wouldn't she get known around town as a slut? An easy lay? I know that, if I saw a woman coming into a club on a regular basis and leaving with a different man each time, I wouldn't touch her or have any respect for her. How can she respect herself — after all those men have had her? These guys might even pass the word around that she is a no-strings-attached lay."

Anne-Marie shrugged. "That's their problem, not hers."

Marion was outraged. "I don't believe it *is* just their problem! She's giving it away for free. She puts up with all the dangers of disease, violence, rape, and she isn't even getting the satisfaction of payment that prostitutes get."

"That's the point! She doesn't do it for the *men*. She isn't just giving, she's taking too. She's enjoying herself. She *uses* the men."

"That girl needs a man to love her. To show her that sex is more than just sensation. It's emotional too, something to share with someone you love. It's an experience you have to build on. How much love is she gonna get once a fortnight?"

"And what man is going to want her, when he finds out she's had more guys inside her than the Dog and Duck?" Errol added, and Marion nodded.

"You see…" Anne-Marie gestured at both of them with an open palm. "Even in the nineties, attitudes haven't changed. A man can sleep around and his woman just calls him 'experienced'. But society sees the women who do it as reckless and irresponsible. She's not going to get a pat on the back for bedding twenty men in a year."

"But do women want to be like men?" Errol asked.

"Some of us just want the freedom of choice men have. Society still frowns on women who don't want children."

"Good point," Errol said. "It's about fulfilling your potential as an individual with aims, ambitions and a life to live for yourself — not your man."

"I've managed to have it all, and I'm happy," Marion interjected. "But no one can live contentedly without love."

"You could only reach fulfilment through having it all, Marion," Anne-Marie said. "You *wanted* kids, you *wanted* to be a journalist — as a bonus you're a TV star too. You wanted love from a good man. In fact you're one big success story!" she added with a grin and a pat on Marion's hand.

"Thank you." Marion smiled, unsure whether Anne-Marie's congratulations were genuine or not.

Errol knew that what Anne-Marie was saying was true. He didn't condone men sleeping around, playing with people's feelings. And he knew that any woman who'd deliberately pick up a new man every time she wanted sex was heading for trouble. Why not just find a steady, reliable sexual partner, as he had? You agree on the boundaries, and if one or the other wants to break it up, it's up for discussion.

"So, what made you decide to stay a bachelor?" Anne-

Marie asked.

Errol dipped his eyes and appeared to study something in his drink. "Circumstance. I'm an ambitious, career-minded person. I haven't got time to fall in love and give a relationship what it deserves."

"Is that all?"

"Yeah. And in case you're wondering, it's not a physical problem."

A wry grin appeared on Anne-Marie's face. "But of course not! You are a black man."

Marion laughed as Errol's mouth dropped open. She knew that it was the AIDS-related death of one of his friends that had made him more careful with his sex life. And she was the only one who knew. Errol trusted her.

He quickly changed the subject. "Now Marion's nabbed you for her show I suppose I'll have to wait until the second book comes out before I can get you on mine."

"The public can wait, Errol. You can have me anytime…"

She still had that smirk on her face. Errol was sure she was scheming something.

Embarrassed for him, Marion cleared her throat. "Anyone for dessert?"

"Not for me, I'm dieting again."

Marion gave Anne-Marie a look, but didn't say anything.

Errol ordered his favourite hot chocolate fudge cake with cream, and then excused himself to go to the gents.

Anne-Marie couldn't wait for him to disappear from sight before quizzing Marion. "What do you think of Errol?"

Marion raised her eyebrows. "Errol?"

"Yes." Anne-Marie crossed one leg over the other and leaned back on her chair, her eyes turning to the ceiling dreamily. "Do you think he's interested in me?"

It wasn't the first time Anne-Marie had brought up the subject, but now it was beginning to get annoying.

Marion's brow creased. "I know you're interested…"

"That obvious, eh?"

"Anne-Marie, you can't stop talking about him!"

Anne-Marie sat forward on her chair, her elbows on her

knees. "But does he talk about me?"

Marion tutted and rolled her eyes. "Errol is a very private person. He wouldn't tell me who he's seeing or who he likes. As far as I know he's single and will stay that way until he meets a woman he can trust to fall in love with."

"So he's not gay then? Maybe he could do with a counsellor, a personal therapist. You know, to help him come to terms with opening up."

Again Marion frowned. This girl was *not* the one for Errol. "Errol is a close friend of mine, Anne-Marie. Leave him alone."

Anne-Marie smiled indulgently. "*Moi*? I wouldn't hurt a hair on his pretty head. I just want to know a little more about Mister Cool; it's my profession. He intrigues me."

"Just don't do anything underhand. If you're going to use him for your studies, make sure he knows about it."

Anne-Marie laughed sarcastically as she lifted her cappuccino to her lips.

Marion decided to let it go. "This psychologist you told me about — for the eating disorder programme…" Errol's a big boy, she was thinking — he can take care of himself.

Anne-Marie wasn't the first admirer, and most certainly she would not be the last.

When Errol returned to the table, Marion filled him in on what he had missed. "I was telling Anne-Marie about Black Networkers With Attitude. She's interested in joining."

"Yeah? Good. We can do with opinionated women."

"Well, I do speak my mind…"

"So I discovered." Errol caught her eyes again and felt the same bolt that had hit him that first morning. He wasn't sure what it was about Anne-Marie… something intriguing, something in her eyes. It wasn't a physical attraction, as he had first thought, but it was an attraction.

Marion felt a pang of jealousy. Errol had never looked at her like that. Anne-Marie wasn't even that pretty…

She stopped the train of thought. What was her problem? She was engaged to Paul.

She sighed. She and Errol were just good friends.

FOUR

"So where are we going again?" Karen flicked her cigarette butt out of the car and turned to the driver.

Yvette sighed exasperatedly. "We're gonna go back to look at that house in Croydon."

"What, the mansion?"

Yvette giggled and wound down the window, letting out the cigarette fumes that had accumulated inside her Cabriolet. "All right, so it's bigger than I was going for… but don't you think it suits me?"

"You mean like a leotard or a Lycra dress suits you?"

"Shut up, Kaz! I just have to see the inside of dat place, man. Read out what it says on that property sheet again."

Karen screwed up her mouth and gave her friend a crazy look, but she did as she was told, and reached behind her to retrieve the pages from the back seat. "Right, here we are…" She held the page in both hands, trying to steady it as Yvette took a corner at thirty miles an hour. "Built 1898… probably haunted," she mumbled.

"Just read the damned thing!"

"Semi-detached, halls adjoining, four storeys with mezzanine… Boy, it's one ah dem house wid stairs you don't need, innit?" She sucked her teeth and continued. "Four storeys, cellar… A cellar! In a house that old it's probably got bodies buried down there…"

"Will you stop criticising it until we actually see it!"

"Awright, awright. Chill…" Karen almost laughed. Her friend was so eager to get her own place and it had to be just right. Boy, this was worse than shopping for clothes with her! "Where was I? Yeah — cellar, lounge fifteen by fourteen, dining room, kitchen stroke breakfast room, four bedrooms, double-glazed and centrally heated… Like I said, a mansion. What you gonna do with four bedrooms?"

"You don't think I deserve a mansion?"

Karen raised her eyebrows and stared at her friend. "It's

not that, baby. You can't afford it."

"No harm in browsing." Yvette pulled a Tina Turner pout. "Even if it is to see what I'm missing."

The September wind whipped at their coats as they stepped out of the car. Yvette's dream house stood opposite, and for a few seconds they stood side by side and just stared at it.

"Well?"

Karen raised her hand to her hair, holding it back from her face. "Not bad, if you like that kind of thing."

Yvette hiked up her sleeve and checked her watch. "They're not going to be expecting us now, you know. But who cares? They wanna sell their house, don't they?"

They linked arms and crossed the road.

The door was answered by a woman in her forties with grey hair that dropped to her shoulders in a stylish bob. She looked down her nose at them. "Can I help you?"

Yvette put on her very best negotiating accent. "The estate agent sent us. Sorry we're late, we had a few to see today."

The woman was obviously taken in by it. "Oh, of course…" A smile cracked her face. "I'm afraid my husband isn't here, but I suppose I can show you around."

She stepped back to admit them into the gloomy hallway.

Brown wallpaper! Green doors! Who *were* these people — naturalists?

Karen turned to whisper to Yvette. "I suppose you could always brighten it up by painting a mural on it."

"Ha ha."

"We'll start upstairs, shall we? There's a lot to see."

They followed her up a flight of stairs to the first floor and the woman showed them a bedroom and a bathroom. "We had three children," she explained. "The last one left a year ago. The place is just too big for us now."

She opened the door to another, darker room. The walls were grey and the faded purple carpet was stained and worn. There was no furniture, just bags and boxes, packed and ready for removal. Yvette was thinking ahead. This could be a store room — too small for a bedroom, and not enough light for a study.

Karen gingerly lifted the grey net curtain that covered the small window, and got a view of the most beautiful garden she'd seen in a while. An apple tree stood in one corner, opposite a pond with love seats on either side. Despite a recent change in the weather, the lawn was still green. Because of the slope of the hill behind the house, you could see for miles over the tops of the other houses.

"You have a view."

Yvette rushed over and looked down at what Karen was excited about. "Wow!"

The bathroom was small, a tub and wash basin only, but the next floor up was more promising. Two rooms — one presumably a sitting room, the other a bedroom.

My bedroom, and study, Yvette thought. God, this is just so perfect!

The sitting room cum bedroom looked out onto the street from all four windows. It was at least fifteen foot by eighteen.

The woman went ahead of them, opening doors. On the top floor were the other bedrooms and another bathroom, fully equipped with a shower.

Back on the ground floor was a very quaint "country" kitchen, recently furnished with new cupboards and units and a fitted cooker and oven. Yvette nearly wet herself with excitement when she saw the basement. It spanned the length of the house. The floors were stripped and polished wood, as were the walls and ceiling. A gym — in her own home! With a bit of renovation she could even build a sauna!

Karen could see the euphoria on her friend's face as they drove back home. "You know it's going to cost a fortune to do up properly."

"Look at the outlay as a long-term investment," said Yvette. "I might never get another chance like this."

"And just where are you gonna get the extra ten grand?"

"I'll find it. My brother—"

"Your brother told you you were up to your limit in

loans, and the business can only handle the forty thousand for the shared ownership..." Karen suddenly grabbed Yvette's arm. "What are we thinking of? Why don't you just get lover-boy to move in?"

"Errol?"

"Mr Errol Wright himself. He's got money. You've been seeing him for... what, a year? Haven't you thought of living together?"

"Not really. It's not that kind of relationship."

"And why not? Do his feet smell? Don't he take care of you? He hates kids? What?"

"He's got his own house, and I've got my independence. It just never came up."

"Well bring it up, girl. You want that house, don't you? Tyrone would love it! You'd be a family again, in your dream home."

God damn it, Karen was right! Why hadn't she thought of going into this with Errol before? It would be the perfect arrangement.

Errol Wright, you are in for the treat of your life.

The Channel 6 building was modest by Canary Wharf standards, standing only ten storeys high, but every floor was taken up with the station's industries. Hundreds of offices, thousands of people, all sheltered under the Channel 6 umbrella.

The lights were on to dispel the September gloom, and for a second Anne-Marie felt a shiver of doubt as she stood outside, a sudden unnerving loss of confidence. She had previously only come to this building as a guest; never as an employee. A real, honest-to-goodness television researcher.

Squaring her shoulders, she walked through the familiar foyer. She was greeted by the security guard and the pretty-faced, expensively dressed woman who looked up from the reception desk and chimed, "Good morning."

She smiled back. She belonged here.

Sitting at her new desk, relaxing in a huge leather swivel

chair, she was thinking, This is it. Finally she had got into the world of television. Maybe it was behind the scenes, but there was always the chance — if she made the right contacts, and with her qualifications — of getting on the other side of the camera.

Her desk was heaped high with forms, files, reports, books, pens and notepaper. Such was the life of a researcher. Still, it hadn't been hard — with her references, her published book and her brilliant CV.

She had won a place as one of the programme's researchers. She shared an office with two others — but that wasn't a problem. After all, she didn't plan to be stuck behind a desk the whole time she was here.

Errol's dressing room was one floor beneath her.

She smiled to herself. Hers was a smile that made people want to smile back at her, but underneath it was a scheme — a scheme to get a man who was convinced he couldn't be got.

She had asked around about Errol Wright. No one knew who he was seeing. A very private man, he didn't socialise with anyone at work unless he had to. He did, in fact, live alone... even if he was seeing that bimbo from the wedding. But she was no match for Anne-Marie, a woman who knew how to get what she wanted.

Without Errol, this job meant nothing. The men she had been with in the past meant nothing.

But this one would. In her heart and soul she could feel it was right.

Errol's secretary Helen arrived promptly at half past nine every other weekday. She worked in Errol's self-made study, a small, light room upstairs, where she opened fan letters and other requests by mail, made phone calls and wrote letters that Errol didn't have time to do personally, and took messages off the answerphone, filtering any through to Errol that she thought he needed to deal with. She was extremely efficient. In her late forties, she had two grown-up children and an ex-husband. She had worked in the media field before, and so was perfectly experienced to deal with things on her own.

Errol got on with her very well. They even compared notes on the quick, easy recipes that their lifestyles required. She fitted into his life with ease. He was always interested in her stories about herself. She seemed to have led such a full life. She was a school governor, took regular keep-fit classes, held afternoon teas at her house, and was also a hospital volunteer and carer for housebound patients.

Wednesday's work was sorting the post into piles of fan mail, fan mail that needed a reply, requests for appearances, and refusals. Errol always liked to go through the correspondence with her once it was sorted.

That Wednesday was also the cleaner's morning in. Mrs Donaldson came only twice a week, on request. She was a strong-looking, slim woman in her mid sixties, with salt-and-pepper hair that she kept tied back in a bunny-rabbit ponytail and skin that could have been borrowed from a baby, it was so smooth.

That morning she didn't appear in a good mood. "What a mawnin!" she moaned. "Couldn't put me feet dem outta bed dis mawnin'. Cold! Times like dis me waan go 'ome."

Errol smiled warmly, used as he was to Mrs Donaldson's moans and groans. He was dressed in a cool linen shirt, worn loose outside his beige Armani trousers; his feet were slipped into beach sandals: his relaxing attire. "I was going to say 'Good morning', but I suppose it isn't for you."

She followed him down the hall to the kitchen, shrugging off the oversized coat she wore. Mrs Donaldson had been offered the job on the strength of the fact that she knew his family. She had cleaned for his mother, and had been given first refusal for whenever he needed a cleaner. So here he was, stuck with Mrs Chatterbox Gossip UK.

"Boy, de floor need a good scrub, eeh? Wha'appen? Yuh 'ave anudder party?"

"No, just Aaron."

"Ah, dat boy! Him mussi big now. My pickney, dem big

but dem nah leave 'ome. Big man, but dem love dem 'ome comfort. Boy, I was so tired dis mawnin' I coulda just stay in me warm bed. But you know I don't let nobody down if me healt' allow. You 'ave yuh breakfast yet? 'Cause if you want I can do the living room first an' come back in 'ere later…"

"As you wish. I'll be upstairs." Errol hurriedly exited and joined Helen reading through the mail.

"Looks as though someone's in love," she said as he walked into the room.

Errol raised an eyebrow. He couldn't imagine who she meant.

She held up a letter. "You have a new admirer."

Taking it from her hand, Errol sat at his desk. It was a laser-printed A4 sheet of pink paper, signed simply, "Yours":

> I don't quite know how to start, Errol. All I know for certain at the moment is that I love you. I know how that sounds, you're probably thinking who is this woman and what have you done to provoke the emotions I feel for you. It's simple. I am your number one fan, and you are my Mr Wright.
>
> The only problem is that it is much too early for me to introduce myself to you. But soon, I promise, we will be together.

Errol ran a hand over his bald head. "You're right. Any more like that?"

Helen stretched a hand out, palm down, and rocked it. "Some, but none proclaiming love."

"Bin job?"

"You might have thought that, but no. I have a file for the weird ones. You know, just in case it gets a little heavy… Some of them are totally harmless, but—"

"You mean I could be a celebrity with a stalker?" Now Errol laughed.

"Who knows? Trevor Macdonald has one."

He laughed louder. "Okay. File it, just in case."

A few minutes later, Errol was suddenly in need of a cup of coffee. He was about to send Helen, but when he looked up he saw she was far too busy. He would have to go downstairs himself and endure Mrs Donaldson's company.

She had finished the dishes and was scrubbing the floor on her hands and knees. As soon as she saw Errol in the doorway she began talking again as though she had just been switched on.

"Errol, you know what you need? One ah dem Vax, sump'n. Clean, polish, hoover, suck up water — everyt'ing. Me poor knee dem, every time me haffe get up again it tek a few minute before me feel right in the leg dem. An' the danger... I could slip an' cause serious damage to me ol' body."

"I'll look into it, okay?"

"You're a lovely man," she said, straightening herself with a palm in the centre of her back. "Not like de las' man I clean for. Ungrateful? Bwoy! 'Im couldn' even manage a fifty-pence bonus at Chris'mus time. An' 'im pickney did rude! The crying an' carry on..." She shook her head. "His wife did work at a college, I feget which one. I don't t'ink she did right in de head. Never see 'er widout a glass in 'er 'and and she wasn't drinking water—"

Errol poured hot water into his coffee. "Really..."

"They had tenants, treat the house like Deptford Market. De stink! Oh Lawd, if me did 'ave anudder job me woulda stop work fe dem."

Errol removed himself silently.

FIVE

John Everett sat at his desk, a cup of coffee and the *Daily Mail* in front of him, as Errol entered the office for his early-morning editorial meeting.

"Ah, Errol…" John, a young forty-something, looked up from his paper. "I have good news… the show has been re-commissioned for the spring."

"Well!" Errol grinned, unable to conceal his joy. "Shouldn't we be celebrating? Where's the rest of the team?"

"This is just between me and you for now. There are going to be a few changes…" John shifted uncomfortably.

Errol raised an eyebrow. "Changes?"

"New director, new team, new style, new slot."

Errol was perplexed, but it was still good news. "You know what's best. So long as my job's safe…"

"Certainly. You're our star. We'll have a full editorial meeting after I've briefed the individuals concerned. But I thought you should be the first to know. Now, let's talk about the guests for next week's show…"

Errol settled back and listened to his producer. The man had brought him this far and had plans to take him further. He couldn't knock it.

Later that day Errol was hurrying along, late for a pre-recording and trying to avoid the rain that was about to pour from the gathering storm clouds, when a female voice hailed him just as he reached the entrance to the studio building. Reluctantly he slowed and turned round.

Anne-Marie was hurrying up to him, high-heeled boots clacking on the concrete paving. His brow furrowed briefly before he eased his face into a relaxed smile.

"Hi! Fancy seeing you here."

"Hi yourself. I'm glad I caught up with you before the meeting this afternoon."

"The meeting… with the production team?"

"Yes."

Errol's eyes questioned her as they entered the lobby of the glass-fronted building.

"I've been offered a freelance job with the programme."

"*My* programme?"

"Yes."

Errol shrugged. It was already a small world, and as far as Anne-Marie Simms was concerned it was getting smaller.

"Well… being a qualified psychologist and author isn't all it's cracked up to be. I wanted to branch out."

"And Channel Six offered you a post?"

"We might be working together on a couple of proposed shows," Anne-Marie said as they stepped into the lift.

As the lift rose, Errol began to suspect that this was more than coincidence. Or was he becoming paranoid? All right, so she was Colin's ex, she knew Marion, and happened to get a job on his show's production team. Coincidence?

But Errol wasn't so full of himself to think that this woman was deliberately interweaving her life with his own. They stepped out into the corridor. "I'm going straight to studio two to do an audio recording," he said.

"Do you mind if I sit in? I'll be as quiet as a mouse."

She gave him that half-smile again, and Errol relaxed. She was one of the friendliest people he knew. It seemed she could fit in anywhere. What was his problem?

When they got to the studio Errol realised that he had forgotten part of the script he needed for the voice-over.

"Didn't you memorise it?" Anne-Marie asked.

"I wish," he sighed, running a hand over his head.

"Give me your keys. I'll go and pick it up if you like."

"Would you? Anne-Marie, you're a saint!" He fished his keys out of his pocket. "This is for the deadlock. The code for the alarm is…" He whispered, "one-seven-four-five."

"Okay everybody, let's start the editorial meeting…"

John Everett smiled briefly, took his seat and opened the

folder in front of him. The meeting was being held in a small conference room. Around the table sat the production staff (including the recently recruited Anne-Marie Simms), and Errol Wright.

Anne-Marie had been late, because she'd spent ten minutes in the ladies' getting her look just right. She'd wanted to look her best, to make an impression at her first meeting, and also to catch Errol's eye. Just yesterday she had relaxed her hair and bought some new make-up. She had power-dressed in a short red dress and suit jacket. Her hair was worn straight to her shoulders with a side parting, and she had ventured to wear heels. She had to admit she looked extremely confident.

Errol smirked but didn't say a word. He'd noticed Anne-Marie's transformation when she'd entered the room, and he had to admit that the woman had style and taste. Anyone could see it.

"First of all let me introduce to you the newest member of our research team, Anne-Marie Simms," John said.

He paused while everyone welcomed her, then continued. "With all the news in the media at the moment about stalkers, we're going to do a programme titled, Is Love a Disease? We'll be talking to people who have become obsessed with a partner, and examining the difference between healthy relationships and damaging ones."

There were nods from the team. Anne-Marie was smiling. It had been her idea.

"Aren't we covering old ground?" one of the production assistants said. "The love angle's been done over and over."

John looked at him. They were all looking at him.

Anne-Marie swallowed nervously. She'd imagined the idea would have the same thrill for them that it had for her. "Actually it hasn't ever been approached as an illness on a talk-show," she said. "Some shows have skirted around the issue, but never in any depth."

"I like it." Errol spoke up. "We could bring on the ordinary couples first, do a love at first sight angle then follow that with people who it went sour for, both the loved and the in love — and the obsessed…"

"Okay, what about an author?" another researcher asked. "A psychiatrist, maybe, and one of those people from marriage guidance — a counsellor. I've seen a book called *Women Who Love Too Much* — the author may be available."

"Yes!" John brought his hands together excitedly. "That's the right idea. Anne-Marie, you're a published psychiatrist, you must know a lot about this subject. "

"I do have quite a bit of material on it already," Anne-Marie said, trying to keep her expression neutral even though she was bubbling inside. "I'll see what I can dig up."

"Great! Theresa, let me have a list of potential guests A.S.A.P. Errol, are you okay with this?"

"Sure, John, this is exactly what the show needs. It certainly won't do the ratings any harm."

Anne-Marie gazed at him as if he'd just given her the honour of a pay rise.

John talked deadlines and times for the next meeting, then the team filed out, full of chatter, most of them making their way to the kettle. Anne-Marie waited by the door as Errol finished a conversation with John.

"Hi," she said, flipping her hair over her shoulder deliberately.

"Hello," Errol said gently. "How are you settling in?"

Anne-Marie switched her folder to her other arm and they walked towards the lifts together. "Pretty good. They seem a very organised team."

"Only the best. And you know you wouldn't have got the job if they didn't feel you would fit in."

They joined the small queue by the elevators. Anne-Marie was looking at his strong chin, and as he turned to face her she averted her eyes, suddenly unable to take the full force of his weakening gaze.

"How are you fixed for tomorrow night?" she asked.

Errol flipped open the organiser he was carrying. "I'm free," he said, somewhat surprised. These days the words "free time" hardly ever entered his vocabulary.

"Well, how about that dinner you promised me?"

She was asking him out; this time there was no mistake. Errol actually froze for a few seconds as his brain processed this information. He'd be going against the lessons he had taught himself. "Tomorrow night…"

"I thought we could discuss the programme. You could fill me in on what it entails — you know, from first-hand experience. If it's too short notice—"

"No. No, it'll be fine." It was work. he told himself. Work, dinner, and good company. No problem. "You know where I live. Shall we say seven thirty?"

"Great. I'll bring a bottle."

The elevator arrived and Errol stepped in. Turning round, he smiled at her. "See you then."

She waved her fingers at him as the lift closed, leaving her staring at her own reflection in the door.

Yvette looked across the dinner table at her son. Tyrone was shovelling spaghetti bolognese into his mouth and hardly chewing before swallowing.

"Tyrone, I got a call from your school today."

The boy looked up from the comic by his plate, one eyebrow raised in question.

"You know why, don't you?"

Tyrone sighed, and then continued to chew indifferently.

"Tyrone, I'm talking to you."

"Yeah, I know."

Yvette dropped her fork on her plate. This wasn't like her son at all, being so unresponsive and rude. She grabbed the comic from under his eyes and dashed it towards the bin. "Then explain yourself!"

Tyrone wasn't sure how to respond. Torn between continuing with his dinner and leaving the table, he stared stubbornly at his mother.

"You've been hopping classes. Why?"

He shrugged. "Boring."

"Boring! What exactly do you find so boring?"

He shrugged again.

"You have a nervous twitch or sump'n?"

No response.

"Tyrone!" his mother warned.

"I just can't take some classes."

"You can't take them? What's stopping you?"

"I just don't like them."

"Are you being bullied?"

He looked at her as if she were asking him if he'd wet himself. "Course not."

"Then I don't care how boring the classes are — you have no choice in it. If you're having trouble with what you're being taught, or the teacher, then talk to someone. Your headmaster, for instance—"

"He's a batty man."

Yvette raised an eyebrow. "Don't use that language in front of me! I don't care if he's from Mars and sleeps with sheep. His job is to teach, and he's concerned about you."

"Yeah, well…"

"Well what?"

"I won't skip any more classes, okay?"

"You promise?"

He nodded.

"Good, 'cause I don't want to have to follow you around school to make sure you go. But if I get any more calls like this, that's exactly what I'm going to do."

Tyrone knew his mum wasn't messing. She never made threats; she promised — and never broke her promises. "Can I go now?"

"One more thing. I've asked Mr Peters to send home the work you've missed over the past month, which means extra homework."

"Mum!"

"What? Did you expect to get away with it?"

He stamped his way out of the kitchen.

"Make sure you do your homework before you do anything else," Yvette called after him. "I want to see it before you go to bed!"

She started to clear the table. Bringing up a young man

on her own wasn't easy. Tyrone was very moody and withdrawn these days. Also he was shooting up in height. She had no idea how she was going to cope with him when he became a teenager, an adolescent, a man…

She would just have to take it in her stride; after all, she was his mother.

Errol gave his evening squash game his all, and by the end of the session he was aching. It felt good, though; he'd needed a release of tension, and that was what he had got.

His partner Chris Stevens always gave him a good match. He was a fitter player than Errol, and tonight he was surprised at his opponent's vigour. "I know you said you was feeling good tonight, but you really had me running back there. Something happen today?"

"I'll give you one guess."

"It's a woman, ain't it?"

Errol looked at his friend as though he were a mind-reader. "This is between me and you, okay?"

"Okay. You know I was planning to call the tabloids up as soon as I left this place," Chris laughed. "You still seeing Yvette?"

"Yeah, and everything's going good."

"Yeah, so it's Yvette that's given you a high?"

"I ain't saying I'm seeing someone else…"

"So what *are* you saying?"

"There's this woman — at work. She's got a body that is so… I don't know, feminine, you know. She has this air of vulnerability, but she's also cool, detached. All we've done so far is have lunch and talked, but I feel so good around her… and it's not sexual. She makes me feel special."

Now Chris was intrigued. "What — we talking falling in love here?"

"Hey man, you know me better than that."

"Then we're talking sex?"

"No… I don't know." Errol knew how it must sound. He was still confused about how Anne-Marie affected him. He knew it was something he hadn't felt before, not even with Yvette. It was weird. "I'm not saying I wouldn't sleep with her. She's *fine*! But I'm seeing Yvette. This woman is just going to be a friend, a colleague. She's coming to dinner at my house, and nothing is going to happen."

"You know how many times I hear guys say that? 'We just gonna chat.' Next thing you know they're getting married."

"Chris — listen to me, man. I can't read the future, but you know my motto..."

"Yeah, yeah: never get involved with colleagues. But I know men, like you know women. You can't 'just be friends' with a woman. It might happen by accident — you know, your arm brushes against her breast, you both bend down to pick something up and accidently come into contact, you fall asleep with each other and wake up naked..."

Errol was shaking his head.

"I'm serious!" Chris insisted. "Once it's happened — if it was any good — there's no reason why it shouldn't happen again. I think you should find out exactly what she wants from you before you make the assumption that all she wants is to be friends." He slapped Errol on his bare shoulder. "Why do you keep trying to be friends with them, man?"

"Because I *know* them, I listen to them. I know what a woman wants, and they can sense that. Why shouldn't men and women be friends?"

"If you succeed in this new venture of yours, you should write a book: *How To Be 'Just Good Friends'*. You could be rich, man..."

Chris pulled his shirt down over his torso. He could already see the outcome of this little liaison: "tears and swears" was what he would call it, the swears being the man swearing he'll never get involved again, the woman providing all the tears.

62

SIX

"Daddy, where's all my toys gone? I can't find nothing."

Errol wiped his hands on his striped apron and put the wooden spoon down in a saucer. He turned to his seven year old son. "Aaron, I told you. I have bought you a toy box — the one shaped like a bench, with the clowns on it. They're all in there."

A grin spread on Aaron's face and he shoved his hands into his jeans pockets before replying shyly, "Thank you," then turning and dashing up the stairs to his room. Fair-skinned, like his mother, with the miniaturised figure of his father, Aaron was a very handsome boy. And he was always dressed in the most up-to-date fashion. Money was nothing when it came to Errol Wright's son.

Aaron had been dropped off by his mother an hour ago, even though Errol had told her he had a date tonight.

"Are you actually going out?" she'd demanded.

"No," he had answered.

"So why can't you have him? It's not as though he'll be any bother. Jus' make him promise to keep out of the way. I do."

Tanya was being her usual self-centred self. Errol had agreed to look after him for the night and take him back in the morning. It meant that the boy would have to eat with him and Anne-Marie — which was really no problem, since they were doing nothing more than having dinner and a pleasant evening of conversation.

He could have done without the extra work, though. It had been a hard enough day in the studio, recording another show. He'd gone back to his dressing room afterwards, and had frozen in the doorway. There, on the counter cluttered with tubes and jars of make-up, boxes of tissues and cotton wool, paper cups and bottles of water, had sat a huge bouquet of flowers. Errol had smiled as he'd slowly opened the envelope, thinking they had to be from an admirer, maybe Marion or Yvette.

Two words. That was all. No signature, no name.

"Soon, Errol."

He'd dropped the card in the bin and left the flowers there. Maybe one of the cleaners would appreciate them.

Errol removed the lid from a pot of meat, and the steam escaped as the memory faded. So, he had a fan with money. No problem.

The doorbell rang, and as Errol looked at his watch he heard Aaron's feet on the stairs.

"I'll get it, Dad!"

"Aaron! You don't know who it is." He untied his striped apron and hung it on the hook behind the kitchen door. Rubbing his hands together, he went to let his guest in.

Anne-Marie turned to face him as he swung the door open.

"Good evening."

She wore a long overcoat and matching hat. Errol stepped back to let her into his home and she handed him the bottle she held in her gloved hands.

"Thank you. I'm afraid we have an extra guest for dinner. This is Aaron, my son."

Aaron was now standing behind his father, trying to get a good look at Anne-Marie before she spotted him. With surprise in her eyes, Anne-Marie stretched out a hand to the little boy.

"Hi! My name is Anne-Marie."

Aaron looked up at his dad, waiting for the nod that said it was okay to shake.

She helped Errol prepare the vegetables for dinner while she chatted about her relatives' cooking and her own cooking skills. Over dinner Errol quizzed her on her interviewing skills.

"Well, one vital ingredient is to be prepared — know the subject inside out."

Errol swallowed a mouthful of wine to wash some of the salmon starter down. "Good one. I learnt that from John. I always try to do a little research myself, however many researchers I have on the show."

"What are your secret tips for interviewing?" she asked him.

Errol put his fork down and picked up his glass, resting his elbow on the table. "Well, you've got to *like* people — or find something about each person to like. I think that's the key. Once people know you like them it comes across. People will forgive you even the toughest questions, *and* they will answer them. Have enthusiasm, curiosity, and the ability to laugh, especially at yourself. And be as open as possible. I occasionally reveal bits of myself on screen..."

Anne-Marie giggled.

"... Not physical bits, of course, but personal things. Look at Oprah's empathy. She's accessible. It's the same with Rikki Lake."

They had been so deep in conversation that they hadn't noticed Aaron nodding off. His face was nearly resting on his half-empty plate.

Errol looked at his watch. "It's well past his bedtime."

He told the sleepy boy to go and get ready for bed, and to give him a shout when he was ready.

Anne-Marie touched her napkin to the corner of her mouth as she watched the youngster make his way out of the room. "Can I read to him? He likes bedtime stories, doesn't he?"

"Of course. Although his mother and I don't get too much time to read to him."

"My parents were the same. You don't mind, do you? I mean, you can sit in on it if you like."

"No, that's okay. He'll enjoy it — you go ahead."

Errol began to clear the table and loaded the dishwasher.

Anne-Marie was gone for half an hour. Every now and then Errol would hear Aaron laugh. He smiled, glad that his son was taking to Anne-Marie. She was turning out to be a good friend to have — and she wasn't bad to look at.

Relaxing in the living room after Aaron had gone to sleep, they started to talk more personally as they finished off a second bottle of Chablis.

"He's a great kid. Just like his dad."

"Thank you. Did he do that kiss thing he does — where he pretends he's going to kiss your cheek and then smooches you?"

"Yeah, he did." Anne-Marie smiled. "I suppose you taught him that one."

Errol laughed, giving away nothing.

"Do you remember your first kiss?" she asked, her legs stretched out on the sofa, her stockinged toes pointing to the ceiling.

"Yes, as a matter of fact I do," Errol said from his spot on the floor, his back against the armchair. "It was with a very young-looking two year old with pigtails. My mum made me kiss her so she could take a picture of us. I was about four or five at the time."

Anne-Marie giggled and jabbed a finger at him in jest. "You cad! Taking advantage of the young, even at that age…"

"Who me?" He laughed with her. "No, but seriously — my first teenage kiss was with Tracey Cole, at about… thirteen. I'd fancied her for ages, you know, since we'd started secondary. She was one of these girls who was the leader of the gang." Errol's eyes turned to the ceiling as he reminisced. "Always had the latest fashion, family had two cars, she wore about three gold chains round her neck, fastest on the track… You know the type — the most popular girl in school."

"I know the type," Anne-Marie said with feeling. It had been that type of girl who'd bullied her and made her an outcast. She remembered her schooldays well. "And I suppose you were the school's most popular boy?"

He smiled coyly, "Well, you know… not far off it."

"So, how did this first kiss happen?"

"We used to hang out together after school. I'd wait outside the gates with my boys and she would come along with her girls and we would all walk together, catch joke, check them out, you know."

"But all the while you were trying to get close to her?"

"Yeah." He shook his head and smiled at the memory. "One night I casually asked her to meet me outside the chippy after dinner. She asked if she should bring a friend, and I said no. I remember I had this real serious look on my face, you know, like I was trying to psyche her into reading my mind. Well it must have worked, 'cause she came alone."

Anne-Marie turned over on her side to face him.

"We just went for a walk round the park. I bought her chips and a Coke and boasted about what my family had. We had that in common, at least — our families were both professionals. By the end of the night, standing at her front door, I knew I wanted to kiss her, that I couldn't let her go without kissing her."

"Did you ask permission?"

"Naw, man! That woulda been death to my credibility. She turned round to say goodnight and I just dived at her face, nearly breaking both our noses."

They laughed together as Errol refilled their glasses.

"What about you? When was yours?"

"Oh, I was a lot older than thirteen. I kissed my first man at the ripe old age of twenty."

"*No!* What — a looker like you?"

"It's nice of you to say so, but it took hard work to get to look this good. Mum wouldn't let me wear make-up or relax my hair. She wouldn't let me out if she suspected I was seeing a man."

"Strict upbringing. Exactly how I would bring up my daughter."

Anne-Marie grabbed a cushion and threw it across at him. "Luckily I had no brothers, so I couldn't judge whether I was being treated unfairly by my parents. But when the other girls at school or at college would brag about their dates and their boyfriends buying them gifts, I would become insanely jealous."

"Describe your first kiss."

"Do I have to? I promise you it was nothing spectacular."

"Have you ever had a spectacular kiss?"

"Of course! Anyone who has been in love has had a spectacular kiss."

"Then describe that one to me."

"Errol Wright! What is this — research for your show?"

He shrugged, his face now serious. "Maybe. Stand up for me."

She gave him a look of curiosity, but stood up anyway.

He followed. "I am going to describe a perfect kiss to you. Just how a first kiss should be. Do you trust me?"

"Errol, you're a man, I'm a woman, practically alone and drunk... Of course I don't trust you."

"Then pretend to trust me just for a couple of minutes." He took her hand and led her to the middle of the floor. She wondered what he was up to but didn't want to break the spell. Something was happening here, and if he was feeling what she was feeling she wanted it to carry on happening.

"Close your eyes," he told her.

Anne-Marie giggled. "Why, what are you going to do? Walk out of the room and leave me standing here?"

"Trust me. Close your eyes — or I'll have to find a blindfold."

Anne-Marie breathed deeply, feeling a chilling excitement. She did as she was told with a sigh.

"Okay. Ready?"

She nodded.

"It starts here," Errol said, gently touching her lips with his fingers. "And here..." He placed the palm of one hand on her heart, just above her nipple. "And here..." A glancing touch against her belly. His voice was low, persuasively calming. She could feel his breath on her face, sweetly scented with wine.

"Think about a kiss..." He moved closer, so close his body was almost touching hers.

"I am," she replied. God, was she thinking about it.

His warm hands cupped her face, fingers gently stroking the curve of her cheeks. She shivered, wanting to press herself closer to him.

"When a boy wants a girl, when he wonders if that girl

wants him, he kisses her first with his eyes, tests the texture of her skin, the shape of her lips, matching it mentally to his own…" His hands moved to her neck. "Kissing your body with his eyes, tasting you in his mind…" His hands were on her shoulders. "Exploring you…" His hands moved down her arms, so impossibly light through the satin of her blouse that it was somehow more erotic than if he were touching her skin. She could feel the hairs on the back of her neck rising.

"He's wondering what lies underneath," Errol continued, "picturing your breasts, sucking them in his mind, feeling your nipples harden to the touch of his tongue."

She couldn't see him, but Errol had a wicked smirk on his lips and an erection that was aching in his pants. He remained, however, firmly in control. His hands, now on her hips, began to rise again, retracing his steps over her upper arms and shoulders, just missing her nipples. He could feel every tremor of her body. The vibrations coming from her felt almost like electricity.

Anne-Marie's breathing was deep and erratic. Her fingers clenched and unclenched, wanting to reach out for him — but this was his game, he played the lead. He had barely touched the silky satin over her breasts, but her nipples were hard, aching for his mouth. She could feel herself getting wet, a swelling heat between her legs.

"He'll be teasing you just a little, daring you…" His hands moved down, flirting with the waistband of her trousers, roving lower to the swell of her sex. "… tonguing you with his eyes, finding the curves your clothes hide, wondering how you will taste when he finally licks you…"

Anne-Marie audibly moaned and pushed her mound into the palm of his hand, but he was already moving on. His hands ran over the swell of her hips, then slipped gently away to trace the line of her thigh, the slender length of her calf. He knelt down in front of her, his head now level with her belly, his mouth so close she could feel his breath on her skin.

He watched her face from where he rested on knees. His voice was so soft now that she had to strain to hear it. "... Screwing you with his eyes before he kisses you with his mouth."

She felt a sudden impulse to reach out and touch him, draw his head between her thighs, knowing that his whispers against her sex would be enough to make her come instantly.

Almost as though he was reading her mind, Errol rose and took her hands in his. They stood with their lips almost touching. She could sense the heat of his body; she knew that the first touch of his lips would have the same effect as if he had gone down on her.

"See? You can get all those things from a single glance, a look."

She was shivering with physical intensity.

"So that's it," he said matter-of-factly. "A first kiss. Open your eyes, Anne-Marie."

She did as he asked, suddenly too aware that he wasn't going to complete his demonstration.

He was smiling ironically as he walked across the room and sat down, crossing his legs. Seething with frustration she took a sip of wine and excused herself to go to the bathroom.

Did he *know* what he'd just done? Was this a game — his form of foreplay? Because if it was, he was very good at it and she couldn't wait to get back downstairs for more.

She splashed her face with water, dried it and freshened herself up.

Thinking Errol would be waiting in anticipation for her downstairs, she exited the bathroom to find him waiting in the hall.

"I've put the electric blanket on in the spare room, and put towels on the bed for you."

Noticing the puzzled look on her face, he added, "You're welcome to stay; I wouldn't let you have to wait around for a cab." He kissed her cheek. "Good-night. I'll see you in the morning."

And he was gone before she could even reply.

The next morning Errol woke slowly to the smell of cooking. He made his way downstairs, pulling on his short white dressing gown, and experienced a curious feeling of *déjà vu* as he entered the kitchen. Anne-Marie had her back to him; she was wearing the shirt he'd had on last night, and was singing as she cooked eggs. Her relaxed hair had been brushed smooth so that it hung straight to her shoulders, the morning sun making it appear lighter in colour. His eyes travelled down past her buttocks to her very strokable bare legs. He was tempted to creep up behind her and put his arms round her, but he knew by now that he should fight temptation.

"Good morning," he said, leaning against the door jamb.

"Good morning! How do you like your eggs?"

"None for me, thanks. Look, I think you ought to go. You know — with Aaron here I don't want him to get the wrong idea."

"What possible idea could a seven year old get? Besides, can't a friend cook a friend breakfast now?"

"Yes, but—"

"No buts. You cooked me a delicious dinner, and I want to repay you."

"That's not necessary. Besides, we had a late night and I'm sure you want to go home and freshen up... before work, I mean."

She stepped seductively towards him. "We both know you don't want me to leave."

This wasn't what he'd intended. He should give up the drink — sometimes it made him a little too loose. He knew he had been giving off the wrong signs last night. Maybe Chris was right: you couldn't just be friends with a woman. "We both have work..." he said.

"Okay," she laughed, "then why don't I fix us a packed lunch? Cooked meats, cold salads, French bread..."

"Sounds more like a picnic to me."

"It can be whatever you want it to be. And Aaron would love it."

Errol sighed and took a step back. She was obviously after more than a platonic friendship. "I'm taking him home today. I'll drop you off after I drop him if you like."

Anne-Marie's face clouded over.

"I don't think your being here is a good idea."

"Too much too soon?"

He shrugged non-commitingly, though he knew he was hurting her feelings.

"No problem," she said, and left him to get dressed.

Throughout a man's adult life he has to put up with rejection time and time again. Any man who has had to ask a woman for a dance in a nightclub knows the feeling. The women who do the rejecting seem unaware of the harm they are doing, and yet when it comes to their turn they can't handle it. It is as though the man should feel so honoured to be offered her body that he shouldn't be able to refuse.

Well, sometimes things don't happen that way.
Errol wished he had put Anne-Marie in a cab last night. What had he been thinking?

They drove most of the way to Tanya's home in silence. Errol stayed in the car as he watched Aaron knock on the front door and wait. A minute later the boy's mother answered it. Errol waved his son goodbye, and the door closed behind him.

Anne-Marie tried to make conversation as they drove on, but Errol wasn't in the mood. He liked her — she was a good conversationalist, and they had some laughs together; it also helped that she got along with his son — but there was Yvette to consider.

SEVEN

"You hear 'bout Predator?"

Dean looked up from his cards. "What?"

"Went to Nations las' week…" Fits of laughter from Colin. "… Come out wid six numbers and thought it was 'im lucky night!" He rolled about on the sofa.

"Nations! Naw, you know what dem call dat place, innit? Dungeons and Dragons!"

"Me know, me know! The guy called t'ree ah dem an' all were mashed, guy!" Colin 'licked' wood.

"What did I tell you about that place? Only desperados rave in Nations. Night pretties paradise." Dean threw his legs over the side of the armchair. "One gyal I know was boastin' how she come out wid nuff numbers. I turn roun' and show her how easy it was. Called this gyal over from 'cross de road, y'know? Didn't even bother wid any chat, an' she han' over her number quick-time. Soon as her back was turn me dash it weh. Easy, man. Nation!" He wrinkled his brow in disgust.

"It's true! You ever hear of anyone meeting their woman in there?"

"No! A ride, yes — but you could nevah tek one out seriously."

"You know Predator. The guy's probably still trying the other t'ree numbers."

"He needs to fix himself up and tek care ah dat bad breat' before he even t'ink about checkin' woman."

Dean never minced words. If you wanted an honest opinion, just ask him. There had been times when his down-to-earth, blatant comments had lost him friends, but he didn't care; as far as he was concerned, if they didn't want to hear the truth they shouldn't ask.

Dean's flat was a cosy bachelor pad in Elephant and Castle. The living room and kitchen took up one space, separated only by a counter. The other rooms in the flat were the bathroom and bedroom. Still, it suited him just fine — he was planning on living on his own for as long as possible.

His apartment had seen more women come and go than hot dinners. Standing six foot one, with a caramel complexion, perfectly squared jaw and elongated almond-shaped eyes (he described himself as a Chinese black man), Dean knew he was irresistible to women even before they heard his deep, gravelly voice. Unfortunately his attitude occasionally got the better of him, and women sometimes didn't stick around for very long, whether he wanted them to or not.

He poured himself another shot of Cockspur and leant back against the sofa. "So, Errol say he's coming tonight?"

"Yeah, man."

Dean picked up the remote control and started the CD playing again, and the cool tones of Adina Howard floated through the room. "Y'know what he said to me the other day? The reason he don't rave too tough now is cause he's always getting noticed. He can't relax."

Dean, who had known Errol since school, missed the old times. He had enjoyed their old kick-back-roll-a-spliff-and-check-gyal days. Everyone seemed to be pairing off, meeting their soul mates, getting important jobs, buying property, taking on responsibility and cutting themselves off from their old lives. And soon, he surmised, he'd be raving alone — unless *he* met a soul mate too.

"He's bullshitting," Colin said. "He loves all dat. He's still raving, jus' moving wid a diff'rent crowd." He took a gulp of wine, shaking his head. "No, man. Errol ain't into that high-and-mighty t'ing. He's still my homie, y'know what I'm saying?"

"He may be dat, but my man ain't checking de punnany no more."

"Who tell you dat?" Colin's tone showed he was ready to defend his long-time spar against any derogatory remark.

"You don't hear what people are saying? He ain't sticking it to women."

Colin shot straight up, rum spilling onto his fingers from

his glass. "I know my man. He's got a woman!"

Dean laughed, deep and resonant. "You should see your face!" He swung his legs to the floor. "Boy oh boy!" He shook his head, still chuckling as he crossed to the kitchen area.

Colin visibly relaxed. Dean was always winding people up. He swung the peak of his baseball cap to the back of his head and breathed out. "Errol's checking all right. He's just keeping it under cover 'cause of his career."

Dean pulled open the fridge. "You wanna sandwich?"

"What you got?"

"What you t'ink this is, a restaurant?"

"I don't eat everything, you know, not like you guts," Colin retorted.

Dean wasn't a fussy eater, and he ate plenty. But dressed in a string vest and boxer shorts he showed not an ounce of fat.

"Ham, cheese, or both?"

"You doin' it in that toasting thing?"

"Sandwich maker, yeah."

"Gimme ham and cheese then."

Colin reached for the cable control, but before his fingers could touch it Dean blasted him: "Leff it deh! How many time me haffe tell you nuh touch me t'ings!"

"I was only—"

"I don't care! Anyt'ing goes wrong wid it I've gotta replace de damn t'ing, so leff it!"

"Bwoy, you're worse than a woman..."

Dean didn't give a damn about Colin's opinion. He'd grown up in a house with three elder brothers, and everything he'd ever had had belonged to all of them before, including his clothes. Now he had his own possessions he made sure no one took liberties with them.

The intercom buzzed and Colin looked to Dean before even thinking of answering it.

"Get the door nuh!"

Dean slapped a slice of ham on top of a slab of cheese and completed the sandwich with another slice of bread. He heard two men's conversation as they came back into the living room: Colin's excited and full of news; Errol's cheerful, laughing.

Errol appeared in the doorway dressed in a cream sweater and black jeans, jacket slung over his shoulder. He looked ready to go out raving. "Dean…" He nodded at his mate before hanging his jacket on the back of the door.

"Awright, man. Long time…"

"You know how it goes."

"I wish," Dean humphed.

"Hear dis, brudda. You t'ink what I do is easy?"

"Easier than lugging wood all day. You get paid to ponce about in a suit and chat to heartbroken people. Gimme dat any day."

"Jus' walk t'rough the door an' this is what I get!" Errol threw himself onto the sofa. "So, what we having for dinner?"

"Dinner! I jus' done tell dis brudda dis ain't no restaurant. The only reason he's getting food is 'cause I don't eat without offering. You come too late, man." Dean put Colin's sandwich on a plate and chucked it onto the counter, signalling his friend to come and get it.

Errol let it go. "Bring us a glass when you're coming — I might as well get a drink. By the way, whose turn is it to drive?"

"It ain't me!" Dean said, sure of himself. "Since we ain't been nowhere wid you fe months, you can." He watched Errol's hand drop from the bottle of rum, his face drop with it.

"Naw, man. You can't do this. I need a drink."

"Look, jus' cool. I'll drive, all right?" Colin offered.

"You pussy!" Dean spat. He handed Errol a glass and resumed his favourite chair.

"Wha' you dissing the man for? If he wants to drive, let him. You gonna argue wid that, you drive!"

"You know he's only doing it to suck up to you."

"Suck up… Wha'!" Colin spluttered. "Errol an' me go way back! He'd do the same for me."

"Yeah, whatever, man. Cho…" Dean bit into his sandwich and swung his legs back over the arm of the chair.

"Why don't you get a recliner?" Errol suggested.

"You payin' for it?"

Errol cocked an eyebrow but didn't answer. He knew Dean well enough to recognise that, despite his brash attitude, he was a good mate. They were guaranteed a good time with him in tow.

When they were at college together, Errol and Dean had found that between them they made one massive talking machine. The both of them were tall, good-looking and intelligent, with sex appeal that didn't need turning on. While Errol had studied hard, Dean had studied woman. He'd had no problem in getting them, and he had taken advantage of his God-given talent… until he'd met Pauline. Pauline had been hard to land, and when he'd finally got her she'd told him that their affair was to be no fling. She'd heard about his reputation and wasn't planning on being just another lay. Before long he was totally hers.

After a year or so his friends had started telling him he'd got it bad. He'd brushed their comments aside. Two years, and he'd begun to realise that he was in love. Three, and they were living together.

Eight years, and Dean's life fell apart. Pauline's best friend had told him that his girlfriend was having an affair. She'd said she liked Dean too much to carry on lying for her.

Dean had confronted Pauline, she'd admitted it, and he'd moved out. Her best friend was the first bedding of his new, swinging bachelor life.

"So, where's this place we're going?" Errol looked from one man to the other.

Colin licked crumbs from his lips. "Earl's."

"The wine bar?"

"Yeah. It's a nightclub and restaurant too. It's all right, you know. I was there about a month ago."

"Yeah, I hear it's kicking some nights." Errol leant back and studied Colin's profile. His friend was thirty, married, and he looked good on it. Not that there's anything wrong with the way I look, he told himself — but it just showed that settling down doesn't do you any harm.

"So, Mister Superstar, nice to see you still 'ave time fe we lickle people," Dean teased.

"Time! The only thing I know 'bout time is dat I don't have any to myself any more."

"I hear dat," Colin put in. Dean cut his eye after him.

"You know," Errol continued, "it's like I get up, grab two food, then head out. I got meetings, rehearsals, recordings, interviews, photo sessions, more meetings... plus I gotta find time for my women and my son. My whole life is one big schedule."

Dean chuckled sarcastically.

"You wanna say somet'ing, D?"

"No, not really... but I'm just making an observation here, right?"

Errol opened his arms as if to say, "Go on."

"You're living in a three-bedroom house in Mitcham, right? You drive a brand new car, you have over ten set ah suit an' a pair ah shoes fe go wid each ah dem. You're wining and dining models and TV stars, you 'ave woman ready fe drop dem baggy fe you. Correct me if I'm wrong..."

"Yeah — so?"

"What the hell yuh ah worry 'bout time for?"

Errol had to laugh. Looking at his life from someone else's perspective was a great exercise. He had to admit he enjoyed his work, and the money was giving him and his family a life of luxury. For the first time in his life he had something in the bank. If his only worry was finding time to sit and think, then compared to most people he had none.

"I know what Errol is saying." Colin, who had been quietly taking it all in, knew what not having time for yourself felt like. "When me and the guys were touring with the football team, I had two evenings a week to myself, that is nothing. An' in those two nights all I wanted to do was sleep."

Errol was nodding.

"I didn't want to call up my spar or woman to come keep

me comp'ny; all I wanted was my bed."

Dean snorted. "People like you don't deserve to have money and fame. You cyan't handle it. Now, if it was me, I'd be on the ball twenty-four-seven wid me stamina an' t'ing. I wouldn't care if I never see my bed again, 'cause all it would mean is dat I'd be sharing someone else's."

Errol and Colin shared a laugh. Dean was jealous. It was so obvious it was pitiful. But they couldn't tell him that — he'd only twist it up and throw it back at them.

The countdown had reached five minutes. Dressed in a short red velvet dress, the woman poured two glasses of wine then replaced the bottle in the refrigerator. On her way through the hallway she checked her hair in the mirror. She liked it this way; she'd noticed men liked it too. Every Wednesday was her day at the hairdresser's. Her appointment gave her enough time to get back home so that she wouldn't miss him.

Satisfied that she looked good, she entered her living room. The curtains were drawn against the night, and the only light came from the television screen. The commercials were still running — yet another advert for yet another fast car. The type of car *he'd* drive.

Her favourite armchair was directly facing the TV. A small cocktail table stood on the floor next to it. On this she placed a glass of wine before sitting in the empty chair and curling her legs into its warm comfort.

Holding the stem of her glass between two fingers, she sipped the chilled liquid. Impatiently she watched yet another gimmicky ad, then finally the multi-coloured trademark of Channel 6 came on the screen. She reached for the remote control with a delicate hand, holding down the volume button until the surround sound engulfed her.

The signature tune of *Do the Wright Thing* sent goosebumps prickling their way over her bare arms. Then there he was. Still shots of the man she craved flickered on the screen, smart visual effects making them spin, flip over and change in an instant.

She hadn't realised, but her pulse rate had quickened and her breathing had become a touch heavier.

The show started. The studio audience, not realising how lucky they were to be in the same room as him, applauded, whistled and cheered as Errol Wright appeared on the stage.

She shivered with anticipation. Here was the man of her dreams, everything she had always wanted. He was heartbreakingly handsome, caring, sensitive, mature… and with it, humorous and open. His body was that of an athlete — finely toned, the skin smooth and fresh-looking. He was smiling modestly as he sauntered across the screen to greet his audience. The camera came in for a close-up, and Errol Wright raised the microphone to his mouth.

The woman found her throat had gone dry, and she lifted her glass to sip again from the wine.

"Good evening… and thank you…" Errol Wright addressed both studio audience and camera. "… Thank you for joining me once again on the most talked-about show since Oprah."

His voice was that of a trained journalist and entertainer: demanding, coercing his audience's attention with ease. If only he knew how much she wanted him.

She stood slowly, almost like a snake uncoiling and moving in for the kill. Her glass still in her hand, she smoothed her dress over her hips and padded barefoot across the room until she was standing in front of the screen, where Errol Wright had begun to introduce his guests.

She knelt, her nose a few inches from the glass. "Tell me what you like, baby," she whispered. "Tell me what you want from me. I want to be your everything."

Oblivious to his admirer's lust, Errol was chatting to a young black man who was about to confess to his best friend that he was gay.

Tears formed in her eyes and trickled down her cheeks. A single drop fell into her glass, causing no more than a tiny ripple.

"I'll make you notice me!" she wailed. "Why can't you

see me?"

"Bobby, I've got something to tell you," the young man was saying. He swallowed and looked to Errol, who reassured him with a nod and a smile. "Bobby, the reason you never see me with no women is 'cause... I'm... I'm gay."

Bobby jumped away from the young man as though it was catching.

Gulping the rest of her wine, the woman screamed at the television, where the audience had gone wild: "Love me, damn you! I... love... you!"

Finally, exhausted by her emotions, Anne-Marie crumpled into a sobbing heap in front of the television, ruining her new hairdo, and the glass fell from her hands.

The scenario had been the same ever since Errol's first show. It had originally started with a photograph in *The Voice* newspaper. Anne-Marie recognised the handsome new TV personality and had racked her brain to remember where from, becoming more desperate to meet him the more she tried to recall where she'd seen the guy. When it had finally come to her it had all seemed so easy: she simply had to get in touch with Colin, tell him how lonely she was, and remind him that she wasn't doing anything at weekends, tell him she was available for parties, get togethers... oh, and whatever happened to that friend of yours, Errol Wright?

She had known all along that he was destined to be part of her life. And it was up to her to make it so.

The weekend had passed with thoughts of Errol never far from Anne-Marie's consciousness. Her moods had swung from joy to confusion to pure lust. She had to know what was going on. Was he or was he not interested in her? She knew how she felt.

Marion had taken her out on Sunday night — dinner with an old friend and guests. It had been so... pally. Marion was a very friendly person who had decided to make Anne-Marie part of her circle of colleagues and friends. She'd introduced her to a couple of people in the same line of work, and everyone had seemed interested in her... and yet all she had been able to think about was Errol. Why hadn't he been invited?

She'd slept badly, and woke at seven with her eyes puffy and red from tiredness and the amount of wine she'd drunk the night before. She rose slowly, feeling unusual aches and pains in her back. Was this what getting to thirty meant? She knew she should exercise, start going to a class or swimming. Did Errol swim? Maybe she'd ask him — they could go together, make it a regular thing.

Breakfast was black coffee and toast, eaten alone in her living room with the TV on. She always watched television with a pad somewhere nearby. It was a habit from her days at college. Being a researcher, there was usually some piece of information she found useful. Even if she didn't realise it at the time, it might come in handy later on.

She was still thinking of Errol as she went to buy her morning paper. Another stalker story had stolen the headlines. She folded it and stuck it into her bag as she headed for the station.

Maybe she needed to make the first move with him. She had been too subtle so far. Play the right moves with a man, any man, and no matter if he's gay, married or committed to the church, you can get him to want you. Women are used to being pursued, to having their space invaded; men aren't, and so they struggle against it more. But Anne-Marie's philosophy was that persistence pays.

She was passing the florists when the idea came to her. She'd send him flowers. He'd like that.

EIGHT

"You know what we need round here?"

"A swimming pool?" Yvette suggested sarcastically.

"Where would we put a swimming pool?"

"On the roof."

Yvette and her brother were sitting in her office. She was casually draped over a soft cloth armchair, dressed in her work gear — Lycra leggings and a crop top. Her brother Conrad, her silent partner, had been going through the books as he did once a month, making sure his money was being put to good use and that they weren't losing profits. A man of slight build with quick, inquisitive eyes and a sensuous, small mouth, Conrad was always smartly dressed, had his hair neatly trimmed once a fortnight, and also had a brain that never seemed to rest. Everything he did had a purpose, and he was constantly on the lookout for opportunities. When people asked him what he did, they regretted it when half an hour later he'd still be telling them.

When she had first decided to go into the beauty and fitness business, Yvette had had no idea what an enormous undertaking it was going to be. She soon understood what Conrad had meant when he'd talked of building a company out of your own sweat. Now she had done it, and she was making it work.

"No, I'll tell you what we need," Conrad said. "Men."

"We get men in here. They use the gym every day of the week, especially the weekends."

"But we don't want them just using the gym. The gym costs one price and they use it for hours. And why do we only have female instructors and trainers? Men can do step aerobics too; why don't we have a male instructor?"

Yvette shrugged and frowned.

Conrad quickly hid a grin. He knew his little sister didn't welcome any interference in the business. She was good at her job, but advice wouldn't hurt. "The idea came to me when I was at the Black Youth Achievement awards last week," he told her. "This guy was on stage — a fitness instructor, black guy with bleached blonde hair, and toned until he couldn't be toned any more…"

"So you chatted him up, got his number and promised him a job. Now you want to install him at my club."

Conrad was a closet gay. The only people who knew were his sister and his closest friends. Their mother had her suspicions, but would never voice them.

"No, sis, this isn't personal. I didn't even talk to him. But this man did a routine that was out of this world. There was six of them on stage, each with a step. I'm not talking one-up-one-down — this was a routine with attitude. They were twisting, spinning, jumping, doing the shimmy and clapping all at the same time. This was like no step routine I've ever seen in my life."

Yvette hadn't seen her brother so excited about anything since they'd made their first thousand-pound profit on this place. "Better than mine?"

"Eve, you know you're good. But this guy—"

"All right, I get the picture. But if you didn't talk to him how am I supposed to contact him?"

"I got the name of the promoter, he'll put you in touch."

He whipped a folded flyer out of his pocket and passed it to Yvette. She unfolded it. Now she was smiling.

"Goldie? That's the aerobics guy?"

"That's him."

"And you don't fancy him?" she asked studying his face.

"Yvette, he's not my type," Conrad said honestly. "I think they call it step-cardiovascular funk."

"Okay. I'll get in touch, give him an audition."

"Good. I'm not saying it will just have more men doing aerobics, look at the big picture your female clientele will be flocking in here too to get a look at him too. Only they'll have to pay to do it."

"You know, sometimes, Con…"

"What?"

"I think you really care about me."

He threw his head back and laughed.

Anne-Marie sat at her desk and sighed, the computer's monitor casting an eerie glow on her features. She was writing a running order for the programme "Is Love an Illness?"

She was thinking about the other night at Errol's house. The photo she had "borrowed" from his son's room sat in a small wooden frame on the desk. Staring at it, she found her concentration lapsing and she daydreamed.

As she stared at her computer she imagined Errol appearing behind her. She could see his reflection in the screen, standing behind her. He bent to kiss her neck and she shivered, feeling goosebumps prickle all over her body. Then he unzipped her dress and ran his tongue down her back, stopping every now and then to suck and kiss her flesh. She shifted to the edge of her chair. In her fantasy he sank to the floor in front of her, turning on his back as he shuffled under her chair, his body between its legs. His head came up between her parted legs, he looked once into her eyes, and then focused on her swelling lower lips. He took her clitoris between his lips and lightly sucked.

She gasped. He was manipulating her to orgasm, sucking her to ecstasy. He was feeding on her juices like a thirsty man.

She reached down and ran her hands through his hair. His head wasn't bald any more; it had tight, wiry hair, and her fingers were getting wet.

Her pulse was racing and she breathed heavily as she exploded into orgasm.

"Oh Errol…"

It wasn't enough. Anne-Marie wanted the real thing.

She got up and put her coat on.

The phone rang just as Errol was about to leave. Yvette had been on his mind all day and, although he didn't usually turn up without calling first, tonight he wanted to surprise her.

He picked up the receiver in his living room. "Hello?" he answered wearily.

Silence.

"Hello?" he said again.

"Errol Wright?" a nondescript female voice asked.

"Yes, can I help you?"

"I'm watching you."

Errol held the phone away from his ear for a moment and glared at it, as if his anger could somehow be silently transmitted to the caller. When he listened again he could hear soft breathing. "Who *is* this?"

"I'm watching you."

"Oh yeah? Then what am I doing?"

"You'd just switched the lights off and were making your way out of the front door when the phone rang."

This time Errol's response wasn't so swift. He looked towards his curtained windows. Other colleagues had received calls like this. It was an occupational hazard.

He was about to speak but the caller got in first.

"I'll be waiting for you, Errol," and there was a click as the line was disconnected. He was left with the dial tone.

Slowly he replaced the receiver and decided to forget it. Probably a one-off. He wouldn't let it bother him. Not yet. If he had been a defenceless woman he wouldn't set foot outside the door, but Errol Wright could take care of himself.

Hidden in the shadows across the road, a woman pulled her coat tighter around her and slipped her mobile phone back into her pocket.

Yvette was playing cards with Tyrone in the kitchen when the doorbell rang.

"I'll get it!" Tyrone rushed to the door, cards in hand.

Yvette looked up at the clock. She wasn't expecting anyone. She heard Errol's voice before her son announced, "Mum, it's Errol!" Turning back to Errol, the boy showed him his hand. "Look at this."

"You're in big trouble, Mum." Errol grinned wickedly at Yvette as he made his entrance to the kitchen.

She rose from the table, smiled, but was clearly not pleased. "We weren't expecting you, were we?"

"No. I just got the urge to be here," he said, one hand reaching for her waist. This woman never ceased to look sexy, even when she wasn't expecting company. She was dressed in blue: a short cut-off top and a tight mini.

Tyrone was tapping his cards impatiently.

"We'll pick the game up later, Ty," Yvette said, removing Errol's hand from her body.

Tyrone breathed heavily in exasperation. "But I was gonna beat you!"

"Later, okay? Look, why don't you do the dishes for me? I'm gonna take a break."

Tyrone dashed his cards on the table and threw Errol a truculent look.

Yvette glared at Errol. "See? All that could have been avoided if someone knew how to use the phone."

They went into the living room. "Maybe I should have called first," Errol said. "But I thought Tyrone would be doing his homework or something."

Yvette sucked air through her teeth. The liberties some people take! She had an agreement with him that under no circumstances was he to turn up at her house unannounced. She liked to be prepared.

"So? I might have been busy." She left no doubt to what she was talking about; after all, they were supposed to be having an open relationship.

"Well *are* you?" Errol asked, taking a seat as she poured some drinks.

"No," she said over her shoulder. "Tonight I'm spending quality time with my son."

"I'm sorry."

She crossed the room and stood in front of him. "A woman has needs," she said.

His head was level with her most intimate spot, and he

looked up to meet her eyes, sensing a new game. "Tell me about it," he said, pulling her down to him. His voice was low and sexy, a tone she knew very well.

"Hey, my son's in the next room," she said, gently pushing him away and handing him his glass.

"I want you," he whispered, reaching for her buttocks.

She smiled knowingly. "Maybe. But I'm not performing in front of my son. Now, if you'd called, we might have had the place to ourselves…"

Errol sighed and let his hand drop away. He looked like a sad puppy. Yvette was sure he needed her for something, but what was it?

"So, you came round on the spur of the moment for sex?"

Errol shook his head, taking a sip of his drink. "No, I came round to be with you. The sex is a bonus." His eyes followed her as she crossed the room to the armchair.

She changed tack. "So — how was your day?"

Surprised by the question, Errol didn't answer.

"I know you didn't come here to talk about work," she sighed, "but we have to have some kind of conversation."

He got up and walked across to her. "Why would you want me to talk about work? This is about us."

"I just feel that we don't really talk any more. I have to read about your glamourous lifestyle in the papers."

"Why didn't you say so?"

"I *am* saying so. Sometimes I feel you only want me for one thing — just a playmate."

He touched her chin, raising her face to meet his eyes. "I do want you as a playmate — we have fun together — but that's far from being all I want. I just don't want you to become like Tanya. She got hungry for the celebrity life and the power, the money and the glamour, and she stopped caring about us." He was staring at her intensely. "When I'm with you I want to leave all that behind. I spend enough of my life belonging to everyone else; I just want to be yours."

Oh boy, this man had a way with words! Yvette grabbed the back of his neck and brought his lips down to hers, thinking, You don't know how much I want the same thing.

NINE

"Symptoms: rapid heartbeat, stomach cramps, extreme mood swings, erratic behaviour…" Errol came down the steps in the audience, microphone in hand. He wore a light-blue satin waistcoat over a collarless navy-blue shirt. "It causes you to spend money you ain't got, including running up your phone bill. Does this sound like an illness? That's what we're here to discuss. 'Is Love an Illness?' "

The audience applauded as the title spun onto the screen.

"My guests are all couples 'suffering' from love. Also here is my resident psychologist Anne-Marie Simms, author of *Internal Bleeding*. Please, welcome them to the show!"

The audience applauded the guests, who were already seated on stage. Errol continued. "First, let me introduce Mark. Mark was hit by the thunderbolt ten years ago. The moment he laid eyes on Letitia he knew she was for him…"

He paused as women whistled in the audience.

"Mark, tell us about it."

Mark wasn't a tall man. He was stout, with a tidy haircut and cute cheeks with dimples. He wore a red sweatshirt under a black leather waistcoat and black jeans. "We met at college. When I first saw her, she was looking at me, you know, like watching me." He grinned at the memory. "I was hit here…" He pounded a fist on his chest. "I just knew, and I told her that on our first date the next day. She didn't take me seriously, though. But now we're engaged, and as soon as we're both financially stable we'll get married."

Errol clapped and the audience whistled, stamped their feet and applauded.

When the noise had died down Errol turned back to his guest. "How'd it feel to bare your soul to a woman on her first date? I mean, I'm a man — I know how difficult it is to say things like that, even to my mum." He glanced round to the audience who made sympathetic noises, before addressing Mark again. "Now, you didn't know this woman from a serial killer. So how did you know you loved Letitia enough to tell her that? Describe it for me."

Mark shifted uneasily in his seat, clasping his hands in his lap to stop from fidgeting. "It was just there, like I said before. It hit me. There was something like a magnetic force, a chemistry... I know they say opposites attract but we're actually a lot alike. Our birthdays are a day apart; we're aquarians with the same surname..."

There was a murmur from the audience.

"... We're a year apart in age; we want all the same things in life. She sometimes finishes sentences for me, or I'll answer a question she was just about to ask me. And we always know when the other needs a cuddle, a chat, togetherness..." Mark gave a huge dimpled smile. "It's like fate brought us together."

"That's amazing! And since you've been together you still feel the same? Knowing Letitia hasn't changed that... magnetism?"

"No. If anything the feeling has become deeper. Anyone who knows 'Tish knows that you can only grow to love her. She's a fantastic human being."

"There's a man in love!"

The audience took their cue and gave Mark a warm round of applause, until Errol motioned them to stop and started speaking. "Later we'll meet Mark's intended, Letitia..." The camera panned to the seat next to Mark, where a young woman with gelled hair sat. "Next we have Cheryl, who lives with her boyfriend, Curtis. Curtis and Cheryl are in love, but can't stop arguing..." The audience laughed. "A case of can't live with him, can't live without him for Cheryl."

He turned to his second guest and gave her a warm smile. "Cheryl, tell us about it."

"Let me just put you right there first, Errol. Curtis only lives with me when he feels like it, okay? When we have a disagreement he runs back to his mum's house." Again the audience erupted. "But, Errol — I love the man, you know? We been together t'ree years but he's jus' so stubborn."

"How's that?"

"I'll give you an example, right? If I wanna go out, he'll says 'Where d'you wanna go?' I say, 'Surprise me — you choose.' " She kissed her teeth and slapped her hands on her big thighs. "Then he tells me to choose, and we end up going nowhere… And he's always sulking…"

"Don't you ever feel that these arguments might be *your* fault?" Errol asked, raising an eyebrow.

"Naw, man! I'm into discussing t'ings, you know? I give the guy so many chances, 'cause I love him. All I get back is sorry! What good is sorry when he goes and does the same t'ings again? When we first met he used to always turn up when he said he would, he'd never come empty-handed. He used to always say, 'Anything you want, just ask, I wanna take care of you…' Anyway, we used to make love, including foreplay…" The studio now filled with whoops of laughter, as the women in the audience dug their boyfriends in the sides. "Now we jus' 'ave sex, see? It ain't nuttin'."

Errol laughed too, but remained professional. "Why put up with him? Why not just dump him and start again?"

"I been there," she said, lifting her hands. "Being with him is like a drug. Despite his faults and my complaints, being with him is like a fix and I can't live without it."

Errol turned to his resident psychiatrist. "Anne-Marie, would you care to comment on what you've heard so far?"

"Well, Errol, Mark seems to know exactly how he feels. But what I find interesting is that, ten years on, this whirlwind affair is still little more than an affair." She turned to Mark. "You love each other, you're living together… Usually after this long a couple that have made the commitment to get engaged are making plans to get married and have children."

"And Cheryl?" Errol asked.

"How do you live with someone you're constantly arguing with? Doesn't your love suffer? You need to find someone you're compatible with, someone who wants to be more than a part-time lover." The studio erupted in agreement. "But — and this is a big but — if you two decide that you really want to be together, I'll give you some tips on constructive arguing. Yes, there is such a thing!"

Letitia sat beside Mark. Errol turned to her for her side of the story. She looked at Mark with apologetic eyes.

"I love Mark — and it's true what he said about us being soul mates — but I do think that Mark loves *too* much."

Mark's mouth fell open and he turned sideways in his chair to glare at her. The audience was silent.

Letitia continued. "When we first started going out I loved all the attention. He was always on the other end of the phone, ready to cheer me up. But now that we live together it's sometimes claustrophobic—"

"Hold on," Mark interrupted. "What do you mean 'claustrophobic'? I give you all the space you want!"

Errol jumped in before Letitia could answer. "Now, this is where communication comes in. Letitia, do you tell Mark when you feel like this?"

"Well, I try. The thing is with Mark, because he feels so strongly about me he thinks I feel exactly the same. He wants us to do everything together. If I'm going out he wants to go too; even if it's a girl's night out, he'll get his mates and turn up at the venue, like he doesn't trust me."

Mark was now sullen. He'd let go of her hand and was staring at his shoes.

"I'm very independent and, though I love him, I don't want him in my life twenty-four-seven."

The audience was loving it; the women were nodding and even some of the men were whispering to their girlfriends, "You see?"

Curtis, Cheryl's boyfriend, came on next. Cheryl wanted more than he was offering, but thought she could make him want her more by being the perfect woman. "And there isn't any such thing," he said.

It was Anne-Marie's turn to speak. "First off, never believe you can change someone... Cheryl argues with Curtis in public. Do it behind closed doors..."

Anne-Marie was enjoying herself. "When you're unhappy about something, keep calm... Your relationship is not worth wrecking over one silly disagreement.

"I'll conclude by saying to Mark and Letitia, you've stayed together this long because Letitia doesn't want to hurt your feelings, Mark. She needs her space. Now that you know this, maybe you could give her some. It may be hard, but try asking her occasionally, 'Do you want to… ?' 'Is it all right if… ?' Believe me, you won't lose someone who truly wants to be with you by giving them a little space."

Goldie stepped into the gym and stood just inside the doorway. Yvette stood across the room from him, watching, hands on hips, one leg stuck out to the side, foot pointed.

He wore a bandanna around his head, a tie-dyed jacket, and trousers so baggy that MC Hammer would have been jealous. His skin was dark, in stark contrast to his bleached-blonde hair. She couldn't see what his body looked like under all that gear, but so far he had her imagination going.

"So, are you as good as your reputation?" she asked suggestively as she approached him.

He smirked, dropping his gym bag to the floor and shrugging off the cotton jacket. "Better… Put me to the test."

Her eyes drifted over his taut chest and the tight skin on his muscular arms. "I intend to."

She turned to the tape machine and started the instrumental tape she used for her classes.

"I brought my own music," Goldie told her.

She raised an eyebrow, but stretched her hand out for the tape none the less. A mixture of James Brown funk and hip-hop burst out.

Behind her, Goldie had removed his track-suit bottoms so he was down to short shorts stretched over tight buttocks and a thin, athletic vest. He positioned himself ballet-like on the step in front of the two-way mirror.

"You ready?"

She stepped beside him, gave him a sideways look in the mirror, and said, "Okay."

"First we're gonna warm you up a little, and then a lot,

until you're feeling hot, hot, hot!"

Yvette rolled her eyes as he took her through the first steps of the warm-up. They stretched their necks, shoulders and arms. Easy stuff. Then they used the step to warm up their legs and calf muscles, keeping their arms moving up and down from the elbows.

The second stage was a little more rigorous, and before Yvette realised it they were dancing and using the step at the same time. It felt great, energetic and fun. There was bum slapping, clapping, triple sequences... Every now and then Goldie would add a "Woo!" to his instructions.

"Oh yeah! Keep it going — step off, and kick... I know you're feeling hot now. Stay with me. I know that feels good. Let me move ya... Oh yeah! Now we got a change coming up — you're gonna do a three-count repeater, knee up, hamstring, then a kick..."

By the end of the hour Yvette was glistening with sweat. Goldie was no different, but he looked less out of breath.

He mopped himself down with a towel. "That was the beginners routine. Shall we go for the advanced?"

"Are you kidding?"

Goldie put his hands on his hips and rolled his head on his neck. "I thought you were a fitness instructor."

Yvette jumped up off the bench. "Bwoy, that sounds like a challenge to me. Get back up here. Give it to me."

So they went again for a second hour. This time the pace was faster, not so sequenced, and they were up and down quicker than yo-yos, arms doing windmills as their bodies twirled on and off the bench.

When they finished Yvette sunk to the floor where she stood, struggling to get her breathing back to normal, while Goldie paced the hall keeping his muscles going while he cooled down. She had had a hard time keeping up with him. She hadn't realised how much of her training she had forgotten over the years, how stale her routines had become.

"Yeah!" Yvette shouted almost like an hallelujah. "I found my man! When can you start?"

TEN

"You do date, don't you Errol?"

"Meaning do I go out with women? The answer is yes. I'm just not into seeing anyone seriously at the moment."

The moment it left Errol's lips, he wondered why he had said that. What would Yvette think of being nobody serious?

Anne-Marie smiled into the telephone handset. "Listen, I enjoyed the other night so much I was wondering if we could do it again. On neutral ground this time. I'll drive."

There. She had made the first step and asked Errol out.

He hesitated, and it threw her for a moment, but eventually he came through. "Fine — so long as you understand we are just friends. Where are you taking me?"

"I know the very place. We can have a chat, a drink, a little food… and the waiters are very friendly."

"Right pick me up at… say eight?"

"Great. See you then."

Errol replaced the handset and frown. He wasn't so sure this was a good idea. Picking up the phone again, he dialled Marion's phone number. After some chit-chat, he got to the point. "Are you and Paul doing anything tomorrow night?"

"Why? You wanna borrow our place for a wild party?"

He laughed nervously. Marion was his closest female friend, but she was also a woman. Could he trust her? "I need a favour."

"I thought so," she chuckled.

"I wouldn't ask, except… I'm running out of excuses."

"Excuse me?"

He sighed. "It's Anne-Marie. She's been phoning me at least twice a day since I invited her round for dinner last week. When I told her I was tired she offered to come round, run a bath, wash my back and curl up with me… Well, now I've kinda promised to go out with her tomorrow night."

"You made your bed, boy…"

Errol went silent.

Marion agreed to a double date. If it took that to get Anne-Marie off Errol's back, then it would be worth it. She had suspected there was more to the girl's intentions than simple friendship, but had he listened? No.

She put the phone down and sipped at her lukewarm coffee. Errol was a level-headed man — maybe he was working his way up to dropping her gently.

It was Friday night, and the busy wine bar in Paddington had its usual trendy crowd in. The four of them walked in together, girls first, boys following. The women went to find a table while the men bought the drinks.

Anne-Marie shrugged her jacket off and hung it over the back of a chair. Marion immediately noticed the garment she wore underneath. It was the shirt she had bought for Errol last Christmas. Blue silk. What right did she think she had to wear it like some kind of prize?

"Nice shirt," she said with a smile that was almost a grin. "It looks exactly like one I bought for Errol."

Anne-Marie took the seat opposite her and smiled warmly. "*You* bought it? Well, you have good taste. Errol lent it to me." Her eyes flitted up to meet Errol's as the men came back to the table.

Marion's eyes were also on him. The look on his face confirmed that he hadn't known she'd borrowed the shirt until just now. What was she up to? Marion waited for Errol to make a scene or to pull Anne-Marie aside, but it never happened. He simply gave her a questioning look and sat down, placing the drinks on the table.

They were sitting in a quiet corner, out of the way of passers-by. Paul and Errol discussed politics, Anne-Marie anxious to join in, while Marion couldn't get her mind off the fact that this woman was wearing the shirt *she'd* bought him. No — not only was she wearing it, she had *stolen* it!

"Well, let me think… I did want to be a fireman when I was five years old," Errol was saying. His laughter brought Anne-Marie back to reality. She had been daydreaming about what it would be like to be undressed by him. She was finding it difficult to concentrate on what he was saying, more interested trying to find out whether his friendliness was masking lustful intentions. He was *so* masculine, so astonishingly attractive, so at ease with himself. He looked more like a male model than a talk-show host.

"What did you want to be?" Paul asked her.

"Oh, I... a nurse," she laughed.

Paul smiled. "I bet you dressed up as a nurse a lot when you were a kid."

Anne-Marie smiled coyly. "How did you guess?" Then her expression became serious. "Of course, I had no idea then how far it would go. I graduated in clinical psychology, specialising in psychopathology. That was when I began making notes for my book. I've always been interested in researching the human psyche, and so I decided that the way women's minds work was to be my first study."

"I guess being a woman helped," Errol joked, showing his attractively dimpled smile.

Anne-Marie wanted to run her fingers along his silky eyebrows. "I still had to do a lot of research. In your job, you must get into so many people's minds. Don't you find that interesting?"

"I guess it is. Sometimes it can be a little scary too — you know, when we have murderers or child molesters on. You don't wanna go into those people's minds, in case it rubs off... But then you get people on with a zest for life, like the show we did on over-fifties acting like twenty year olds..."

Once Errol started discussing his show, it was difficult to get him to talk about anything else. Anne-Marie was captivated by his enthusiasm, his opinions, his likes and dislikes.

After about twenty minutes they ordered the food. Marion had lost her appetite and Anne-Marie ordered just a salad, but the men tucked into steak, fries and side salads.

It was the first time Anne-Marie had met Paul, and she liked him. Marion was being unusually quiet. But that was all academic; what she really wanted was to get Errol alone.

Anne-Marie was eager to weave Errol's private life into the conversation. Finally she thought of an innocuous opening line. "You seem to be putting in a lot of hours, Errol," she observed. "Do you find time for a social life?"

"I'm here, aren't I?"

Paul slapped him on the back. "You make time for drink and food, but when was the last time you were at my club?"

"I'm getting there, man. I'm making time slowly. This is just the start of my career, and I think I need to make a good impression." He shrugged his irresistible shoulders. "I can see the admiration in the eyes of the research assistants and journalists, and I know I've achieved an all but impossible task. Eventually I know I'll have time to go away on holiday, safe in the knowledge that I can still come back to a job."

"And just what kind of holiday does Errol Wright take?" Anne-Marie crooned.

He gazed shyly into his drink. "Naw, you'd laugh…"

"Oh, come on! This is me you're talking to. I want to know all about what makes you tick."

His eyes rose to meet hers, and for the first time that night Anne-Marie got the distinct feeling that there was a spark of attraction between them. Errol was ideal fantasy material, and she hungered for closer contact with him.

"You really wanna know?"

"Please."

Errol shook his head and smiled into his lager. "I want to lock myself away in a secluded cabin on a mountain somewhere." His eyes took on a faraway look. "Somewhere with lots of snow and nothing else for miles."

Paul and Marion both rolled their eyes and laughed, but Anne-Marie was watching him seriously, her eyes widening and her mouth dropping open.

This man was more man than she could have guessed. She had to have him.

"See! You're too stunned even to laugh."

"No! No. God, that is just so… I don't know. What a perfect holiday! I mean, you cut yourself off from everything, everyone. Give yourself time to think, to recuperate and plan. Perfect... And from the lips of a man... Well, you amaze me!" Anne-Marie could have sworn that he blushed as she stared at him adoringly.

Marion pulled a face and mimicked Anne-Marie's breathless voice: "... from the lips of a man... you amaze me!"

Errol — and Anne-Marie — ignored her. "Thank you," he said. "Coming from a woman, I'll take that as a compliment." And they laughed together.

She wanted to reach out and touch his dimpled cheek, and had to sit on her hands to control them.

Marion kept throwing Errol glances across the table. He seemed to be enjoying himself, but he wouldn't meet her eyes.

As everybody finished their meal and chatted away, having a good time, Errol's arm found its way behind Anne-Marie and rested on her chair, and every now and again her hand would drop below the table and onto his leg.

Outside the restaurant, Anne-Marie suggested they go dancing. One of her favourite nightspots wasn't far away. Marion and Paul said they had to get back to the babysitter, adding that they had enjoyed the night out. Errol was unsure, but after Anne-Marie challenged him there was no turning back.

Marion stood and watched them hail a cab, anger at his stupidity boiling up inside her.

As soon as she was alone with Paul she let rip. What the hell did Errol think he was doing? If he didn't want anything to happen between himself and Anne-Marie, why was he playing up to her like this — straight into her hands? And why had he sat throughout the meal next to a woman who had stolen his shirt — and heaven knows what else! — when he already had a girlfriend?

"What was he supposed to do?" Paul said in his defence. "Argue with her in front of everyone?"

"Why not? I bet if it was me or you he would've. Now she's got away with that, there's no telling what she'll do! I mean, taking her out with two of his closest friends—"

"Are you jealous?"

Marion threw her hands up. "Me! Jealous!"

"Yes, you! I know you and Errol are close—"

"You know that I care about Errol like a brother. I don't want someone like her getting her claws into him."

"You're over-reacting. What is it exactly that riles you about Anne-Marie? I liked her. Errol could do a lot worse."

Marion had clammed up, so Paul continued. "She's well spoken, intelligent, attractive…"

Men! They all stuck together when it came to attractive women!

"Leave it, okay?"

She didn't bother to mention the fact that Errol had told her he wasn't interested in Anne-Marie, then turned round and done the complete opposite.

This girl was a lot more powerful than she was letting on.

By three in the morning, after spending hours on his feet in a hot, smoky atmosphere, Errol was open to any suggestions.

"Why don't you come back to my place? I never did get a chance to give you that signed copy of my book."

"Well…" he began, knowing that Yvette was expecting him to go back to hers tonight.

"Oh, come on. I promise I won't bite."

Almost a challenge.

Errol went along with it.

She led him into her spacious lounge. He followed numbly, having had a little too much to drink, stupidly commenting on the weather they'd been having.

"What can I get you to drink?"

"Coffee would be fine, thanks."

Errol took a seat on her cream leather sofa. She smiled. She could sense his apprehension from across the room, and took it as a sign of an imminent conquest. His nervousness would make him just that little bit more vulnerable, easier to handle, more susceptible to the powder…

Errol watched her move about in the kitchen from where he sat on the sofa. Her every move was made with sinuous grace. He shook his head again at the injustice of not being able to have this woman.

"You live here alone?" he asked, for the sake of something to say.

"Yes. After my mother died I wanted a place of my own." She removed a sachet of powder from a small container and carefully shook the contents into his coffee cup before pouring on hot water and stirring. Then she poured herself a glass of wine and brought the drinks into the living room.

"Here. It's quite special. I hope you like it."

"Thank you. You're not having any?"

"No, I need something a little stronger." She placed the silver tray on the coffee table and helped herself to a handful of nuts. Errol sipped the coffee and repressed a shudder. It was terrible. How could so sophisticated a lady have such terrible taste in coffee? No wonder she was drinking wine. Oh well, he would have to drink it to show his appreciation.

"To us," she said, holding her glass aloft.

"If you like." Errol followed her action, and was forced to take another gulp of the vile brew before placing it on the table between them.

"This is nice, don't you think?"

Errol raised his eyebrows in question.

"The two of us — here, alone. Dimmed lights, jazz music, intelligent conversation…"

"Yeah, it is nice," he said. He reached for his cup and took a swig. It was still awful. He winced, and decided to down the rest quickly without tasting it.

"Why haven't you got a husband already, a boyfriend at least?" he asked as he replaced the cup on the table.

"I did… have a boyfriend, I mean — until a month ago."

"Oh?"

"I finished with him. I'd been trying to ditch him for ages, but he would always threaten suicide. Once he slit his wrists; another time he overdosed on Paracetamol. I caught him in time and had him pumped out. Then he drove my car into a tree, wrecking the car but walking away without a scratch. Emotional blackmail…" She sighed and shrugged. "Now I'm young, single, and available again."

Errol nodded, turning his attention to the aquarium at the other end of the room. "Seems you've been through a lot."

"I suppose so, but I'm a fighter. Always have been." She paused. "Marion is very protective of you. Did you know that?"

"Marion?"

"Yes, she seems to think that you're delicate."

Errol laughed a hollow laugh. Was it getting hot in here? He could feel an undefined warmth snaking through his veins and centring in his groin. He crossed his legs. "I can't think why. Ah, she might… feel…" He stumbled a little over his words.

She finished for him. "That you need protecting?"

"Well… we do know a lot about each other…" As he spoke he was removing his jacket.

"You're warm. Maybe I should open a window."

Errol's eyes roamed over Anne-Marie's body as she crossed to the window. He took in the way her breasts pushed out the material, her nipples straining to be noticed, the lean, flat stomach, situated just above her—

"Errol, are you okay?"

He was swaying a little and undoing the top button of his shirt. "I… I'm not sure. Could I get a glass of water?"

"Of course."

It was becoming increasingly difficult for him to think of anything but sex… sex with Anne-Marie. He wanted to touch her, feel her skin against his, press himself against her.

"There you go." She handed him a glass and sat beside him on the sofa.

Errol gulped it down. She was so close he could smell her perfume, the wine she'd been sipping, even the soap she had used this evening. Every sense in his body seemed to have been heightened. An erection ached and strained against his trousers. Suddenly he needed to be naked.

102

Anne-Marie studied him, trying to control her delight. "How do you feel now?"

"Sensations... so hot."

Had he said that out loud? He couldn't be sure.

"I think you've had too much to drink," she said lightly.

Legs tightening around his waist... shivering... beautiful, bobbing breasts...

"Why, Errol, I'm surprised at you!"

He barely heard her as he reached for her, his senses on fire. He slipped a hand under the shirt, *his* shirt, and touched her shoulder, squeezing the warm flesh. "You... *do* something to me..." Her skin was as smooth as he had imagined it. Leaning forward, he pulled her close. Gently, tentatively, he kissed her neck. His lips felt hot, tingling, but numb.

His breath was warm against her skin. She sighed deeply. Hadn't she dreamed of this very moment over and over again, ever since she had first met him? "Errol, are you sure you know what you're doing?"she said.

He was beyond listening, beyond caring. He caught her in his arms, stood up and pressed her against the length of his body. Restless, impatient hands roamed over her body, her throat, her arms, her breasts her back and buttocks.

Anne-Marie couldn't believe how good it felt. This was one of her night-time fantasies come true. She warmed to his touch, becoming loose and pliant under his fingers. She knew it was just the effect of the powerful aphrodisiac, but why not enjoy it? One hand moved slowly down to her belly, glancing off her nipples, while his other hand raised her short skirt, found her thighs and then her crotch, teasing the flesh there until it quivered.

Errol dimly realised he was out of control, but he was beyond turning back. It was as if his life depended on seeing this through to its climax. His mouth nibbled an earlobe hungrily, then his tongue traced the outline of her ear, his pelvis thrusting against her groin, mimicking penetration.

She followed the motion, rubbing herself against the massive bulk of his erection...

Until suddenly he pulled back.

Summoning the last ounce of his flagging self-control, he looked directly into her eyes.

To Anne-Marie his eyes looked unfocused, almost as if he were looking though her. The warmth of her arousal was chilled a little from the look he gave her. This wasn't the Errol she knew. It was as if some devilish, dangerous stranger had taken over. But she told herself it was just the drug. She forced his head back towards hers, mouth open, waiting for the touch of his lips.

And he responded again, bruising her mouth with his urgency, forcing his tongue around hers as though he was dying for the breath from her body.

She was aching all over now, a liquid ache that throbbed between her legs. She gasped for breath. "Errol, I'm—"

"Now!" he growled, cutting off her words. "I need you *now!*"

Her shirt and skirt were loosened it seemed in one movement, and she let them fall to the floor. Instantly his mouth was on her breasts. She held his head to her as he suckled like a hungry infant, breathing heavily. She groaned with the jolts of electricity coursing through her, the pressure in her groin now close to pain.

His hands were rough as he tugged at her skimpy panties and threw them aside, the expression on his face intense as he threw her body onto the sofa and stood above her, throwing off the clothes that had hindered his release.

Anne-Marie was powerless to slow him down. As he climbed on top of her she arched towards him. He found her wet and ready as he drove into her without hesitation. He was massive, almost too big; she could feel him in her belly, filling her lungs, her throat.

Harder and harder, deeper and deeper, his rhythm was powerful and relentless. While she squirmed and bucked under him, her nails clawing his back and shoulders, she felt herself rushing towards orgasm.

Suddenly he stopped again. His head was buried in her neck, his breathing was erratic.

"God, we were so close," she whispered. "Not finished yet, big boy…" She slid from under him and rolled him onto his back. Now it was her turn.

"I'm in control now, Errol…" She climbed astride his supine body. "And I'm going to drive you over the edge."

She closed her eyes and pushed against him. Errol groaned as she impaled herself on his shaft, his groping hands clamped onto her breasts.

"Oh, Errol. Errol…" Within moments she was arching her back and quivering with the first tremors of an orgasm. She increased her pace until she was bouncing furiously, impatient for the climax she could feel rippling through her.

Errol's hands moved to grasp her firmly by the the hips and he matched her rhythm with his own, thrusting upwards to her every plunge. Finally she sank down on top of him with her full weight, and with his hot, thick length buried deep inside her she came in a flood, spasms, shakes and all. He felt her throb and tighten around him, and it sent him spiralling over the edge in a dark frenzy. With a cry he shot into her, spurting out his warm fluid in great jerks before collapsing and falling into unconsciousness.

Anne-Marie sighed contentedly, the aftershocks of the orgasm still shuddering through her. She lay perfectly still for several minutes before opening her eyes to look at him.

"Errol? Errol, honey?"

Even in sleep he was irresistible. She placed a kiss on his mouth before slipping off his limp body.

She bent to retrieve the garments he'd tossed to the floor in haste. As she picked up his jacket his wallet fell to the floor. She picked it up and flicked it open. Inside was a picture of a little boy, about six years old, she recognised: his son. She scanned the other contents, committing certain items to memory before returning them to his pockets.

She neatly laid out his clothes on the seat, then fetched a pillow and a sheet from the airing cupboard in the hallway, making him comfortable before retiring to her bedroom.

ELEVEN

He had made some mistakes in his life, but sleeping with Anne-Marie would probably be his stupidest. He worked with her, she was his best friend's ex, she was an acquaintance of Marion, his best female friend...

All the way home Errol scolded himself. How could he have let this happen? If there was one thing he knew, it was that he would make it up to her — somehow. But at the same time he would have to make it clear that it would never happen again, and that nobody was to know about it.

He had woken up aching all over and with a splitting headache. Disoriented, he'd had no idea where he was until a faint memory of a date with Anne-Marie had come to him. Lifting the duvet, he'd found himself naked. Slowly he'd got up and realised what must have happened. In less than five minutes he had dressed himself, quickly scribbled a note and left, closing the door noiselessly behind him.

At home he headed straight for the kitchen and made himself a cup of strong coffee. He sat at the table clutching the mug, trying to remember what had happened — but even after the coffee everything seemed a blur. No wonder she'd left him on the sofa.

Shit, they must have done it on the sofa. He could still smell her on him. He had to wash all traces of the night away. He felt ashamed, embarrassed. It just wasn't like him.

Under the shower, he heard the phone ring. The answering machine was on. He wasn't expecting any important calls today.

Later he would have to go and pick up Aaron for the weekend. Maybe he could postpone his guilt until Monday morning... when she came in to work.

After his shower he fell across the bed and closed his eyes. The phone rang again. This time he picked it up without thinking.

"What happened? I woke up and you weren't there."

"I'm sorry… I didn't want to wake you. We had a very late night…"

"And wasn't it worth it?"

He could hear the smile in Anne-Marie's voice.

"I don't know. I can't remember much after we got back to your place. I'm sorry… Boy, I didn't realise how much I drank! And… er, what happened shouldn't have. You know I try not to mix business with pleasure…"

More answers to questions not asked. She knew it, and ignored it. He was *there*. Here. "We were great last night. It's this morning that's the problem."

"This morning I wasn't thinking clearly. I apologise for the way it looked—"

"Why do you keep saying sorry? Are you trying to say it was all a mistake?"

"Anne… Anne-Marie, I don't know what to say…" He transferred the phone to his other ear.

"Say that you enjoyed it too and want to do it again."

"I think we should meet and talk about this… But I can't this weekend. How about I call you tomorrow night?"

Errol couldn't see it, but Anne-Marie was grinning. "Okay. I'll talk to you tomorrow."

He held the handset to his chest and breathed out deeply. Holy shit, what had he done?

Karen shut the bedroom door and placed the tray on the desk by the window. Yvette was stretched out on her double bed, watching the television.

Karen handed her a drink, then reached for her cigarettes. "I know you're only watching this for that black surfer guy…"

The programme was *Sunset Beach*, and Yvette tried to catch it whenever she had a chance. On Saturdays they broadcast the whole week's shows in one long omnibus.

"He's a lifeguard. And no, I don't need to ogle a fictitious man — I've got one of my own—"

"Please! You've got *half* a man…"

"Don't start on me, Karen."

"What — reality too much for you? I seem to remember a certain woman calling me and cussing the man she's sleeping with because he won't talk commitment."

Yvette's eyes stayed on the box. "It's not easy, Kaz..."

"Why not? You have a mouth, don't you? If he won't bring it up, then *you* do it." Karen dropped heavily onto the bed beside Yvette, spilling a little of her drink.

Yvette kissed her teeth. "Has it ever occured to you that this was *your* idea? We could be making a mistake. Okay, we've been seeing each other long enough, but we've never spent much time together. Living together... it's a big step."

"Is that what *he* said?"

"No! You don't know him like I do. Errol has a way with words. He always manages to say the right thing — we talk, and then it isn't until after he's gone that I realise I didn't get the answer I wanted. I don't know how he does it..."

"Actions speak louder than words. Don't let him get away with it. As soon as you realise he's wormed his way out of an argument, pull him up on it."

Yvette sat up on the bed. "For example, I asked him why he never takes me to any functions but has escorts instead, he says..." Yvette put on Errol's voice: " 'Baby, you wouldn't enjoy it — a lot of air kissing, hoity-toity luvvie darlings. Besides, you'd be too distracting for me...' "

Karen shrieked with laughter, rocking back and forth on the bed. "I love that bit on the end! Boy, he's slick!"

"You see what I mean, though."

"Okay... Let's do a role-play! I'll be you..."

"*What?*"

"Humour me." Karen cleared her throat and put on Yvette's assertive voice: " 'Now, Errol, you remember I asked you if you would buy a house with me... ?"

" 'Aah.' " Yvette slipped into character. " 'Yes I do.' "

" 'Are you still interested?' "

" 'Of course, baby. I mean, we have to talk about it.' "

" 'How about we view the house tomorrow?' "

" 'Tomorrow? Oh, I have work tomorrow.' "

" 'In the evening,' " Karen pressed, still in character.

" 'I'd rather see it in the day... Does it need any work?' "

" 'Some...' " Karen was beginning to crack.

" 'That means decorators, estimates, time...' "

Unable to keep it up any longer, Karen laughed. "I see what you mean! So... I suggest we plan it out now."

"Plan what?"

Karen hopped off the bed and came back with a pen and pad. "What you're gonna ask him: when he's free to view the place, when he's going to put his place up for sale—"

Yvette laughed. "You don't think that's a little pushy?"

"No! He's had time. If he cares for you he'll give it a go."

Yvette sighed. Karen was always right.

To be, or not to be, that was the question.

Errol grabbed a trolley and strolled into Sainsbury's in his 'regular Joe' disguise: black track-suit bottoms, cream sweater, expensive trainers, baseball cap turned backwards and sunglasses. He would be picking up Aaron later, and wanted to make sure he had all his son's favourites in. Usually he would leave a list for Helen or Mrs Donaldson, but occasionally he took a perverse pleasure in walking among his viewers without being recognised.

Besides, he needed time to think. He had a decision to make — a decision that would affect not just his own life but those of a woman and her son as well.

He didn't want to lose Yvette. She meant a lot more to him than he'd ever let on. She was more than a lover, more than a friend. And Tyrone was like a younger brother to him. Errol had gotten used to being with them. That stability in his life helped him to stay normal.

If only there was a way of finding out if it would work before moving in with them. He'd made enough mistakes in his life — Anne-Marie, for one.

He'd never stayed with Yvette longer than a night, leaving early in the morning, making sure that no attachments were made. Now, all of a sudden, they were supposed to become a full-time family, bound by the commitment of buying property.

Not only that, but being a full time father... He wasn't even that to his own son!

Every time he'd spoken to Yvette over the past few days he'd avoided talking about the house. Sometimes he was sure he could feel her wanting to bring the subject up, wanting *him* to bring the subject up. But he wouldn't. Maybe she'd get the message from his apprehension; maybe she'd have second thoughts and go ahead on her own. But if she did that, would she still want him, knowing that he found it hard to make big decisions?

Would she see that, in the long run, he was probably doing her favour? After all, he had a past history — Tanya and their son — she would have to take that on. And heaven knows how Tanya would take the news that every time he took Aaron it was to stay with another mother figure.

His career wasn't exactly stable either. The show could be cut at any time, leaving him redundant...

Now a new thought occured to him. He was well known all over the country. Women wanted him, temptation lay on every corner. If he chose to, he could forget about Yvette altogether, date a socialite instead... Hell, he could marry one and be made for life!

But would anyone else be able to make him feel the way Yvette did? He realised that, if he said no to her now, he could lose her for ever. Finished!

She had turned a corner in her life. She was ready to move upwards, and wanted to take him with her. He should feel honoured. She was looking for commitment. Could he, Errol Wright, give it to her? The only thing he'd been committed to over the past few years had been himself.

And could she cope as a celebrity wife? She was a working-class girl from Streatham. Okay, so she was also a business women. But that didn't prepare her for being photographed and hounded...

As Errol queued at the checkout, he knew he had been making excuses. This matter could be resolved only if he talked to Yvette about it. Talked to her, that is, without hurting her feelings — one thing he didn't want to do was hurt her feelings.

Errol reversed the car into the only parking space on the narrow street. Only five doors away from her house tonight. There had been times when he'd had to walk back two streets or risk getting a ticket.

The house was lit up, as if it were warding off evil spirits, the lights shining onto the dark street from the windows upstairs and downstairs. Didn't she realise electricity costs money? There were only the two of them in there. He supposed she'd be asking him to pay for it in extra maintenance. Ever since the show had taken off she'd expected more money; all of a sudden things had needed replacing and Aaron had started growing a lot more quickly.

He rang the bell to the right of the newly painted front door. He could see a distorted image of his face in the gloss.

More money.

Not that Errol begrudged giving to his son — it was *her*. Tanya knew nothing about money except how to take it and hand it to a hairdresser, or a boutique or a furniture retailer.

The door was answered by an extremely attractive fair-skinned woman, dressed in a figure-hugging body suit and ski pants. Her long, jet-black hair was pulled back into a ponytail. She had a face that needed no make-up and a figure that needed no exercise. Tanya had men begging for her attention, and she knew just how to play them. She'd had Errol eating out of her hands... until his money had started to mean more to her than he did. Then, suddenly, her spell had broken and he had seen her for who she really was.

"On time — for a change." She turned her back on him and sashayed down the hallway.

Errol entered his ex-home and closed the door behind him. The hall carpet was covered with see-through plastic throughout, an effort to prolong the life-span of the expensive carpet.

"Is Aaron ready?"

"He's getting changed." Tanya entered the living room. "Don't forget to take your shoes off before coming in here."

"I won't come in." Errol stood uncomfortably in the doorway, glancing around the room. Nothing new caught his eye. This made a change — over the past six months the whole room had been altered beyond recognition. Tanya had gone for the art deco look — and an interior decorator friend of hers had designed the layout: uplighter lamps, obscure prints, unusually shaped shelving. Now the room looked like an ad for Ikea. The suite was made entirely of pine and leather. The floor, which had been concrete and carpet before, was now a polished wooden expanse with expensive rugs strategically placed to give warmth. The television was a massive screen built into its own cabinet. Exotic plants stood sentry-like each side of the patio doors, which Tanya had had built in to open out to the garden.

"Looking for anything in particular?" Her tone was frosty.

Errol threw her an annoyed gaze. "Just looking at the luxury I'm helping you live in."

She immediately went on the defensive, her big Spanish eyes catching fire. "I work too, you know…"

"Yeah, but a shop assistant's salary wouldn't pay for all this in six months."

"All you have to worry about, Mister Superstar, is that your son is being fed and clothed properly. He's getting everything he needs."

"I suppose he's banned from this room now. Am I right?"

Tanya stepped forward, hands on hips, and stared him straight in the eyes. "He has his own TV, right? His own room. And we have a dining room." She poked a finger at him, her black eyes flashing. "So don't come into my house trying to make me feel bad about having something for myself, right?"

"Who said I was trying to make you feel bad? I just

wanted to see how my son lives. You've been squeezing me for cash, and all I can see it going on is this house…"

"This house, in case you'd forgotten, is where your son lives! I ain't spending it on nothing he ain't sharing! Ask 'im yourself — anything he wants he gets… And d'you think dat does 'im any good?" she screamed.

"What you raising your voice for? I'm not arguing with you. Unless you've got a guilty conscience, we've got nothing to argue about any more."

Tanya's mouth opened then shut again, as if she'd been about to counter-attack and changed her mind.

Errol turned away to see his son at the top of the staircase in his baseball cap and his yellow denim outfit.

"All right, son?"

"Yeah, Dad." Aaron looked past his father at his mum, then back to his dad again. "Are we going out?"

"Course — like always. Your granny wants us to call her…"

Tanya's mouth drew into a tight line at the mention of Errol's mother. She turned and headed for her easy chair in front of the TV.

Aaron skipped down the stairs to stand next to his father, his rucksack hanging from one shoulder. "I'm going then, Mum," he said. He knew he couldn't cross the threshold of the living room in his shoes, so he waited for her attention.

She got up and bent down in front of him. "Bye, baby. Have a good time, yeah?"

Aaron was already heading for the door. "All right, Mum."

Errol turned to Tanya. "We'll be back around eight tomorrow."

"No later, Errol. Remember—"

"He has school on Monday — I know that."

Again the hostile air. Every fortnight it was the same thing. Whenever he took Aaron on a Sunday she reminded him that the boy had school the next day — as if he didn't know.

What was her problem? Whatever it was, it had stood in

the way of Errol making Tanya his wife.

They'd had everything; they'd been a stunning couple, meant for each other physically. The physical attraction had made it last seven years. But compromise didn't exist for Tanya. She always had to have her way.

Errol was already seated at the table when Yvette walked in. She was wearing a short black dress, and a choker with three rows of mock pearls adorned her long, graceful neck. Her two-tone hair extensions were piled loosely on her head. The look was simple but highly effective, and heads turned as she crossed the floor to join him.

Errol stood, a wide smile on his face. "You look good enough to eat," he whispered in her ear as he kissed her cheek.

"Yeah, well you don't look too bad yourself — but then you can afford to."

Errol grinned, pulling out her chair for her before resuming his own. "I've been thinking about you all day."

Yvette indulged him. "And I bet I know what those thoughts were."

"Actually, you're wrong."

"You mean you *weren't* thinking of my body?"

Errol smirked. "Well, you know — that as well. But mostly I thought just of you being you."

He was telling the truth. Ever since the call from Anne-Marie and the realisation of what he had done, he could think of nothing else but being with Yvette. He'd felt an incredible urge to talk to his mother, and had called the USA and spoken to her just before she left for work. She'd sounded so good that it brought home how much he missed her, how much he missed having a woman in his life who cared about him, cared for him. His mother was a very young looking fifty year old, in the league of Shirley Bassey or Diana Ross. He realised now, as he looked over at Yvette, that she and his mother were the fittest women he knew.

She spread a napkin on her lap and picked up the menu.

"It's a coincidence, but I was thinking about you too," she said from behind the raised card.

"You can't look me in the eyes and say that?"

Yvette met his gaze and held it. "I've been thinking about you too."

He smiled. God, she was so sexy.

He signalled the waiter. "Let's eat."

Yvette ordered steak with two different salads and fries. Tonight she felt she could eat everything in sight, but being the lady she was she controlled her appetite.

"So, do we have the evening to ourselves?" Errol asked.

"Mm-hm." Yvette answered through a mouthful of salad. "Now we just have to decide what to do with it."

"I've missed you, Eve."

She looked up at him, licking her lips, but said nothing. Secretly she was extremely pleased. Errol rarely said anything that gave her a clue about how he felt about her; it had always been a meeting of bodies, not minds. This approach was new, and she found it quite exciting…

"I want to devour you." He rubbed her leg under the table. "This is what I'm hungry for."

But this was more like it. She put her fork down and picked up her glass of wine. She could feel the ache between her legs instantly. "You sex maniac. You'll have us arrested."

"Handcuffs and uniforms… That might be fun," he said, his eyes dancing, his voice low and seductive.

Yvette laughed. "You should be ashamed of yourself."

"The only thing I'd be ashamed of would be not pleasing you."

Yvette slipped her shoe off and found his crotch with her toes. "Don't worry. I'm pleased. You've just bought me steak, and later I'm gonna have some more meat, hopefully…" She lowered her voice. "… deep inside me."

The waiter approached their table again. "Everything fine?"

Yvette straightened up in her seat self-consciously. "Yes… yes, very good."

Behind the waiter's back, they giggled like schoolkids.

"He knew what you were up to."

"You think so?"

"Yes, and I bet he's as jealous as hell — just like all the other men in here."

"You're too much!" she laughed through a mouthful of food.

"Why not test me right here, under the table? We could put on a show, give these people some entertainment."

"Just let me eat this and you can give me a private showing," she said quickly.

They passed the rest of the meal almost in silence, each knowing exactly what they wanted to do to the other, then they left the restaurant in something of a hurry.

Errol's house always impressed Yvette. It was filled with expensive furnishings and unusual antiques that she would not have expected a bachelor to own. In the living room, the overstuffed leather two-seater sofa and its two armchairs were surrounded by sculptures and art objects, every item in its place. In the centre of the room was a glass table, four sculpted marble mermaids forming its legs. He'd told her the piece had cost him two and a half thousand pounds.

He kept the place immaculately tidy. No glass stood around without a coaster, no dirty dishes were heaped in the sink, no unmade beds, no towels tossed on the floor...

As soon as they arrived, Errol bustled about creating the mood. He lit a fire in the fireplace and went to open a bottle of wine. Yvette yawned as he re-entered the room.

"Didn't know I was away so long. You need to sleep?"

She kissed him as he stood beside her, tasting the wine on his lips. "You're what I need."

"Oh really?" he said, massaging her back through her dress. He loved a woman with a strong back. "You feel so good," he said into her neck. Gently he pulled the neckline of her dress down until her shoulders were exposed. Then he kissed each one and ran a finger along her collarbone. "I love this body: your skin, your bone structure, your nose..." He kissed her nose, then her lips. "Your mouth..."

Yvette moaned and leaned back, letting him work on her.

116

She hadn't worn a bra, and soon she was nude from the waist up, the fire's warmth against her back. She fumbled with the buttons on his shirt, so excited she couldn't open them fast enough. They stared at each other in the dim light of the fire, then pressed their chests together in an embrace.

"Beautiful breasts," Errol said, reaching to take one nipple in his mouth while his hand roamed over the other. And in one easy moment they were on the plush carpet, her dress tossed aside, leaving her in her navy-blue g-string.

Errol had bought her underwear before; he loved watching her parade about in silk slips and panties that always left something to the imagination. Now he ran his eyes over her body.

"Beautiful," he said again.

She lay eyes closed on her back listening to the fire crackle a few feet away, as his hands roamed, the wine heightening her senses, loosening her reserve. A quality man was making love to her. Nothing else mattered.

As he spread her legs and bent his head between them her whole body tensed, knowing what was coming and preparing to be taken to the heights of pleasure. He held her in place with his arms, and her body responded, arching up to meet the downward strokes of his tongue. After a minute of his caresses she felt she couldn't take any more, so close was she to an orgasm. She tried to pull him on top of her but he resisted.

"I wanna do you like you've never been done."

The pleasure was overwhelming, building deep inside her body. She was out of control, powerless, high, and yet ecstatically aware.

"I need to feel you inside me. Please, Errol..." she begged.

Finally he came up for air and stretched out on the floor next to her. Instantly she was upon him.

"Ride me," he said hoarsely, his eyes filled with lust.

She let him plunge deep inside her, his hands gripping her buttocks, forcing her to rock with him. Her inner muscles burst into spasms as she gripped him tightly then released him, over and over again. She would rise, so that they were nearly disconnected, then push back down and backwards, arching her body, making him gasp aloud. His hands flitted over her nipples, then moved down to her hips, her flat, hard stomach, and finally found her clitoris.

"Oh, God. Oh, man…" she cried out, riding him fast and hard, their bodies wet with perspiration. "I love you…" As the tidal wave of her first orgasm washed over her she collapsed on his chest, spent.

He rolled over with her, still connected, brought her legs up and draped them over his shoulders, plunging inside her again and again. His eyes were shut, engrossed as he was in the power of the moment. His breathing came in shorts pants as he finally climaxed, body trembling, gripping her arms as he slowed, lowering himself, still moving inside her but gently now, back and forth… until at last he stopped.

They lay quite still for a time as their breathing slowed. Then Yvette gently eased herself from under him.

He rolled onto his side, facing her. "You sapped me, girl. Don't think you're getting any more out of me tonight.'

Yvette laughed, cuddling up closer. "Old age catching up with you?"

"So I'm getting old. Leave me alone."

She laid her head in the crook between his shoulder and his neck. "Errol, remember I mentioned us living together?"

"Mmm." He stroked the back of her head.

"I've found a place, it's beautiful — perfect. For us. And Tyrone. Aaron would love it too. So… what do you think?"

Errol was on the brink of sleep. "Sounds nice…" He sounded far away.

"Are you in, then?"

"Whatever makes you happy."

"You want to live with me?"

"Who wouldn't?" He kissed her forehead and drew her closer. "We'll talk about it later."

Yvette grinned in the dark. He was going to be hers. They were going to be a family. She sighed, taking the scent of their lovemaking deep into her lungs.

TWELVE

She was thirty, and had been in control of her life now for two years. Her previous life had been one of prescription and routine. But now, she was a woman of shrewd premeditation with a degree in psychology to prove it.

Several men had hurt her over the two years and she had come to the conclusion that she was better off being alone. Until Errol Wright came along. She knew if anyone could heal her completely it would be him.

But she needed him to fall for her too.

Anne-Marie Simms stood up in the bath and held out her hands in front of her, palms up. The scars on her wrists and forearms criss-crossed each other. Some had been deep cuts but were no more apparent now than thin stretch-marks.

Her self-mutilation was brought on by the lack of attention she'd received from her parents. Cutting her arms had made them notice her. Errol, she knew, felt the same. His mother and father had been far too busy to devote any time to him. She wondered how he had dealt with it.

Sometimes she thought about her past, wondering if she had subconsciously invited bullies to pick on her at school. Had she deliberately made herself different, distant and unfriendly, to provoke them? It had certainly got her the attention she craved.

Painful memories.

Daddy left home on her twelfth birthday and never came back. Anne-Marie blamed her mother at first, and then herself. She had begun hurting herself soon after that.

Men had been leaving her ever since.

But this time, with this man, she would not lose control. This time there would be no unconscious, reckless action.

She had set out to get Errol Wright, she had had him, and she was going to keep him.

It was another weekend. God, how she hated weekends! Saturday night. Couples would be going out together, holding hands, laughing, being close, then going home and getting into bed together, making love… And where would she be? At home in her tiny flat, in front of the telly, alone.

There was a note from Marion tacked to Errol's dressing room door when he came into work:

> *Congratulations — you passed me in the ratings once, now watch your back!"*

He sighed contentedly. Everything seemed to be working out… Well, everything except his private life. Apart from the little problem of his infidelity, he was a success.

Another bunch of roses sat on the dresser. This time he knew who they were from, and he was not amused. The note said, "You're mine. What was meant to be can't be undone."

After the morning's recorded interview, Errol left the studio hurriedly. He was pacing through the foyer with his head down when the voice that he had been dreading all day called out from somewhere above him.

"Errol! Errol!"

Anne-Marie ran down the stairs. He turned slowly to face her and forced something resembling a smile on his lips. "Anne-Marie…"

"I waited for your call," she whispered, looking around as though they were being watched.

"I'm sorry." He shook his head, touching his temple. "I had my son until late. When I got home I just crashed out."

"I just want to know where I stand."

"I don't know what to say. It shouldn't have happened."

"You're all the same, aren't you?" she hissed.

"Now don't try to put that one over on me. I never once tried to seduce you before—"

"And why not? Wasn't I good enough?"

"You're one of the most sensual creatures I know, but…"

She put a hand on her hip and tapped her foot impatiently. "I knew there'd be a 'but'."

"You know my lifestyle… I've been trying to avoid this." He was pleading with his eyes for her to let it drop.

"Can we go somewhere and talk?"

Errol looked at his watch. Maybe they should get it all out now. "Okay, I've got a few minutes."

He led the way. Anne-Marie followed, heels clacking on the pavement. He found a wine bar and selected a secluded table. Anne-Marie sat opposite, smiling. She shrugged off her coat. "It's really good seeing you again. I missed you."

Errol opened his mouth to speak but clamped it shut again. He ran a hand over his shaved head nervously, feeling light perspiration at his temples.

"Let's start again." She was still smiling. "How are you?"

"I'm fine. You know, the usual… busy."

"You work too hard." She touched his hand with warm fingers and he drew away as if she'd stung him.

"Anne-Marie, we can't see each other," he blurted out.

"Like what?"

"I don't know. What happened the other night… Maybe it was too much drink, maybe it was a mixture of the mood and the drink, I don't know. But what I do know is that I can't have a relationship with you."

Anne-Marie visibly bristled. "It's *me* you don't want, not just any woman. Is that what you're saying?"

"Not exactly, no. I like you, I have since I first met you… I'm just not ready for something so intense with someone so close to home." He thought about another way to put it. "Relationships are just too much hard work right now."

"Ours wouldn't be, Errol. I *more* than like you. In fact, I think I love you…"

He shook his head disbelievingly. She was smiling again. He recalled briefly how he had been unable to drag himself away from that smile. "You can't be. You hardly know me."

"Errol," she said, slowly, as if to a child, "this is a feeling beyond our control. I can't sleep at nights, wondering who you're with, what you're doing. I want to be with you…"

"I'm sorry. I don't feel the same way." He wanted to tell her he was already seeing someone, but he knew she wouldn't believe him. He'd already said he was single and free. Besides, wouldn't that make him not only a liar but a cheat as well? "I don't see the point in pretending to save your feelings. This simply isn't going to happen."

"Oh, but it already has…"

"What?"

"You may not remember the other night, but I do. You wanted me then. You came on to me, in fact; I think I've still got the bite-marks. You took advantage of my feelings…"

"Feelings?"

"Don't tell me you didn't know how I felt. You knew what you were doing."

"*Knew*? I don't even remember touching you."

Anne-Marie spoke in a quiet tone. "This is getting ugly. I didn't mean for this to happen. I only have myself to blame. I have this habit of going for men that are unavailable…"

He wrinkled his brow, thrown off guard by the change.

She stood up. "So, a sexual relationship is out. How about friends?"

He lowered his eyes. "I don't know. The way you feel, I think it would be better to have a clean break."

"You know that's impossible."

Errol jumped up and faced her. "Impossible? Have I no right to my own life now?"

She smiled. "I meant — we work together."

"Oh! Oh, I see what you mean. Well… we'll just stay out of each other's way then. Okay?"

"Whatever you say, Errol. I must be going. I'm supposed to be in the library."

"Acquaintances?"

"Yeah."

She held out her hand and he shook it. Then she stepped closer and threw her arms around him, embracing him. "I knew you were a bigger man than most," she whispered.

Then she left, leaving him standing there, dumbfounded.

THIRTEEN

Yvette had woken early — Errol was still snoring gently — and had decided to have a quick work-out in her mini gym to start the day. She was half-way through her cool-down when he came in, scratching his head.

"What's wrong with you?" he said. "You need to burn energy, why didn't you wake me?"

She grinned. "Why don't you join me?"

"You know, I haven't had a better offer all day."

In seconds he was stripped down to his underwear and on top of her.

She pushed him off. "I think you've got to cool down, boy. You know what they say about a good exercise routine."

"No, what?"

"You should always warm up first and cool down after."

"What about the middle bit?"

She smiled seductively. "Let's get dressed and go for a walk — we'll discuss it."

Errol was used to Yvette's intrigue and unpredictability. It was one of the biggest attractions of her personality. He never knew what lay around the corner.

He pulled his track suit back on and Yvette dressed in a long skirt. They took the short-cut up to the park, laughing and sharing experiences and memories as they walked. It was still very early, and the lack of people around made them feel as though they had the streets to themselves. Yvette bent forwards from the waist at one point, trying to entice a squirrel to take a cashew nut from her fingers. Beneath her skirt Errol could see the smooth outline of her deliciously perfect buttocks, inviting, made for his hands, and he knew he was ready to accept her challenge.

"Well? Do you want to?"

His hard-on pulsed and pushed for escape. "What — here?"

"Yes, here. Now do you want me or not?"

Did he want her? There was smoke coming out of his ears!

He wasted no time in showing her how much. He reached out for her and pulled her, half-laughing, half-protesting, through the taller shrubs and greenery that surrounded the rose garden, running his hands up her thighs to to her naked buttocks as they went.

"You've got no panties on!"

"Oh!" she said in mock astonishment. "Was I going to need them?"

"You could get arrested for going around without them." He drew her close and pressed her mound against his thickening erection.

"You could get arrested for carrying such a lethal weapon — but I won't tell if you won't," she giggled. Helping him to drop his trousers, she eased them over his buttocks and his erection sprang forth. She turned her back to him so he had a clear view of the tight, dark globes that had been inviting him all morning, placed her palms against a tree trunk, and splayed her legs. His penis throbbed with anticipation as he eased it steadily into her vagina, where she was wet, warm and ready for him.

Brockwell Park was unusually quiet at this time of day. Except for the couple making love in the shrubbery and the occasional dog walker and the squirrels, the only other person braving the chilly morning air was the woman in the trenchcoat and dark glasses.

Twenty minutes previously she had been sitting in her car outside the woman's house, to which she had followed Errol the night before. She had dozed on and off through the night, but had been awake for two hours when at seven o'clock the front door had opened and the woman had come out. Errol had followed her, and they'd linked arms and made off up the road. After they had passed, their observer had considered following them in the car, but thought it too conspicuous, so she'd left the car and followed them on foot, down Acre Lane to central Brixton.

She stopped beneath a low sycamore tree and wiped her dark glasses on her coat, scanning the park and the path she had just come down. There was nothing. Up here even the traffic was barely audible.

The couple had turned a corner ahead of her and the trees had appeared to close behind them. An illusion, a trick of the curving path. She quickened her step, but walked with caution as she didn't want to come face to face with them.

Suddenly there was a squeal from the slope to her right and she stopped again, cocked her head and waited. Now all she could hear was the rustling of the leaves and the roar of a bus on the distant street. She took another step and there was more noise: a thrashing of branches and then a whispered conversation, none of it loud enough for her to hear what they were saying.

She crept silently into the shrubbery beside the path. Now she could see them, could see what they were doing. She crouched down and watched, not moving a muscle until their muted moans of ecstasy told her that the show was over. Then she crept away, a plan already forming in her mind. If only she had thought to bring a camera. But maybe actual physical evidence wouldn't be necessary.

The weekend had passed quickly, but for Errol it had been a memorable one, and he carried these memories into work with him on Monday morning.

The internal phone rang as he was getting ready to leave his dressing room for the studio. He picked it up and said casually, "Errol Wright speaking."

"Errol?"

Damn. She had been put through to his dressing room from the switchboard. He must have a word with the receptionist. "Anne-Marie."

"I'm alone for lunch today. If you're not busy, why don't

you join me?"

"Well, actually I do have a business lunch today…"

"Well then, how about dinner?"

Errol searched his mind for another excuse. "I don't know…"

"It's really important that I talk to you… and soon."

"Right," he said, resigned. They fixed a time and a place and Errol rang off, putting his head in his hands. He hoped she wasn't still playing games; he'd had just about enough of them, and his life was full enough as it was.

Errol arrived at the restaurant ten minutes late, but there was no sign of her. Recognising him, the waiter rushed over and led him to the reserved table in the window, where he could be seen by the other diners and any passers-by. He didn't complain; she would be here soon, and he'd make sure they got out as quickly as possible.

As he sat down he realised the waiter wasn't the only one to have recognised him. Some of his fellow diners were turning to give him a smile or a nod; others were more guarded, and whispered to their partners who glanced at him from the corner of an eye.

He had worked out a golden rule for dealing with autograph hunters and fans: never catch anyone's eye in public. Look ahead when you're walking, and always have something to read when you're sitting down in a public place. So he picked up the menu and pored over it with mock concentration. He ordered a mineral water and waited, glancing at his watch every few minutes.

At twenty past eight he was getting ready to leave when Anne-Marie arrived, smiling. She had dressed seductively for the occasion in a short, red swing dress and a choker of pearls, her hair tied up with a few ringlets allowed to hang free, framing her face.

"Sorry I'm late. I had to sort a few things out." She kissed him brazenly on the cheek, and he noticed that most of the eyes in the room were upon them. Obviously the word had got around. He glared at her as the waiter came to their table.

"Can I get you a drink, madam?"

"It's mademoiselle. Yes, you can: I'll have a white wine spritzer," she answered, never breaking eye contact with Errol. Then he glanced quickly round the room. "I keep forgetting how famous you are. I shouldn't have left you alone for so long."

She reached across the table for his hand, which he drew back.

"What is this, Anne-Marie? What do you want from me, money?"

She laughed. "Of course not! Can you imagine if someone got photos of us together? We'd make the front pages of the tabloids. I can see it now…"

He stared at her. Was she stark staring mad? "You haven't told anyone about us, have you?"

Anne-Marie twirled a finger in one of her ringlets. "Relax," she smiled, "I'm not ready to go public yet."

"*Yet*! Cho'! I'm leaving," He half-stood and quick as a flash she had grabbed his wrist.

"I don't think so, Errol." She looked round the restaurant again. "Unless you want me to make a scene you'll sit down and have a meal with me."

Slowly he took his seat again, shaking his head defeatedly. A little vein in his temple pulsed.

"Don't give me a hard time, Errol. I can make life very difficult for you and those who care about you."

"Why would you want to do this, Anne-Marie? What have I done to you?"

She picked up a menu and leant towards him, ignoring his question. "You enjoy fucking like an animal in the woods, don't you?"

His throat closed. He said nothing.

A shadow of vulnerability had crept into his eyes, giving her confidence and a little extra knowledge of his weakness.

"Photographs leaked to the press of your little liaison in the park wouldn't do your career much good, would they?

127

Just think about that before you turn me down again."

He held her eyes defiantly for a minute. She didn't allow her gaze to drop for an instant.

"Let's eat," he said finally. The sooner he got this over with the better. He'd just have to make sure she never put him in this situation again.

During the meal she gave him a gift. She'd seen it in a shop, she enthused, and just had to buy it for him. She insisted he open it straight away. It was a blue silk tie, exquisitely made, the pattern running through it composed of capital Es.

She managed to manipulate him into giving her a lift home. He sat behind the steering wheel in stony silence, wanting her to know beyond any doubt that he was not enjoying himself.

"I hope you realise that this is just the beginning, Errol," she said as they sat in the car outside her flat.

"Your threats don't frighten me, Anne-Marie. You can't force me to feel for you."

"Wanna bet?" She got out of the car and walked quickly to her door.

Errol didn't wait to see her inside. He was angry, and determined not to be manipulated again.

The phone rang at midnight. Errol had been in bed for over an hour, but he was still awake. Even the hot Milo hadn't helped.

"I want you, Errol."

"Yvette?" he said, sitting up, the sheet dropping from his chest.

"When am I going to see you again?"

He sighed. Anne-Marie.

"Are you still there?"

"Yes. I'm disappointed in you, though, Anne-Marie…"

"Disappointed?"

"From the strong, independent woman I met, to a woman who can't let go of a man she had sex with once…"

"I thought that was what being a strong woman was about: going for what she wants and getting it by any means necessary."

"What will it take to get through to you that I'm not interested?"

"If you just give us a chance, a weekend away... Let me treat you. We could fly to Paris, take in a show, stay in an upmarket hotel. I could—"

Errol hung up.

The phone rang again a few hours later. Errol was almost asleep this time, and as he reached out for it he saw Bart Simpson telling him it was four in the morning.

"Yeah?" he answered groggily.

"Mr Wright? Mr Errol Wright?"

"Yes, that's me."

"Mr Wright, this is Dr Kate Trimble from King's College Hospital. We were given your name by your fiancé a few minutes ago—"

"My *fiancé*?" He bolted upright.

"She has been admitted into our accident and emergency. Could you get down here as soon as possible?"

"Is she all right? What happened?"

"She's stable, but I really do think you should get here as soon as possible..."

Errol had already dropped the phone and was dragging his clothes on. Yvette, in hospital. What had happened? They didn't tell you anything. And what about Tyrone? God, this time of the morning the boy would definitely have been with her.

He was out of the door within five minutes, his mind racing ahead of him to the hospital. He could picture her lying on one of those cots, bandaged, weak, moaning, calling for him.

Parking the car haphazardly he dashed into the hospital's reception and blurted out the information he'd been given on the phone.

"No, we don't have anyone by the name of Yvette Barker registered," the young man behind the desk told him.

"She's here, I tell you! I was called a few minutes ago by a... Dr Trimble."

"I'll get the doctor for you."

Seconds later Kate Trimble came to reception and led him to a row of cubicles. "She's doing okay, a little sleepy... but fifteen minutes later and she wouldn't have made it."

She drew back a curtain and he saw her in the bed, lying on her side with her back to him. He rushed to the bedside, and at his touch she turned round.

Anne-Marie smiled weakly and reached out a hand to him. Both her wrists were tightly bandaged.

"I'll let her explain," the doctor said in a tight voice, "but she's going to be fine." She walked away, pulling the curtain closed behind her

Errol slapped a hand to his forehead. "What the *hell* are you playing at now?" he hissed angrily. "I thought..." He broke off and started pacing up and down beside the bed.

Easing herself up on the pillows, she stared at him. Half-asleep and with a frightened look in his eyes, he was still the most gorgeous man she knew. "You thought what?"

He nodded towards her bandaged wrists, curious. "What happened?"

She lifted her arms. "I cut my wrists," she said, almost proudly. "Only I didn't do it properly. I was in agony for half an hour before I dialled for an ambulance."

"You're pathetic," he said, a look of scorn on his face.

"I didn't mean to put you through this. But I needed you, Errol..."

"You don't get it. You just don't get it, do you?"

Her eyes filled with tears. "I know how I feel..."

"You're sad, you know that? Lonely, and very sad." He leant on the bed with his knuckles and stared into her face. "I pity you."

"Is that why you slept with me?"

"Don't give me that. You drugged me and you know it."

She grinned. It was a parody of a smile. "But you still

care about me. You're here, aren't you?"

"They didn't give me your name. They just told me my fiancé was in here."

"Do you have a fiancé?"

"That is none of your business."

She reached out and touched his jacket. "I don't think you do. Maybe a lover, that tart I saw you with in the park …"

Errol dragged himself away. "You're sick! Why don't you do us all a favour and see a doctor?"

"Oh, it would suit you to think I'm crazy, wouldn't it?" she screamed at his retreating back. "I couldn't simply have been foolish enough to fall in love with you!"

He was gone, and Anne-Marie knew what she had to do. She had warned him she would go public if necessary. He obviously didn't believe her, saw it as just another threat. Well, she'd show him. She would show him all right.

Two men stepped out in front of Errol as he exited the hospital. One switched on a glaring light, the other aimed a camera at his face. The press! How did they know he was here? Did they know *why*?

"Errol Wright?" The cameraman took several shots.

"Can we have a few minutes?"

Errol, who usually had plenty of time for journalists, was in too much of a hurry to get away. How the hell had it got out that he was here? No doubt some unscrupulous porter had tipped them off.

He was backing off as quickly as he could. "I don't have anything to say to you."

"What have you got to say about the attempted suicide, Errol?"

"That is none of your business."

"That's our job to decide. Who is she — a mistress, an old girlfriend, a relative?"

He slammed the car door and the camera flashed a couple more times as he put his foot down and took off. He knew enough about journalism to know that these hacks had nothing unless they talked to Anne-Marie.

For most people, a day at home usually means relaxation and living the life of Riley, but for Errol Wright it was work on another level. Today though, after a sleepless night, he was having trouble arranging his thoughts. He'd tried to sleep, but last night's fiasco had left him too wary to be tired. Sitting at his desk, he stared absently at Helen's empty chair opposite. He wanted to be able to talk to someone about it, about Anne-Marie. Get some advice.

Helen came back into the room, and for a second he considered telling her. She was used to confidentiality. But this was too personal; besides, she was a woman — she might not see things from his point of view.

"Here, you look like you could do with this." She passed him a steaming cup of coffee and one of her blueberry muffins, then took her seat.

He had opened a book on the desk in front of him, which he now pushed aside. He'd read the first paragraph at least ten times, but still couldn't remember a word.

"Are you okay?"

"I think I've got a headache coming on."

The phone rang and Helen answered it automatically.

"It's for you," she said after a moment, and handed the receiver to him.

He answered distractedly. "Hello?"

"I was expecting a call," Anne-Marie said. "You knew I was all alone in the hospital and you never called."

"Why would I do that?" Errol leant his elbow on the table and cradled his chin in the palm of his hand.

"I needed you, and you just left me there."

"What do you want from me? I've been totally straight with you." Remembering Helen was in the room, he looked up and caught her watching him, a look of concern on her face. She dropped her eyes back to the keyboard.

"Put this call through to my room, will you?" he asked

132

her. "I'll pick it up in there."

In his bedroom he took a deep breath before picking up.
"Well?"

"That was your secretary, was it? Or is *she* there with
you?"

"You seem to know everything about me — you tell me."

"Don't play games with me, Errol. I know you're
sleeping with someone else. You lied to me about it."

"I sleep with whoever I damn well please! I don't have to
justify my actions to you."

"You're such a dog, Errol. A fucking animal who can't
control his own dick. You used me and now you seem to
think you can just throw me aside. I won't let you do that,
Mr Wright." Her voice had lost its pseudo-politeness now.
She sounded angry and frustrated.

"Then tell me what you expect from me. I can't *make*
myself feel something for you. We could have been friends,
Anne-Marie…"

"God, you are so full of shit!"

He felt his own anger rising. "Can't we handle this like
experienced adults? Can't we just agree that it was a mistake
and move on?"

"Why should I?" she screamed, and then suddenly her
voice was quiet, almost a whisper. "How can I? I love you."

Errol positioned his finger over the button on the phone.
He could hear her sobbing as he disconnected.

He suddenly felt very empty, vulnerable. He needed
Yvette at that moment. He wanted sexual healing, but he
knew she was working…

Abruptly he jumped up. Maybe he couldn't have Yvette,
but he could have a work-out. Shouting out to Helen that he
was disappearing for a couple of hours, he stuffed his kit
into his bag, grabbed his mobile, and headed out.

Sweat poured down his forehead as he lifted the weights to
shoulder height one last time. The gym was almost empty
this afternoon. Christmas was just weeks away and keeping

133

fit was on few people's agenda.

The gym door swung open. Errol looked up and smiled.

"Chris! Over here, man!"

"All right?"

"Glad you could make it." Errol tried to sound casual but there was a hint of sarcasm in his voice.

"Boy, you're in a good mood. What's up?"Chris dumped his gym bag by the wall and bent at the waist to begin warming up.

"Domesticity."

Chris took his place on a bench beside Errol and threw him a quizzical look. "Come again?"

"You hear about the call of the wild, but it's the call to domesticity that I don't understand. You know, guys hanging up their boots to become domesticated…"

"Don't knock it until you've tried it," Chris grinned. "You're just feeling hard done by because all the lads have settled down and you're still between girlfriends."

"Get outta here! If… *when* I decide to settle down, I won't let it interfere with me catching up wid my bredrin."

"You're an inspiration to us all," Chris chuckled, shaking his head.

Errol frowned at his friend's sarcasm. Yes, he had two women after him, as well as all his unknown admirers, and still he felt unsatisfied. What was missing? Devotion? Maybe Chris was right; maybe he was jealous that his friends were able to make the decision to stay with the woman they loved.

It was weeks since Yvette had asked him to move in, and he was still undecided. He'd cheated on her, for one thing. And she had a son who was nearly a teenager — could he be a father to him? Would his career allow it? And a shared mortgage — that was a commitment.

What did he have to lose by making the decision? From his point of view, too much.

He put his weights down and joined Chris on the rowing machines. "I've been thinking about this settling down business, you know."

Chris threw him a look but said nothing.

"I been spending more time with Yvette and Tyrone lately, and… well, you know, it's nice."

"Nice! Cosy and welcoming…"

"Yeah, all of that… But I've got a problem…"

What the hell? Errol thought. He had to tell someone. Another man.

"You see, there's this one girl…"

"Woman?"

"Yeah, all right, a woman. She started work at the station, so I saw her kinda regular, you know."

Chris was staring at him intently, already knowing what was coming next.

"Nothing sexual– we were just hanging out. Then one night she got me drunk and slipped something into my drink. The next thing I know I'm waking up naked on her sofa the next morning."

"You did the dirty?"

"I guess we did. But the weird thing is I can't remember actually doing it."

Chris was shaking his head, bursting to say "I told you so".

"Don't laugh, man, this is serious."

Chris could even guess who the woman was. He stopped rowing and twisted on the seat to face his friend. "Do I know her?"

"You know *of* her. You remember the colleague I told you about?"

"How could I forget? I warned you…" There was a smirk on his face that Errol didn't like. "Why'd you do it? You said you might be ready to settle down a moment ago."

"Believe me, I didn't know what I was doing! You know me — would I ever touch a woman I work with? Especially when she's my mates ex…"

"What did she do? Blackmail you?"

"Not financially, but she's done something…"

"*What*?"

"She's following me around, sending me stuff. She's on

135

the phone every day. Just before I called you today she called me."

"And what did she say?"

"How she loves me, can't let me go... I don't know."

"Sounds to me like you've got a nutter on your hands."

"But she seemed so... sure of herself."

"Nutters are pretty good actors."

Errol stopped rowing and rested his arms on his knees. Now that he'd started talking he couldn't stop. He could do that with Chris. He was the only friend who'd listen objectively without judgement. "She slit her wrists the other night and called me to come and see her."

"What!"

"No joke. We had one night together, that's all, and I can't get rid of her."

"She needs a doctor."

"You're not wrong. She's a seriously disturbed fan."

"Fatal Attraction Part Two," Chris chuckled, trying to add a touch of levity to the matter at hand.

But Errol wasn't smiling. "There's something else," he said quietly.

"What? She send you a birthday cake with a knife in it?"

"No." Errol was deadly serious. "She told me she's taken stuff from my house."

"Shit! What did she take?"

"She took a few things, but the only one she'd tell me about was a photograph from Aaron's room. And I know she stole one of my shirts because she wore it on a double date I took her on with Marion and Paul."

"Lawdy, Lawdy!" Chris sighed. "You get it back?"

Errol shook his head.

Even Chris was quiet now.

"I don't know what to do, man. I want to report it to the police but I don't want the papers getting hold of it. I can't let this affect my career or what I have with Yvette."

"You mean Yvette knows nothing?"

"I could hardly tell her, could I? But I'll have to do something soon, before Anne-Marie does."

FOURTEEN

Woolwich was packed with Christmas shoppers. Anne-Marie checked her watch then continued on the other side of the street.

Last night had left her feeling bad. Why was Errol being mean? He liked her — she knew that. They'd had good sex. So what was the problem? It could only be that bitch he'd fucked in the park. She had to eliminate the competition for him to be hers. Simple.

The optician's was quiet, and the girl on the reception looked almost grateful to have custom as she looked up from the magazine she was reading under the counter.

"Can I help you?" She smiled the smile of a toothpaste advert: shiny, healthy teeth surrounded by cherry-red lips.

"No, thank you... I'm just looking for new frames."

The assistant nodded. "Let me know if you need help."

Anne-Marie pretended to browse. A moment later the woman she'd been following appeared at the door to her left. She selected a blue pair from the rack of frames and tried them on. "Not me at all," she said, replacing them.

Anne-Marie smiled. She felt as though she knew this woman. She admired her bold style of dress, such a contrast to her own conservative appearance: the short leather mini-skirt, jacket and knee-length boots, her make up...

The woman must have felt Anne-Marie's eyes on her, because she turned to look directly at her. "You fancy me?"

Anne-Marie immediately averted her eyes. How awful! Surely the woman didn't think she'd been appraising her!

Thankfully the optician walked in at that moment with her results. "Miss Barker..." She spread a prescription on the counter as Yvette approached. "It seems you are slightly short-sighted in your right eye. Nothing serious at the moment. This prescription is for mild correction, but you should have your eyes tested again in maybe two years."

"Really? Short sighted!"

"Believe me, it's nothing to worry about. Will you be paying cash?"

"Mm-hmm. Hold on, let me just find my purse."

As Yvette fumbled in her handbag Anne-Marie approached. "I'm sorry, but do I know you?" she asked.

Yvette frowned. "Pardon me?"

"I'm sure I know you." Anne-Marie touched a finger to her head. "Colin's wedding — right? You were there?"

Yvette visibly relaxed; she recognised her now. "Right. Yes, I was." Then she remembered what she'd just done. "Oh! Listen, sorry about what I said just now. I didn't—"

"You were Errol's guest, right?"

Yvette was delighted to be recognised. "I know, I'm unforgettable. How are ya?"

"Fine."

Yvette paid cash. "Christmas shopping?"

"Not really, I haven't any family to shop for."

"You lucky bitch... Oops! Excuse the French."

Yvette flipped her plaits back with one hand, and Anne-Marie caught sight of her long, scarlet fingernails.

Yvette made to leave. "Well, nice seeing you again..."

"Are you going home?"

"No. Actually I'm meeting a friend for lunch."

"Oh... I see." Anne-Marie turned back to the frames.

"Why don't you come along?"

"Oh, I wouldn't want to intrude..."

"Rubbish! It ain't *that* kind of friend."

Anne-Marie found herself strangely drawn to this woman. There was a friendly vitality about her. Her willingness to talk to complete strangers was intriguing. Anyway, she had no intention of turning her down.

"Why not?"

"Good on ya! Just hold on while I find out about contact lenses. I've always fancied those coloured ones..."

They spent the afternoon in Lewisham, leaving dismal Woolwich for better climes. They were sitting at the café in the middle of the shopping centre when Karen arrived.

"I've seen you somewhere before, haven't I?" she asked Anne-Marie after brief introductions were made.

"Joan's wedding," Yvette answered for her new friend.

Karen took a seat, and they ordered salads all round.

"So who'll get married next, then?" Karen asked as the waitress disappeared. "First Jennifer, then Joan and Colin… I suppose the next impossibility would be me and Phillip!"

Yvette laughed. Jennifer Edwards and Joan Ross had both had difficult relationships with their partners before taking the plunge, and Karen was a die-hard independent woman who had just moved in with her boyfriend.

The food appeared, and they stopped talking as the waitress put down plates. Anne-Marie already felt comfortable in the presence of her new companions. She was itching to probe into Yvette's relationship with Errol, but she controlled herself. The time would come.

"The next one to get married should be Marion," she said, resuming the topic. "She and Paul are engaged."

"You know Marion too?" Karen asked through a mouthful of lettuce.

"We went to school together," Anne-Marie said, reaching for the butter.

"Right. And how long have you known Yvette?"

Yvette looked up. Karen was always this blatant when she wanted information. For her, subtlety didn't exist. She was feeling Anne-Marie out with her eyes, checking where she was coming from.

"We just met… properly," Anne-Marie replied. "We were introduced at Joan's wedding reception, but you know how those thing are, you never remember names." She put down her fork and lifted her glass of mineral water. "How long have you two known each other?"

"A coupla years," Yvette answered.

"And what do you do?" Anne-Marie asked Yvette.

"I run a health centre. A small one, but I'm gonna expand one day. Got big plans, man."

Anne-Marie smiled. Yvette was probably thinking of

using Errol's money to finance it. The leech.

"What d'you do, Anne-Marie?" Karen asked, rubbing the rim of her glass with an index finger.

"At the moment I'm a researcher for a TV show," Anne-Marie said smugly. *Do the Wright Thing.* You know it? I'm the resident psychologist. You might have seen me…"

Neither of them had. Karen caught Yvette's wide-eyed look but didn't let her friend speak. "So you know Errol?"

Anne-Marie became coy. "Well of course we see each other at work…" This wasn't the right time to come clean about her relationship with him.

Yvette was still staring in barely concealed amazement. This latest revelation shed a new light on the mystery girl. Was there something going on here? Errol hadn't mentioned her. Well he wouldn't if he was seeing her on the sly.

As the three women chatted, any anxiety she'd felt about Anne-Marie and Errol quickly faded. She liked the girl.

When they'd finished eating Anne-Marie insisted on paying the bill. She was grateful for Yvette's invitation to join her, and had gleaned enough information to be fairly sure that she posed no real threat.

Karen admired the soft leather wallet Anne-Marie pulled from her purse. It was emerald green, almost like snakeskin. "Can I feel it?" she asked.

Anne-Marie handed it over. It was beautifully made, must have cost a packet. "Expensive?"

"Yes. But my mother left me her house and her savings when she died, so I can afford to treat myself occasionally."

Karen found herself popping open the catch, and was stunned when she came face to face with Errol. She showed the photograph to Yvette, but before her friend could open her mouth she jumped in. "Er, why have you got a picture of Errol Wright in your wallet?"

Anne-Marie looked at the purse and bit her lip, as though she'd forgotten the picture was in there. Then she looked at Yvette and gave a sheepish grin. "You may find this silly," she said, taking back her wallet, "but I really do admire him as a black man who is going places. Who knows, one day he might return my admiration."

Karen screwed up her mouth. "Girl, you're tripping!"she exclaimed.

Anne-Marie smiled, and shook her head slightly as she spoke. "Sorry. Do we have a problem here?"

Yvette was simmering just beneath the surface, but she remained outwardly calm. "Do you suffer from delusions? 'Cause I have to tell you, you're having one right now."

Anne-Marie was still smiling, looking from one to the other. "What are you talking about?"

Karen half-stood and leant towards her innocent-looking face. "Errol's her boyfriend, fool."

Yvette touched her friend's hand. "Karen, keep out of this."

"Oh!" Anne-Marie looked down her nose at Yvette. "That's funny. He never mentions you."

"Whether he does or not, I'm telling you: hands off."

Anne-Marie gave a patronising little laugh. "I think that's between myself and Errol, don't you?"

Karen, unable to help herself, stood up and slammed her palm on the table. One or two diners looked up, hopeful for some entertainment. "Listen, bitch, she just told you—"

"I think you should know something," Anne-Marie interrupted. "Errol and I have been intimate."

Yvette gasped. "Since when?"

"Two weeks ago. Look, I think this is something you should really discuss with Errol. Obviously you've got something going for him, but he can't possibly feel the same way about you. You do realise there are probably dozens of women like you, don't you?"

Karen was practically crawling across the table. She couldn't believe this. She had known Yvette a long time; she knew her friend could open her mouth when necessary. So why was she speechless now? The two of them could take this woman outside and give her what for and the problem would be solved. She couldn't let it go on any longer. "What's wrong with you, Eve? You can't just sit there and take that! Slap her one! Errol ain't cheating on you…"

Yvette wasn't so sure. No wonder he couldn't give her a straight answer about the house. No wonder they hardly ever went anywhere together. No wonder… no wonder.

"Call him and ask him if you don't believe me?" Anne-Marie was saying, waving a mobile phone at her.

As Yvette seemed too stunned to react, Karen snatched it out of her hand. "Yvette, call 'im nuh!"

Yvette and Anne-Marie stared each other out. Anne-Marie looked too confident for Yvette's liking. She didn't want to hear bad news — not in front of Karen.

"You want me to make the call?" Karen pushed.

"No, leave it, man." Yvette took the phone from her and handed it back to Anne-Marie, who rose to leave.

"It's been nice meeting you both," she said. "I must go."

"Stay away from Errol," Yvette warned.

Anne-Marie threw her a superior look. "Listen, why don't we let *him* chose his Mrs Wright?"

Yvette's jaw dropped.

"Scared he'll choose me?"

Yvette shut her mouth and narrowed her eyes. "No!"

"Then we're rivals."

Karen kissed her teeth. "I'll rival your backside."

"Okay…" Yvette stood up and stretched her hand across the table towards her rival. "May the best woman win."

Colin phoned on Tuesday morning. He rarely called during work hours, so Errol knew it had to be important.

"You read *The Voice*?" Colin asked

"Not yet. Why?"

"Then you bes' go and find a copy."

"Am I in there again?" Errol asked casually.

"You're in there all right, but I don't think you're gonna like dis one."

"Why?"

"Go and get the paper. Page twenty-seven."

As soon as he had a chance Errol bought a copy. And there, near the bottom of page twenty-seven, was a photo of him and Anne-Marie, her hand on his, staring intently into his eyes. The heading was "The Wright Woman?"

With mounting irritation, Errol read the caption:

> *TV star Errol Wright, at an intimate dinner with his attractive researcher Anne-Marie Simms. Word has it she's the new Miss in his life.*

That's why she'd reserved a window table; it was a set up.

The telephone in his dressing room was ringing as he walked back in.

"Errol, it's me."

"Yvette."

"Have you read *The Voice* yet?"

She'd seen it. Errol sighed. "Yeah, I did—"

"Is it true? Are you seeing her?" Yvette asked before he could start making excuses.

"Yvette, she's a colleague, we were having lunch…"

"I thought it was dinner."

"Lunch, dinner… It was food," he said matter-of-factly.

"And she needed you to hold her hand to eat, I suppose."

"Eve, I wouldn't lie to you." Errol sat down. "She's a friend. As we were about to get up and go she touched my hand. That was all. They've got it wrong, they always do."

Yvette was furious, but held it down. "Sue them then."

"They haven't libelled me. Listen, honey, I've gotta work. I'll see you later."

Errol hung up. He sat in thought for a moment.

He had been faithful to Yvette for a year. Could that be love? That was how he felt. Now decisions had to be made, and for the first time in his life Errol Wright was confused. Did he follow his heart or his practical mind?

He looked out of the window, directly down to the car park and saw a woman in sunglasses leaning against a dark car. She seemed to be looking straight at him. Was she watching him? It sure felt like it.

First at home, and now here…

Errol rushed out and hurried down the hallway to the lifts, his heart pounding. But by the time he got to the ground floor the parking lot was empty.

Yvette's house, Errol has just arrived and was taking his coat off. "Something smells good."

"Must be my perfume. You bought it for me."

He nuzzled her neck and mumbled, "You *always* smell good. I meant the food."

"New recipe."

Yvette cringed, twisted away from him and headed back to the kitchen. An image of Anne-Marie had come into mind just as Errol had tried to hug her. Did he do that to her too?

"Make yourself at home," she said. "I'll be right there."

Errol watched her walk away from him. "Very nice." He entered the front room. "Where's Tyrone?"

"With my sister. We can do with some privacy."

Yvette had set a table in the living room and the lights were dimmed. Errol inspected her efforts and smiled. What had he done to deserve this?

Yvette wasn't a great cook and so they tended to eat out. He helped himself to a drink and took a seat on the sofa.

Yvette brought the food in dish by dish, and served him first. Everything looked delicious. The main dish was a cheese bake, which they ate with pasta and various vegetables. The meal was going fine until Errol started to choke a little. He took a swig of wine to wash down his food.

"Are you okay?"

He tried to swallow, but his throat felt as though it was constricting. Suddenly his mouth began to salivate. "I'm not sure," he replied hoarsely, coughing again.

"I'll get you some water." Yvette got up and walked to the kitchen while Errol continued to open and close his mouth like a fish gasping for air. By the time she had brought the water back he was pacing up and down, wheezing, retching and looking distinctly red in the face.

"Errol, what is it?" Yvette handed him the water and

144

rubbed his back, gently forcing concern on her face.

As if she didn't know.

"The food, the little pieces of meat… what was it?"

"In the bake?"

He nodded.

"Pork…"

Errol collapsed into the armchair. "I'm allergic."

"Oh God…" Yvette faked mild alarm. "What can I do? Have you got medication?"

"At home."

Her mouth twisted sadistically and she took a deep breath. "Oh God, I'll call you a cab." *Bastard, I hope you die painfully.*

There was nothing she wanted less, but she was so angry.

"No. No time," he gasped. "You'll have to drive me."

Unable to think of a reasonable excuse she conceded.

They took his car, and arrived at his house half an hour later. Once Errol had taken a couple of blasts from his inhaler his breathing began to settle.

Yvette was standing motionless in the hallway as he came out of the kitchen. She wanted him to know it had been a punishment, but how could she? He would hate her.

Revenge was supposed to be sweet but Yvette felt remorse. She prayed he would never find out.

Anne-Marie sat in her car outside Errol's house later that night and cried. Several times she had picked up the phone to call the clinic. She would dial a few numbers and then stop, as flashes of buried memory resurfaced. The waiting rooms with "really sick people" in them; the sterile white or pastel-painted rooms where she was spoken to like a child; the medication that turned her into a zombie.

Besides, this time it was different… wasn't it? She was in love with Errol Wright. She didn't want to hurt him. She just knew that they had to be together. So, if it took a little manipulation, it was worth it.

And they had looked so *good* together in the photo.

FIFTEEN

Errol pulled up outside Nyam Food Caribbean takeaway. He smiled at the thought of Errol Wright, television star, calling into the local takeaway for curry goat and rice and peas, but it was exactly what he fancied now. It had been a hard day. Anne-Marie had called his office repeatedly.

She still hadn't got the message. She seemed to find a thousand excuses to visit him on set, was forever asking to come round and cook him a meal or take him out somewhere, offers on which Errol always took a raincheck.

The other woman in his life had been exceptionally quiet. When he'd made his regular call to her this morning, Yvette had apologised again for the pork. Usually just the smell of the potential danger was enough to warn him off it, but this time the pork had been so heavily buried in cheese that he hadn't even tasted it, much less smelled it.

What he really needed now was a long, hot bath, some good food and a cool, strong drink. He was going to pamper himself tonight, he decided.

Of course, he was recognised instantly, and he received an extra large portion of food on the understanding that he would give Nyam Food a mention on TV.

He drove home without the radio on, determined to keep this rare moment of solitude. As he pulled up outside his house he waved to two of his neighbours' children. The boys grinned back at him before darting indoors. At their age Errol had been the family entertainer. He would perform his impersonation of Michael Jackson for friends and relatives — his party piece. His parents had always been sure he'd end up in showbiz.

Wearily he opened his front door and dropped his briefcase just inside. He put the food in the kitchen before going up to shower.

He drew the already loosened tie from round his neck, draped it over the back of a chair, and stared at his face in the mirror. Looking back at him, he saw a weary black man.

"Boy, you need a holiday…"

Then out of the corner of his eye he saw something out of place: a big, striped box on the bed, tied with ribbon.

It was a gift box! Not unusual in itself, but Errol knew that no one else had a key to his house…

Very carefully he picked it up. It barely weighed a thing. Probably not a bomb, then. He gave it a gentle shake and heard the rustle of tissue paper. Frowning, he pulled at the bow and let the lid fall on the bed. Inside was a smaller parcel with the word "SURPRISE!" written on it in big red letters. It had to be from Yvette. Now excited as a little boy at Christmas time, he ripped the wrapping paper away. A note dropped out, and in his hands he held a silk shirt. Picking up the tiny white envelope, he removed the card and read the handwritten words:

Errol, my love,

This is a replacement for the shirt I borrowed. I've become so attached to it, but I know I had no right to just keep it. Hope you like it. I love giving surprises.
Miss you, see you soon.

Love you,
Anne-Marie

Errol's skin broke out in instantaneous goosebumps. He dropped the shirt and the note as though they were contaminated. She hadn't broken into his house, so she must have let herself in. She must have copied his keys.

He walked around the house, checking every room and storage space. There was nothing apparently missing, no one hiding in the house, so he locked the door on his way back to the kitchen, when the phone rang.

He picked it up and held it just away from his ear.

"Errol?"

Her voice was like a switch, turning on his anger. "Anne-Marie — what the hell do you think you're doing breaking into my home!" he yelled. "I could have you charged—"

"Did you like it?"

"Damn you, stupid woman! Didn't you hear what I just said? I'm calling the police!" He slammed the phone down.

But what would he tell the police? That he was being given presents by a beautiful woman? She hadn't broken in, she hadn't stolen anything or done any criminal damage... He stumbled back into the kitchen, defeated, tired and hungry. Maybe it was better just to ignore her. Surely she would eventually get the message. All he had to do was change the locks and his phone number tomorrow.

Yvette stepped out of the health centre and walked towards Errol's car. She had on a red two-piece suit, the skirt nearly reaching her red court shoes, with a cream blouse underneath, and her braided hair was tied back in a bun.

Errol watched her from the car. She looked extremely uncomfortable, confined. At first he hadn't recognised her. "What's up with the suit?" he asked as she opened the door. "You got an interview?"

"Don't you like it? It's my new image."

"It's nice, but..."

She sighed as she got in. "It's not me."

"Got it in one. Why the change?"

"You know... Coming up to new year I thought I'd try a new, more executive image. To tell the truth I thought you'd like it."

He leant towards her. "Why would you think that? Have I ever complained about the way you dress?"

She shook her head, meeting his eyes only fleetingly.

"I love the way you dress, the way you wear your hair..." He buried his head in her neck. "The way you smell..."

Yvette gently pushed him away. "Let's get home first."

Errol frowned and studied her face. "Something

wrong?"

"No," she replied, much too quickly. "I just want you to myself."

That was no lie. She'd hardly slept for the past two nights, thinking of him and that woman together, doing it, laughing at her behind her back. The outfit had been to see if his attitude toward her would change. He'd taken Anne-Marie to bed, so he must think her sexy, Yvette had reasoned, and this was the way she dressed.

Confident. That was what Anne-Marie was. A lot more confident than Yvette, who at the moment felt little more than confusion. Errol had slept with someone else, and yet he still treated her the same. He didn't look or smell any different; he still took her out, the sex was still overwhelming. He still seemed to want her — or was he just biding his time? What the hell was she doing wrong?

She wanted to scream.

They listened to jazz and ate smoked salmon with garlic bread, home-made by Errol. The light was dimmed and they lay on huge floor-cushions in Yvette's living room.

Yvette was now feeling frustrated as well as anxious. She had spent the last few days tamping down feelings that she felt she shouldn't have to hide, and now the pretence was getting the better of her. It was make-or-break time. To hell with Anne-Marie's competition. She knew she couldn't keep up this charade any longer.

"Errol, we have to talk…"

He met her eyes questioningly. "I thought we were."

"No. Seriously."

"About… ?"

"About us. I'm making plans for my future, and I need to know if you're going to be part of it."

"I'm here, aren't I?"

"You're here *now*. But in a few hours' time you'll be back at home, at work… or maybe with someone else." She hardly dared make the suggestion any more forthright.

149

"*What*? God, why would I want someone else?"

"That's a good question — but then you could also ask yourself why you want me."

"What kind of question is that?'

"A question you can't seem to answer. Aren't I intelligent enough for you? Is my career not good enough, not glamourous enough? Are you ashamed of me?"

Errol propped himself up on an elbow and took one of her hands in his. "I don't know what's provoked this outburst, but it has nothing to do with you."

"Obviously not!"

"Eve, I'm thirty-four and very ambitious. I haven't recently had as much time with you as I'd have liked. Because of this it's hard for me to build a loving relationship. I don't want to end up hurting you... You know that when I settle down it'll be for life."

"So what now?"

He stroked her hand. "What?"

"Is this all there's ever going to be to our relationship — dates and sex? I feel as though I'm still having some kind of sordid affair; we haven't moved on from that. I mean, how many times have you invited me to your house?"

Errol knew she'd been inside his house only a few times, had slept in his bed only once. But he liked his privacy.

Irritated and restless, he pulled his hand away. "Do we have to discuss this now?"

Yvette sighed. She should have guessed this would be his reaction. He hated being cornered. Any minute now, she thought, he's gonna say "This is getting heavy".

He stood up and lowered himself onto the sofa."This is getting heavy."

Yvette sat up on the cushion. The knowledge that she knew him so well made the situation more intolerable. Anger was bubbling up inside her. She desperately needed to know what she meant to him, yet she was having such difficulty confronting him about his other woman, this woman who seemed so convinced that he was her man, so confident that she was willing to compete for him.

Well, Yvette wasn't prepared to play that game any more. She wanted Errol to decide which woman he wanted to be with now. "I've had enough of this…"

"I know what this is about. It's about the house, isn't it? I was supposed to give you a decision—"

"Oh, fuck the house, Errol! This is about *your* infidelities!"

He stopped in his tracks. "My what?"

"I know about Anne-Marie, okay?"

"*What* do you know about Anne-Marie?"

"Don't tek me for no fool, Errol! I bumped into Anne-Marie by accident while I was out shopping. I recognised her from Colin's wedding. She told me all about your undercover affair."

Now Errol was sure. Nothing ever happened by accident with Anne-Marie. He was beginning to wonder if she ever encountered an unplanned incident in her life.

He sank slowly to the floor by her side. "It's not like that," he said, barely audible.

Tears sprang to Yvette's eyes and she wiped them away furiously. Errol would only see them as a sign of weakness, and she most definitely was not weak. She was a woman scorned, and the tears were the result of her frustration and anger. "Then what *was* it like? Don't tell me she carries your picture around in her purse because she's your number-one fan."

The look on Errol's face showed he was every bit as surprised as she had been.

"What's going on, Errol?"

He leant forward on the sofa and took her hand again. "Yvette, I don't want to lose you. This woman's been coming on to me…"

"Coming on to you?"

"Yes. Trying to seduce me. Hear me out, okay? I did go out with Anne-Marie on a purely platonic basis. We worked together, had a couple of the same friends, and I just thought… well, I didn't see any harm in it."

"If you were just friends why couldn't you tell me about

it?"

He shrugged. "I don't tell you about all my friends, do I? I don't come round and say, 'Hey, guess who I had lunch with today... Ben!' She was just someone in my life. I didn't find her particularly fascinating, so I didn't see it as important to tell you about her."

"So nothing happened?"

Errol forced sincerity into his eyes and voice. "Nothing. I wouldn't risk what we have."

"So she's been pestering you?"

"Yeah. She fancies me." He shrugged.

"And you haven't touched her?"

"No!"

"Do you... like her?"

"Yvette, I'm not going to lie to you. When we first met, I did find her attractive. You've met her — she *is* attractive. But she was one of Colin's exes and one of Marion's old school friends — I wouldn't dream of touching her... You don't believe me, do you?"

They fell into a silence that Yvette found impossible to break. That was the big question. Was he worth her dignity? The fact that he was accusing Anne-Marie of lying about it intrigued her. Why would she do that?

But Errol was good. When he turned on the sincerity it was hard not to believe every word. She wanted to believe him. But being Yvette, she wasn't letting him off that easily.

"I need some time to think it over. It could have happened that way. But then again..." and she let the end of her sentence drift away.

"You're honestly willing to let our relationship go because of some story from a stranger?"

"I don't know..."

"Eve, I love you."

Her head sprang up. This was the very first time he'd said it.

"Is it too late for you to buy your house?"

"I think it's still on the market. But it's beyond my reach."

"Not if we go into it together."

"Don't try to blackmail me, Errol—"

"We're good together. Good for each other."

"How can I be sure *she* won't tempt you?"

"Baby, I wouldn't do anything to hurt you."

The look in his eyes and the feeling in her heart told them both all they needed to know. They kissed.

"But no more part-time lover," she warned. "This is going to be a commitment. You're either mine exclusively or we have nothing."

"Fine by me. I don't want anyone else."

As he pulled her towards him, the emotional distance that had stood between them seemed to melt away to be replaced by passion. Suddenly they were kissing, stroking, pushing away all the unanswered questions that remained.

And that was the only answer Yvette needed.

He became her lover again, her gentleman, the man she knew she was in love with.

In the bedroom they made slow, sweet love like never before. Later, before Errol fell into oblivious sleep, a deep realisation came over him. He bent his head to kiss her neck and whispered, "Why didn't you tell me I was in love with you?"

She turned her head so she could see his face in the semi-darkness. "It happened to me a long time ago. I was just waiting for you to catch up."

"I think I realised it then. I just wasn't sure what it was... how to go about putting it into practice."

"And you know now?"

"I think... no, I *know* I do. Believe me, this is just the beginning."

Errol didn't know how right he was.

SIXTEEN

She got back into her car and started the engine. It had taken forty-five minutes to finish her task, and it would be a few more hours before anyone saw them. She sighed. It could be a whole day before Errol knew anything of it.

But when he did... He would start to take her seriously. She was certain of that.

Yvette woke up two hours after Errol had left for work and smiled, satisfied, even happy about waking up in his bed. He finally trusted her alone in his house.

She wasn't the snooping type anyway.

She took a leisurely shower and then sat down to read the paper with a breakfast of muesli and orange juice. Just before she took her first mouthful the doorbell rang.

A uniformed delivery man stood on the porch with a clipboard under his arm, "Parcel for Mr Wright."

"Yeah, yeah — bring it in." Yvette held the door open.

The man went back to his van and returned with a large, flat package that looked like a framed picture.

She signed for it and the man left. Then she took a few moments to stand back and look at it, intrigued. There was an envelope attached, addressed to Errol Wright and written in big, florid handwriting. The writing of a woman — no doubt about it.

She left the package to get dressed, but her mind kept going back to it. There was no return address, no company name or sticker: it didn't say "Personal" or "Private"...

She descended the stairs again and paced in front of it. Curiosity getting the better of her, she peeled the envelope off. Definitely a woman's writing. What would be her excuse for opening it? "I thought it was urgent, and that you might have forgotten it was coming." Something like that.

Before she could talk herself out of it she was ripping the

envelope open as carelessly as a little kid at Christmas.

The words she saw burned themselves into her sight.

"To Errol, in endless admiration…" the note began.

Her heart dropped to the pit of her stomach. Immediately she thought of Anne-Marie.

That was it. She dropped the note and stalked to the kitchen, where she pulled a sharp knife from a drawer. Newspaper and polystyrene beads spilled out onto the floor as she slit three sides of the package, pulling it open.

It was a painting, a canvas of a semi-nude woman whom Yvette thought she recognised. The more she looked the more she became sure: it was Anne-Marie, the woman who had boasted about sleeping with Errol. The woman Errol had denied having any involvement with.

Her mind raced. What the fuck was Anne-Marie whatsername doing sending her man a portrait of herself?

Yvette found the note again. "This is for you," she read, "with my love. Every time I sat for it I thought of you. Can you see it in my eyes? At every stroke of the brush I was creating something endless, everlasting, in memory of our love. Always, Anne-Marie."

Yvette zoomed in on the crucial words: love, everlasting, always, endless…

Anne-Marie and Errol were lovers.

She had fallen for the oldest trick in the book. She had believed a man because she'd wanted to, and because she loved him. You fool, Yvette.

She got dressed quickly. She was getting out of here now.

As she left the house and walked down the path she felt the curious sensation that she was being watched. Was Errol's paranoia rubbing off on her?

She almost laughed out loud. She'd believed that story about him being stalked — she had actually felt sorry for him, but he'd been having an affair all along.

Her thoughts raced. Maybe the affair was over now.

As she hurried down the road she became aware of the yellow posters. First one caught her eye, then another, on the next lamppost. As her eyes focused into the distance she saw that every lamppost and tree along this side of the road had a yellow flyer stuck to it. They'd caught the attention of other passers-by too.

Stopping by the next tree, she read the bold print:

<u>RESIDENTS OF WILSON AVENUE</u>
&
<u>CONCERNED CITIZENS OF BRITAIN</u>

I FEEL IT IS MY DUTY TO INFORM YOU OF WHAT IS GOING ON IN YOUR MIDST. ERROL WRIGHT, OF NO. 30 WILSON AVENUE, IS LIVING IN A DEN OF SIN CREATED BY NONE OTHER THAN HIMSELF.

I WAS LURED THERE UNDER FALSE PRETENCES A COUPLE OF MONTHS AGO, SEDUCED AND ABUSED SEXUALLY, THEN THROWN AWAY LIKE RUBBISH. MAYBE I WASN'T KINKY ENOUGH FOR HIM.

JUST A FEW DAYS AGO I WITNESSED HIM OPENLY HAVING SEX WITH A WOMAN IN A LOCAL PARK. ANYBODY COULD HAVE SEEN THEM, EVEN YOUR CHILDREN.

THIS IS A MAN WHO IS SUPPOSED TO BE A ROLE MODEL TO OUR YOUNG.

I THINK HE SHOULD BE CASTRATED. I LEAVE THE DECISION TO YOU.

Yvette felt faint as the blood drained from her face. She felt a range of emotions, but predominant was disgust. She knew now that Anne-Marie must have been watching the house that morning, must have followed them to the park. With blind rage she tore the paper from the tree, then ran down the road, tearing the posters down. This was pure spite, the senseless degradation of the man she loved. No one deserved to be publicly ridiculed like this.

First the portrait, and then this… Her brain was on overload, her life falling apart around her.

When she was sure she had all the posters she walked back to Errol's house and posted them through his door.

Anne-Marie sat at the back of the crowded studio. Last night Errol's enchanting smile had stayed with her as she'd wandered aimlessly around her flat, drinking wine and staring out of her silent home through the dark living room windows. With his smile she had sunk into a bottle of her favourite claret and eventually into her bed,. That smile had stayed as she'd slept restlessly, and was with her as she woke with a headache on a dull, cold morning.

That had decided her to come. Today's show was about five young men who had set up a new organisation called the Men of Vision, and who intended to change the way black men were perceived in society. She hadn't told Errol she was going to be in the studio; she didn't want him to be any different just because she was in the audience. It would be a surprise if he saw her. But if he didn't then no big deal.

She was wondering if Yvette ever came to see him live, when there was suddenly a ripple of excitement and a few cheers from the audience around her, and she looked immediately to the stage. There he was, wandering into the studio. He had a script, a pen and notebook in his hand, and was discussing something with the floor manager…

Errol had tried several times to call Yvette. She wasn't at his place, nor at the gym and her answering machine wasn't on.

He walked back to the comparative calm of the hospitality room for a last-minute read through and to greet his guests. Feeling ready as he ever would, he returned to fetch a handkerchief from his dressing room. The phone was ringing as he walked in. He impatiently snatched it up.

"Yeah?"

"Errol?"

"Yeah?"

"Errol, have you been home today?"

He gripped the phone tightly. "Anne-Marie?"

"Do you like surprises, Errol? I do."

"Anne, stop this…" He heard a click then a dial tone.

"Shit!" He threw the receiver violently against the wall and dug his fingers into his temples. "Don't do this to me! You have no right to do this to me!"

At precisely six thirty the warm-up man began his routine in front of the seated audience. Errol stood behind the set, listening, deep-breathing.

"Stand by," the floor manager called. "Silent studio, please…"

The countdown began. Errol took two more long, deep breaths, flexed and released his shoulders.

"Fifteen seconds to recording… ten…"

The walk to his chair on the set got longer each time.

"… three… two…"

The signature tune swelled, an out-of-vision voice boomed, "Ladies and Gentlemen, please welcome your host for *Do the Wright Thing*, Errol Wright!"

The audience applauded and his mind suddenly cleared. He was in the spotlight. His smile was real.

This part of his life was untouchable, all his own.

"Thank you…" He waited while the noise died down. "Tonight my special guests are: the sensational author of the best-selling book *Baby Mother*, Andrea Taylor!"

More applause. "And a group of young men who say 'Stop looking at the past and look to the future' to the youths out there. They're here now, please welcome Tyrone, George, Michael and Ricky, the Men of Vision!"

The four men walked in and raised power fists to the audience as they took their seats. They wore black suits, the jackets zipped from bottom to top, and on the back of each

158

were written the words "Open Your Eyes, Men of Vision".

The interview went down extremely well. At the end of it the audience got a chance to throw a few questions in.

"What about women? What are you doing for them?"

Michael, a light-skinned guy with a low fade cut, stood up. "Sister, that's for you to take care of. If we started telling women how we thought they ought to act we would get dissed. There is nothing stopping women getting together and doing what we are doing for young men."

"Is what you do religious?"

"We tell young people what's wrong and right." George rose as Michael sat. He was dark, bulky, and wore shades. "Good and evil is the same thing, but we don't want to preach. We're not militant and we're not dictators."

A middle-aged black man stood up with his hands on his hips. "But is it working? I mean, don't the kids just go out an' carry on the same way once you're gone?"

"We try never to do one-offs. We run programmes and help teachers to understand where our young black men are coming from. We help brothas to feel good about themselves, to respect women."

"What are you doing about the ones already in trouble — on the streets, or in prison?"

Ricky, small and light-skinned with thin, silver-rimmed glasses stood and addressed the questioner. "We're working on that. The trouble with men is that we don't talk about our feelings enough. Who knows when we need help... ?"

Errol couldn't help feeling relieved when finally he ushered the men off the stage in preparation for the arrival of the next guest. He gave a brief, glowing introduction, then faced the main camera. "Please welcome the baby mother with attitude — Miss Andrea Taylor!"

He turned to greet his guest. Andrea Taylor walked on to the stage, smiling, head held high, dressed in a long black dress. Her hair was cut in a short, layered crop that emphasised her cheek bones and dark, cat-like eyes.

She shook Errol's hand before taking a seat. Errol had read her book and was looking forward to this interview. He gave her his sexiest smile, confident he could charm her.

"Andrea, I've heard a rumour that you're now a single woman out of choice. Is this true?"

She laughed modestly. "I am single, Errol, because I haven't met a man who matches up to my criteria: ambition, good looks, charm, generosity, sex appeal, sense of humour, an air of authority…" She was counting the points on her fingers. "… A man who will let me be myself, who will have a willingness to love my children as his own—"

"You don't ask a lot, do you?" Errol joked, and the audience laughed. "So, your book, *Baby Mother* — was that based on your own experience?"

"Every author puts a little of themselves into a novel. *Baby Mother* needed my experience to give it credibility. I've raised two children on my own since their father walked out on me. Like my heroine, Jennifer Edwards, he left while I was pregnant. So, yes, I can identify with the story."

"Was it painful to write — because I know you've been single now for seven years? Dredging up the past must have made you feel some bitterness."

"It was actually hard to remember the bitter feelings," she smiled. "Mostly because I am happy now, and my children are happy and healthy. Although at times it's hard, trying to explain to them why they haven't got a father around, they have adjusted to being in a one-parent family pretty well. I've achieved an ambition that I held since the age of fifteen; I'm a published author now, and the bitterness has gone. Sometimes I even thank him for leaving me, because I don't believe I would have had the inspiration to write if we'd still been together."

"You actually work full-time too, don't you?"

"Yes. I work a nine-to-five job, raise two children, and I'm now writing my second novel."

Errol clapped and the audience joined him, a cheer going up from the women. "So, what's your secret? How do you fit it all in? What's a typical day in your home?"

"Well, my alarm goes off at five forty-five a.m., I get up at six and do half an hour of step aerobics, then I get washed and dressed and get the kids up. I drop the children down to my mum's — she's my child-minder — then I go to work. After work I pick the children up and get them dinner. Then I start writing. How much I do depends on whether I have a deadline to meet and how the story is flowing."

"A pretty packed day!" More applause. "So, when people tell you they want to write but can't find the time, what do you tell them?"

"I'll usually ask them what they do with their evenings and weekends. If they say things like watch TV, sleep, shopping, housework, take care of the children, then obviously writing isn't for them. When you want to write, you *have* to write. Sometimes to me it's more important than sleep; it's like a therapy…"

By the time he got home Errol was almost frantic. He'd tried to call Yvette three times on the way, without success.

As soon as he opened the front door he had an idea why. Somehow, even before he picked up the scraps of yellow paper that littered the hallway's carpet, he knew that Anne-Marie had her finger in this, if not her whole hand. Slowly he pieced some of the larger pieces of poster together until he had the whole message. Now he understood Anne-Marie's phone call earlier.

Then he saw the torn paper, the polystyrene beads, the painting…

He sat in his living room and stared at the four walls. He started off feeling guilty, then angry, then he wanted to punch glass. For the first time in his life he was feeling rage, and he had no idea how to vent it.

Yvette sat at Karen's kitchen table, her hands wrapped around her cup of coffee. Tyrone and Karen's two kids were watching television in the front room. Yvette had been badgered into spending the night and she had agreed, knowing that Errol couldn't possibly contact her here.

She was in a worse state than she'd thought. She seemed to be filled with adolescent emotion that she was unused to.

"Men!" Karen said, filling her glass again. "Why did we think Errol would be any different? Damn! Give them a bit of fame and it goes straight to their damned cock."

"*Why*, though? Shit, I shouldn't have let him get under my skin. I thought I was giving him all he wanted…"

"What are you, blind *and* stupid?" Karen touched Yvette's hand, not wanting her friend to take affront. "I can say that, 'cause we're soul mates. But men *never* have all they want. There's always something missing in their lives."

"But what is it, though…?" She faltered in her speech. "I still love him, you know."

"Then, when he knew he had you where he wanted you — under his thumb…"

Yvette looked up from her coffee. "Maybe I should have given him a chance to explain."

"Now you're sounding like a pushover!" Karen got up, turned her chair round and sat backwards on it, resting her arms on its back. "Baby girl, you did that when you came clean about knowing about her. And what did he do in return? Lie through his teeth! This bitch basically told you she was shagging him. But you chose to believe him."

"So that's it? It's over?"

"Of course it is! Leave him to all them celebs. They're not for us, an' he's one ah dem."

"We had it good, you know. I can't just forget him—"

"It was sex, babe. You told me yourself." Karen looked steadily at her through a haze of cigarette smoke. "It's not love. It might have been good, but you'll get over it."

Yvette was silent.

Her friend watched her, wondering how the woman she knew so well could get into a situation so alien to her nature. "You're not getting ready to forgive him, are you?" she asked sternly.

"I suppose I did over-react…"

Karen opened her mouth to say something.

"No — let me finish. He told me this woman was

162

deranged — you even thought the same thing when we met her. I've had one-night stands, you know — cheap thrills, irresistible circumstances. He never promised to be faithful to me. Neither of us promised that."

"Just 'cause you don't say it doesn't…"

The telephone rang and Karen got up to answer it.

"Jennifer! Girl, you calling from abroad? No! Really…? Course — we got to get together. Where you staying? Donna's… Okay. I'll catch up with you tomorrow. I'll call you… Yeah. Listen, got to go. I've got company."

She looked at her watch as she hung up. "Nearly midnight. She must be in another time zone!"

Yvette yawned. "Speaking of time, I'm tired…"

"Time to walk away from Errol the Irresistible."

Yvette straightened her back. "You're right. We have different ideas about how affairs should be conducted."

"You wanna go to bed…" Karen smiled. "Or we could open some Haagen-Dazs with loads of whipped cream."

They both laughed.

"What would I do without you, Kaz?"

"You'd manage. Not very well, mind you. But you're strong. When he finally finds you and you have to speak to him and hear his excuses, that's when you'll really feel it."

Karen got up to get the ice cream.

Yvette breathed deeply. Tomorrow was another day.

Two days later, Errol woke to find that he'd overslept. He had spent the previous day undergoing excruciating mental torture. Yvette's colleague at the gym had told him she'd taken leave at short notice, and she wasn't picking up the phone at home. When he'd called Karen's, she'd told him that if Yvette wanted to call him she would call him and to stop wasting her time.

So he'd decided to let it go for a while. Let her cool off.

Maybe she didn't love him. He couldn't blame her for reacting the way she had. And now she didn't trust him.

He shuffled through his mail while eating dry toast.

Another love letter from from Anne-Marie — he recognised the handwriting. He didn't bother to open it, but left it aside to go into the file.

Most of his calls that morning were business, except for one from his mother, which perked up his day. She still cared.

Nothing from Yvette.

That night he dined with his good friend Chris Stevens, the only man he felt that understood him.

The waiter poured their wine, then left them to study the menus.

"I think I'm in love with her."

"You! In love?"

"I dunno. Now I've said it, how do I know what love is?"

"Boy, don't ask me, you know. 'Cause I been caught in that is-it-love-or-is-it-lust triangle too many times."

"It's definitely not only lust." Errol took a gulp of wine and leant his elbow on the table lowering his voice a little. "I think about her constantly; I have to hear her voice at odd times during the day or night; she makes me feel good…"

"Yeah, you been bitten."

"It just hit me. One day I was fine being single, doing my own t'ing…" His vocabulary always seemed to slip around his closest friends. "And now, whenever I'm at a loose end, the first person I think about is her. Her opinion matters to me…" He shrugged his shoulders. "I dunno. I guess I was so out of practice, I didn't even realise it was happening."

SEVENTEEN

Yvette had her head in the clouds.

Walking was a favourite pastime of hers. Walking on her own, walking with Errol… It helped clear her head. When Tyrone had been a baby she would often walk for miles, pushing the pushchair. Cheapest way to keep fit, and the baby always slept well afterwards.

She was approaching their restaurant. They'd started to call it "ours" because he'd taken her there many times. They even had their own special table. God, how romantic it used to be… and they would go home and make love, and it would continue all night long.

She shivered with the memory. She still loved that fool.

She stopped by the restaurant door, wanting to go in, to sit at their table and reminisce… No. She was being stupid.

About to walk away, she caught sight of a familiar figure pulling out a chair for a very stylishly dressed woman.

Yvette's mouth fell open and then clamped shut as the blood rushed to her temples. "You really are something, Mr Wright!" she hissed. "Two women not enough for you?"

Arms pumping, she barged into the restaurant. She didn't wait to reach the table before she started to vent her pent-up anger. "Didn't take you long, did it! Got bored of Anne-Marie already?"

Errol's companion looked up in shock. "Excuse me—"

"Do you *know* about him? Can't keep his dick in his pants longer than a couple of hours."

"Yvette…" Errol started.

"There must be some mistake," the woman gasped.

"I'll give him a mistake." Yvette seized a nearly full pint-glass of lager from the table and threw the contents over his head. He collided with his chair, which clattered to the floor behind him, causing muted gasps from inquisitive diners.

Yvette turned and stalked out, still cursing.

Chantelle Wright, Errol's companion, sought an

explanation. "Errol, what is this all about?"

"It's okay, Mum, I'll sort it out."

He followed Yvette's lead, and caught up with her as she threw the door open.

She came to a halt outside the restaurant. Breathing heavily, she could feel his presence at her back. She turned to see him mopping lager from his head and face with a handkerchief that was already sopping wet.

"Your mother?"

He loosened his tie as he answered. "My mother. Arrived this morning unexpectedly. She called from the airport…"

Yvette's hands flew to her head in embarrassment and she backed away from him. "Oh my God! What did I just do?" she gasped. She spun round, almost head-butting Errol in the process. "What the *hell* was I thinking of? I *wasn't* thinking, was I? I was about as crazy as your bloody stalker." She looked at his ruined suit. "I'm sorry. I mean, I'd better go — let you get back to your mother."

She turned away as she felt the tears stinging her eyes, not wanting him to see her bawl.

Errol grabbed her arm and she turned back and looked into his eyes. He pulled her to him. "No, *I'm* sorry…"

Yvette twisted out of his grasp. "I don't want to do this. Just let me walk out of your life now…"

"What are you talking about? I don't want to lose you."

She held her hands up to stop him saying the things he didn't mean. "No. It's not happening, Errol. You're not getting the chance to twist me up again."

He looked pained, his eyes filling with concern. "I don't want to do that. I wouldn't do that." He glanced back to the restaurant. "Come with me. I want you to meet my mum."

She gave him an 'are-you-crazy?' look.

"Then let me bring her out to meet you. She's only here for four days…"

Yvette started to feel a tinge of anger resurfacing. She crossed her arms and tapped one foot, breathing hard to hold on to her emotions. "What about your other woman?"

"There *is* no other woman. Only you."

She let him pull her into his arms this time, and she sobbed into his chest for a minute. Then she turned her back to him. "Maybe another time, eh? I have to go."

She started to walk away.

"Yvette!"

"I'll call you!"

She broke into a run, tears streaming down her face. Their worlds were just too different. She should never have attempted to be something that she wasn't.

Errol Wright's wife? Yeah, right!

As Errol watched the warm-up man's routine on the monitor he recalled how he'd felt just a week before. He'd been so happy. He'd finally decided he had found the woman who could keep him that way. He wasn't after any upper-class snob who couldn't go out unless she had a new designer label. He wanted Yvette Barker: down-to-earth, sexy, ambitious in her own right… and in love with him.

Now he felt completely changed. The happiness had subsided, leaving him feeling vaguely distraught, wishing he'd made firmer decisions about Anne-Marie.

The recording didn't go well. He couldn't concentrate, he forgot lines, missed scripted camera angles, and basically blew his cool image. The studio audience was getting restless with the constant retakes. They began to shift in their seats. The floor manager tried to settle them down.

Someone was sent to check on the reformed drug addict he was about to interview. Then recording continued. The *Do the Wright Thing* theme tune played Errol in, and he announced the guest and stood to greet him.

Errol's heart sank when the young white man stumbled and giggled as he took the single step to the podium. Errol hastily put his hands out for him to steady himself.

"Yikes!" He giggled again. "Who put that step there?"

The show didn't get any better. Errol knew they could bleep out the language afterwards, but his guest was either stoned, brain-dead or had an attitude problem. It was hard work getting a coherent word out of the man at all. A few minutes before the final music, the floor manager began to make signals for him to wind up the interview.

The man was retelling a tale of the night he'd broken down his girlfriend's door while she was out, and stolen anything valuable to get money for drugs.

"Well, Tony, that's a terrifying story — and I'm sure the viewers and our audience are glad to hear that it's all behind you now…"

"Yeah." Tony rubbed his eyes. "Yeah, I… I left all of that now, man." He stood and swayed on his feet. "The only drug I take now is caffeine."

Errol moved swiftly. "Well, Tony, the clocks have caught up with us." He turned to the audience. "Time for me to say thanks to our fascinating guest, Tony Collins!"

Tony was trying to get off the set. He tripped on the step and fell in a tangled heap to the floor.

"Last time I deal with druggies…" Errol headed for his dressing room where he poured himself a stiff brandy.

He held his head in his hands for a few moments, and when he looked up his mother was standing in the doorway.

"Mum!"

"Hi, baby. I saw what happened. You're not having a very good day, are you?"

"Not having a very good life. Period."

Chantelle Wright came into the room and stood behind her son, placing a manicured hand on his shoulder. "Sounds to me like you need a love life."

"I had one — until I ruined it with one stupid mistake."

"We all make mistakes, baby. Each of them is a learning experience. But the only people who learn are the people who do something about making it right again, the people who don't let those mistakes ruin the rest of their lives."

Errol met her eyes in the mirror. His relationship with his mother, a thing of such distance in his childhood, had become stronger and warmer throughout his adult life.

Chantelle held the hair off her face and bent to kiss him on the cheek. "You love that girl, don't you?"

He nodded.

"And she loves you?"

His voice caught in his throat. "She did."

"Boy, don't give me that," she said, gently but firmly. "She's hurt — and she's waiting for you to show her that you're ready to give her devotion and commitment. What went on is none of my business, but I don't want to go home knowing you are unhappy. You go get her."

Errol swivelled his chair to face his mother and circled her waist with his long arms. She was so trim that his arms doubled over, his fingers reaching his elbows.

She held his head to her stomach. "You don't need me to tell you where your heart lies, Errol. Remember, never stop trying for the things you want in life."

He felt so secure in that moment, nestled in his mother's arms. No woman had ever made him feel this secure.

Except Yvette. She cared.

Marion sank against the wall outside Errol's dressing room. She had waited silently in the corridor, and had overheard the conversation. She had seen the elegant older woman earlier and, though she didn't know her, hearing the advice she'd given Errol, Marion felt a resentment growing for her. For the last few days he had come to Marion for advice on relationships and women — one woman in particular: Yvette. She thought he was much better off staying single, and had told him so. Yvette couldn't possibly be right for him. As soon as the going had got tough she'd left. She hadn't stood by him. Errol needed someone stronger.

As soon as this other woman was out of here, Marion decided, she would have to get him on his own again.

First that Anne-Marie and now Yvette screwing with his head… Why couldn't they all just leave him alone?

Errol sat in the car outside Karen's house for fifteen minutes before he had the courage to get out and face the music.

The door was answered by Karen's ten year old daughter. Errol bent down to speak to her.

"Hello. Is your mummy in?"

Without answering she turned round and walked back into the house calling, "Mum! Errol's at the door!"

In the living room Karen put a finger to her lips, indicating to Yvette that she should stay there and keep quiet. "I'll handle it," she whispered.

Yvette got up anyway, and pressed her back to the living room door so she could hear everything. The children watched this little act, bemused for a couple of seconds before turning back to their video game.

"Good evening, Errol. What can I do for you?"

"Hi, Karen." He shoved a hand in his pocket and put on his brightest smile. She didn't invite him in. "Is Yvette here?"

"Errol, you asked me dat yesterday *and* dis morning, and I told you she doesn't want you to contact her."

"If you just let me see her, I might be able to persuade her otherwise."

Karen crossed her arms. She knew he wanted to make amends — but did he have a right to? Yvette was her friend, and she had a duty to protect her.

Errol could see all of this going on through her eyes. It looked like she wasn't going to give in. He pulled an envelope from his pocket. "Do me a favour, then. Give this to her. Please."

Karen took the envelope and glanced at it. "You got it. Anything else?"

Errol started to go and then turned back, looking into Karen's eyes. "Tell her… tell her I love her."

Another sleepless night. Yvette lay on her back on Karen's sofa-bed, Errol's crumpled letter still clutched in her hand.

Karen was a good friend, but there were some decisions a woman had to make on her own. He said he loved her — and Yvette knew how she felt about him. Even after she'd made such a fool of herself in that restaurant, and then the tears afterwards, he cared enough to seek her out and give her this. How many men did she know who could write a real love letter?

What would he be doing now? Thinking of her? She doubted it. But all of a sudden she felt she had to know; she needed to feel wanted. On impulse she got out of bed and picked up the phone.

Dialling his number was hard, but necessary.

"Hello?'

Yvette held the phone to her ear and listened. Are you alone? she wanted to ask. Are you missing me?

"Anne-Marie, is that you?"

Yvette suddenly felt sick. It was *her* he expected to hear. It didn't even occur to him that it could be someone else.

"Haven't you caused enough trouble? I warned you, woman, and I'm not playing any more. You keep out of my life or…"

Yvette hung up and started to shiver, so she lay down and pulled the duvet up around her head. He had sounded so unlike himself… He had been enraged.

That wasn't her Errol. What was this woman doing to him?

Finally she managed to sleep, only to be woken up again by a sudden realisation about her situation. As she lay in the dark her thoughts assembled, and she knew she was right.

This was exactly what Anne-Marie had wanted: for Yvette to walk out and leave the coast clear for her to move in on her man.

"Well she's messing with the wrong couple," she said out loud.

Yvette made up her mind to go back, to see Errol and talk. There was a lot at stake here. Too much of her heart was invested in their relationship. They had a home to get ready to move into before Christmas. She was going to fight for her man. He meant too much to her.

But first she had to build up the courage to face him and lay down some rules.

EIGHTEEN

The club was packed with women, which was usual for Night Moves on a Sunday evening. The men certainly had their pick. But there was only one woman Errol was interested in. He didn't care how much she protested, he was determined to make her see the truth.

He walked tall through the dimly-lit club, trying to look as casual as possible, aware of the stares of recognition.

The first hour was uneventful, but then as he was about to go back to the bar for another drink he saw her. She was swaying to the sound of the gentle soul music, her eyes half-closed. The feeling in his chest was so strong, he thought for a moment he was about to have some kind of seizure.

She didn't notice him until he was standing in front of her, devouring her with his eyes. The music throbbed and pulsed. The beat was almost hypnotising.

Errol registered the shock in her eyes. She had stopped dancing and now faced him square on, her eyes challenging him in her own way.

He accepted the challenge.

He gathered her in his arms. She melted into them, kissing him hard and deep. His hands roamed her bare back, her tight bottom through her tiny satin skirt. They seemed to be barely moving, but where their hips were pressed together they were moving, winding so slowly it was like making love.

The track came to an end and Yvette met his eyes again.

"Let's go," she said.

And they left, leaving Karen watching with amusement. "That girl's got it bad," she said to herself.

The phone woke Errol just before seven o'clock the next morning. He let it ring until the answerphone picked it up. Yvette was snuggled up beside him. He looked down at her, gently removing a few strands of hair from her face. She was back in his life. Last night their lovemaking had been intense, as potent as before, but without the game-playing. It had been the soothing, pacifying love of true lovers.

He kissed her forehead lightly and she woke up. They squeezed each other for a few minutes without saying a word. Then she whispered, "What are you thinking about?"

He kissed her again. "About you — us."

She breathed in the scent of his body. "Me too."

"I've been blind. I didn't realise what I had before now."

She smiled sleepily. "It happens."

He tipped her chin up so that their eyes met. "You won't leave me again, will you?"

"Are you planning to sleep with another woman again?"

Errol tensed and sunk further into his pillow. "Never. Don't wanna be a player no more. The only woman I want is you, Eve."

"I'm glad. 'Cause that's what you got."

As he left the house that morning he marvelled at how warm it was for late November. He was behind the wheel before he saw the note on the windscreen.

Anne-Marie hadn't given up yet.

Yvette was coming down the path, so he scrambled back out and retrieved the note, stuffing it into the glove box and let Yvette in. They were going to view the house.

Errol looked around the empty room. One wall was completely dominated by a huge window overlooking the rooftops of houses and buildings for miles. He could imagine the view at night, twinkling city lights.

Yvette studied him. "Well?"

"Well… It needs a lot of work. A few gallons of paint, miles of carpeting and expensive curtains. To heat this place is gonna break the bank. We won't even be able to move in until we've had all the essential rooms decorated…"

Yvette smiled coyly. "But you like it though, don't you?"

"Elegant squalor."

"You gotta admit it's got potential. Exactly what I want."

"Home sweet home, eh?"

Her shoulders dropped with relief. He liked it, she could tell. She did a twirl in the middle of the wooden floor.

Errol watched her every move. "Okay, we'll buy the house, turn it into a palace…"

She licked her lips, her eyes fixed on his steady stare. "I love it — the house, the view. the garden…"

"Me?"

"Of course you, rude bwoy."

He pressed closer. "How 'bout we christen this room as ours?"

"Oh no, big boy. You just control yourself. We're not doing anything in here until I have my four-poster bed and a shag pile carpet and a fire burning in that grate."

"You drive a hard bargain." He released her hands.

"Only way to keep your man under manners," she said.

Later, after dropping Yvette off at home, Errol remembered the note and removed it from the glove box. It was a single sheet of A4 paper folded in half, typed with large, bold letters. It said, "LOVE HAS NO BOUNDARIES."

Kissing his teeth, he screwed it up and dumped it in the street. The sooner he moved out of here and in with Yvette, the better.

Anne-Marie was searching for aspirin, paracetamol, Nurofen — anything. She always had something available; her long hours of concentrated reading required it.

Giving up, she went back into her living room and stretched out on the sofa, her dress riding up to reveal her soft, feminine thighs.

Waiting. She was waiting for the call. It *would* come, wouldn't it? A few words, just some contact… She glanced at the telephone. Why didn't the damn thing ring? She passionately wanted to hear his voice.

But deep down she knew he wouldn't phone.

It was no good. It was impossible to think of anything else. She needed him. To hear from him. Just to see him. He should have got her messages by now. If not the phone messages, then the one on his car. Trying to get hold of him at work was getting harder, he placed as many barriers in her way as he could. He hadn't even called to bawl her out about the posters; surely he knew about them by now.

The phone rang and her body jerked upright. She dashed across the room, knocking her ankle painfully on the coffee table as she went, and grabbed it on the third ring.

"Hello?" she answered breathlessly.

"Anne-Marie?" A female voice.

"Yes."

"It's Marion. How are you? I haven't heard from you in two weeks."

Marion sounded so cheerful, it was sickening to Anne-Marie's ears.

"Oh, Marion," she sighed.

"Well? What's been happening?"

"Happening?"

"You know — the new job."

Anne-Marie summoned up all her expertise to disguise her disappointment. "Oh, everything's been great. Errol and I have worked on a couple of programmes together. You know, researching, interviewing techniques…"

Marion was fishing for information. "Oh? He never said."

"Well… He's trying to keep our relationship… you know, under wraps."

Marion felt her heart sink to the pit of her stomach. Just who *was* telling the truth here? "Relationship, is it now?"

"We've been seeing each other… intimately."

"You *have*? You and Errol?" Marion asked incredulously. He had only just got back together with Yvette! Marion couldn't believe, with the amount of work he'd spent on doing that, that he would already be two-timing her.

"Is that such a surprise? You know we've been getting on

pretty well. In fact when the phone rang I thought it might have been him. We're going out tonight... or staying in, as the case may be..."

Marion was flabbergasted. This woman could also tell stories — was there no end to her talents? "Well... congratulations! I guess you finally got your man." She tried to keep her voice neutral. "I must admit I'm surprised."

"I told you, all he needed was the right woman. I think he loves me. I know I love him. But, Marion, remember: don't say anything. I would hate for him to get cold feet. We've come so far. He doesn't need any pressure right now."

"Yes... Well, it's none of my business. I really called to ask you to a dinner party to celebrate my birthday. Errol, of course, is also invited. I suppose you could come together."

"When?"

"Next Friday night."

"I'll try. Can I let you know after I've talked to him?"

"Sure."

"I'd love to be there, but Errol's schedule has been a little hectic recently. We may decide to stay in."

"I've already left a message on his answerphone. He never misses my parties."

"We'll be there then."

"Good. I'll get off the line in case he's trying to get through. See you next week."

Anne-Marie's false smile disappeared as she put the receiver down. Her throat felt dry. A couple! She and Errol — a couple? What had got into her? She laughed out loud. Such a good actress! How the hell was she going to pull this off, if the actor was refusing to accept the script?

She had until next week to become Errol's other half.

It wouldn't be too hard. He had already taken the first step.

The blinking light on the answering machine told Errol that he had five messages.

Every message was from her. She had started by simply

asking him to call her, and ended up screaming that she needed to talk to him urgently.

Anne-Marie had drifted off, but being a light sleeper she was fully awake on the second ring. She picked up the phone, and before she could finish saying hello Errol's voice cut her off, cold and insistent.

"I got your messages. And as I've said before, don't call me. Don't send me nothing. I won't be returning your calls. It's over. Take care of yourself. Bye."

The line went dead.

Anne-Marie stared at the receiver, then slammed it down and burst into tears

By Monday Errol was feeling better emotionally, but his workload was giving him no time to enjoy it and he had a dull, persistent headache. He rubbed his eyes with his fingertips and closed the folder that lay in front of him. His eyes drifted to the roses, dumped unceremoniously upside-down in the dustbin in the corner of his dressing room. They had arrived earlier that day with a card from Anne-Marie:

Marry me, Errol. You'll be the happiest man on earth.

What the hell was she playing at? Luckily her stint on his show was over for now.

He had issued an order to his assistant that day: "If Anne-Marie Simms calls I'm very busy, okay? Tell security she's not allowed up to this office."

The phone rang, making him jump, and he was tempted to let it go, but as usual his hand found itself reaching out and picking up the receiver hesitantly, steeling himself against Anne-Marie's voice should it be her.

"Errol?"

"Marion, thank goodness! How are you?'

"Fine. So someone's glad to hear from me…"

"Who wouldn't be glad to hear from you?"

"Well, when was the last time we had a quiet drink together? We used to do it all the time. Anne-Marie wasn't too happy when I called her last night."

That name again. "Yeah?"

"Why didn't you tell me, Errol?"

"Tell you what?"

"That you and she were seeing each other."

Errol was no longer surprised by any revelations concerning Anne-Marie. "Because we're not. What's she been saying?"

"Errol, I know this is none of my business, but she told me you were, in her words, 'Intimate'."

Errol moaned, sagging visibly in his chair. "It's not true."

"That's not what she thinks. The other day she was wearing a diamond ring which she said you'd given her after she spent the night at your house."

"She stole Yvette's ring!" Errol thought he'd mislaid it and had notices everywhere for it to be returned to him.

"That's not how she tells it—"

"Marion you don't know the half of it! The woman's obsessed. All right, I admit we had one night… You know, it was nothing. You know Yvette and I are back together?"

"Does she know about your one-night stand?"

"That's what caused the split — but she believes my side of the story. Yvette trusts me. I can't lose her now. And I couldn't tell you about it; you were just too close to home."

"Maybe you weren't clear enough when you said you weren't interested."

"It wasn't like that! From the start I told her nothing was going on." Errol's headache suddenly throbbed painfully. "Look, Marion, just stay out of my business, okay?"

He hung up and instantly regretted letting off on Marion like that. But why were all these women all of a sudden trying to tell him how to run his life?

As Christmas loomed closer, Errol found himself relaxing

more and more into his relationship with Yvette. For the first time in months he was feeling loved and pampered.

Yvette had convinced herself that the Anne-Marie affair was over, and now at last she felt happy to be in love. She bought sexy underwear and spiced up their already spicy sex life. She was doing *all* the things that women are told they do when in love: cooking, cleaning, constantly phoning when they weren't together.

"You know, there's something about your body in dungarees that's got my mind wandering…" he was saying.

"What?" Yvette carefully half-turned on top of the step ladder, a paint roller in one hand. She was wearing a pair of denim dungarees over a plain white vest; her hair was caught up in a bushy ponytail; a shaft of winter sunlight caught her face sideways on. Errol thought he had never seen her look more beautiful.

"The dungarees… leave a lot to the imagination."

"Turning you on, is it? Maybe I'll start a whole new fashion trend. Painted baggy dungarees." It was a grumble, but her eyes were twinkling.

Errol cocked his head to one side, one paint-splotched hand on his chin. "You you could have something there…"

"Look, you — are we supposed to be decorating or admiring each other's bodies? At this rate we'll still be painting at Christmas."

"What, no ravishing today?" He made a puppy dog face.

Yvette kissed her teeth and turned back to the wall. She was enjoying watching her home take shape. And she found it doubly satisfying to be doing it with her partner — the partner had come so close to losing more than once.

Errol had wanted to get professionals in to do the whole house but Yvette was having none of it. This was her home, and she intended to enjoy doing it up. The walls needed to be stripped and filled, and the skirting boards replaced. The floorboards, they had both agreed, would look wicked sanded and polished. At the end of each "decorating day" they would massage away the aches and pains from their necks, backs and arms. Although they weren't living

179

together yet, they were spending a lot more time together on the house project. In the time they had for breaks they would laugh and kiss and cuddle just like newly-weds.

A few minutes later he dropped his roller back into its tray. "Finished!"

Yvette looked across the hall at the smooth, still wet expanse of wall. "How the hell did you finish before me?"

He threw back his head and laughed. "Jealous?"

"Sure you done it good? I'm gonna check, you know…"

"Sore loser, eh? Want me to finish yours for you?"

"Want to be coloured blue from head to toe?"

"What did I tell you? Sore loser."

He ducked when Yvette turned on him, roller in hand, aimed for flicking, then held held his hands out in appeasement. "Okay! Sorry, babe. You're a good loser. Satisfied? How 'bout some coffee?"

Yvette didn't answer. She dipped the roller into the tray for the last time, and watched the last bit of plaster disappear beneath the cool blue paint. "Perfect!"

It had been a long day, and Errol couldn't wait to get home. But before he called it a day he had a report to write up.

The phone rang, and he cussed in annoyance as he reached for it, saving his document with the other hand.

"Anne-Marie Simms calling again, Mr Wright," the operator told him.

"Again? I thought you told her I'd call back."

"I did, but she's quite insistent."

"Okay, put her on…" He heard the click of the call being put through. "What is it with you?"

"I dreamt about you last night."

A vein throbbed in his forehead. "I'm really not interested in your dreams. Anne-Marie, you're not leaving me much choice but to seek legal advice."

"You shouldn't have thrown away those roses. How do you think it made me feel? I was furious, Errol. So furious I almost forgot how much I love you."

"Goodbye, Anne-Marie."

A few minutes later there was a knock on his office door, and before he could look up Anne-Marie had let herself in.

"So. You won't take my calls, you leave me little choice."

"I have little respect or time for women who continue to throw themselves at me after I've told them I'm not interested. Now will you kindly leave?"

"I'll teach you about respect, Mr Wright." She strolled over to his desk and sat on the edge.

Errol pretended to be engrossed in the computer screen.

"There's a party at Marion's on Friday night. I was wondering if you'd like to go with me."

"No." The single word was sharp and stern.

"Actually I'm not asking you — I'm telling you. We *are* going. I've already told Marion. Yvette won't be there..."

"How the hell would you know that?"

"I know all about you. She dumped you, didn't she?"

"For your information, we're back together. Now get your ass off my desk and go and do some work. That's what you get paid for, I presume," he added with a hint of malice.

"You're making a big mistake, Errol. Would you like to open the Sunday papers and see pictures of us together?"

"*What* pictures?"

"Meet me tonight and I'll show you."

"You're bluffing. I'm not buying it, Anne-Marie."

She slid off the desk and undulated out of the room, slowly turning at the door to blow him a kiss. "We'll see."

Errol was shaking with rage. He slammed his palms down on the desk so hard that he was still feeling the sting an hour later, as he sat across from his producer.

"Errol, my boy! What can I do for you?"

Errol sat up straight and leant towards him, elbows on knees, fingers twined in front of him. "Can I be frank?"

"Sure." John raised his shoulders in a shrug.

Errol breathed out heavily, wondering where to start.

John leant on the desk, subconsciously mimicking the position of Errol's hands. "Trouble?" he asked.

"It's Anne-Marie Simms. Things aren't working out."

"In what way?"

"She's become obsessed with me."

A quirky smile touched John's lips. "Obsessed?"

Errol cleared his throat and fiddled with the knot of his tie. "I had sex with her once and now she won't let it go."

"You want her off the team?"

"I was thinking of something a little more permanent. She's got to be as far away from me as possible."

"You want her fired because she's an ex-girlfriend?"

"John, she was *never* a girlfriend. No — I want her fired because she isn't behaving professionally."

"I'll look into it," John placated. "I won't stand for sexual harassment. I'll do what I can."

As Anne-Marie made her way towards Croydon in her black Fiesta, her face was set in grim determination. Her eyes, though, were expressionless.

She passed the house and parked fifty yards away, turned off the ignition and the lights, and waited. The windows were dark and Yvette's car wasn't there. If she had to confront them both, though, she would. She kept her eyes on the house in the rearview mirror, imagining the rooms. Expensively furnished. Everything picked out by that girlfriend. A thought flitted through her mind: how many times a week did they make love in their four-poster bed?

At around eleven o'clock a taxi pulled up. Anne-Marie peered into the mirror and saw Yvette and her son stepping out. There were no words exchanged between them as they hurried into their home and the taxi pulled away. The front door slammed, and then it was quiet again.

She only had to wait half an hour more before Errol's car pulled into the drive and he almost seemed to leap out of it. He seemed excited, as though he couldn't wait to get inside.

He wouldn't feel so good when he saw her, though. She got out of her car, slamming the door.

Errol looked up to see a woman in a brown suit walking hurriedly towards him.

"Hello, Errol."

"Miss Simms. What can I do for you now."

"I lost my job."

"Is that so?" He turned away from her and walked towards the comfort and warmth of his own home.

"Did you have something to do with it?"

He stopped and turned on his heels. There was a smug smile on his face as he looked Anne-Marie up and down.

"What makes you think that?"

She suddenly came alive and leapt forward, her eyes blazing, voice screeching, "You can't treat me that way!"

Errol remained calm. "I haven't done anything to you."

There were tears in her eyes. "I love you! I want to take care of you, and you just keep pushing me away! Why?"

After all this time, after all she had done, she never ceased to amaze him. "If you had just backed off when I asked you to, maybe you'd still have a job. Give it up!"

"We were lovers—"

"Lovers!" He laughed in her face.

A look of scorn came through her tears. "You can't have forgotten how good it was!"

"Forgotten *what*?" He tapped his forehead. "It's all in your head. There was never anything between us. What will it take for you to leave me alone, a court order?"

The door flew open behind him and Yvette marched out. "What the hell is going on out here?"

Anne-Marie glared. "Keep out of this."

Yvette marched down the steps towards them. "I shoulda given you a slapping from time. Come here telling me what to do!" Yvette flew at her, fists at the ready.

Errol grabbed her and held her from behind. "Leave her! She's not worth it. I'm calling the police."

Defeated, Anne-Marie turned and headed back to the car. She looked back just once, in time to see Errol stroke Yvette's face as he guided her back to the house. Hatred and nausea making her head spin, she leant over at the kerb, bringing up her lunch, and what was left of her dignity.

NINETEEN

It was two days since Anne-Marie had been fired. The whole office had known she had a crush on Errol Wright, and now the gossip was ripe, everyone adding their own details to the tale of a love affair gone wrong.

"What did he do — make a formal complaint?"

"Don't know. He should have had her arrested, though."

"Oh, she's so pathetic! I almost feel sorry for her."

"*Sorry* for her? It was Errol she was harassing…"

Wearing red for confidence she didn't feel, Anne-Marie walked into the office and was aware of her ex-colleagues' heads turning back to work, an abruptly terminated conversation. Under one arm she carried a cardboard box folded flat, over her other shoulder a handbag that matched the shade of her suit. Her hair was pulled back into a loose ponytail. She straightened her back and walked to her desk.

The phone began to ring. She looked at the faces of her ex-colleagues. Most were looking away in embarrassment, and a couple gazed at her in sympathy. She swallowed hard, and for what seemed like a long time she couldn't make another move. The phone continued to ring unanswered. Just as quickly as the paralysis had come over her, it left.

"Will someone answer that phone?" she said loudly and more confidently than she felt. It's all right, she told herself. A job's just a job. It wasn't as though she'd lost everything.

"We were going to post it, but as you're here…" Roger was holding a card out to her.

She reached for it and scanned the short messages and signatures. "Thank you…"

"Errol would have signed it, but we haven't been able to get hold of him." Roger watched her face intently.

The mention of Errol's name, so casually used, was like a bullet to Anne-Marie. She tensed with the memory of her last encounter with him.

"We didn't know about you and Errol," Roger continued

tactlessly. "I mean, it's none of my business…"

"No. You're right — it isn't."

Roger shifted uneasily from foot to foot. "Well, I'll leave you to it. If you need any help, just call."

Anne-Marie raised her heavy eyelids to him and smiled a sickly smile that said she couldn't care less.

Shortly after she left, clutching her box of belongings.

Errol left his guests in the green room and walked with his usual strut towards the staircase. He felt great. Anne-Marie was off the programme. He was free.

When he reached the next floor he saw her standing in front of his dressing room and froze on the spot. For a moment the two of them stared at each other, neither speaking a word. Then Anne-Marie began walking towards him, but her eyes were staring through him, past him. Errol didn't move, unsure whether he could or should say something. Then she brushed past him. He heard the door to the staircase swing open and her footsteps going down.

She'd been so cold, detached…

He continued down the hall and into his dressing room. He unbuttoned his jacket and slung it over the back of a chair. The Donna Karan suit he was wearing for today's show was hanging on a rack at the other end of the room. He pulled it out and gasped as it fell into pieces at his feet.

Rain, sheets of it, blown erratically by the wind, slanted down on to the almost deserted street. It was dark, except for the misty orange glow of the high street lights.

Yvette clung tighter to Errol's arm. "I feel like singing!"

Errol swapped the umbrella to his other hand so he could take Yvette's. "Now there's a cue for a song…"

"I'm si-nging in the rain…" Yvette warbled.

"You'll get us arrested with that voice! They'll think we're mad enough as it is, walking in the rain."

"Well, if I wasn't mad we wouldn't be together."

"Hey!"

Yvette had called him from the station an hour ago. She had been out for a drink with friends, and was feeling in such a good mood that she'd wanted to go for a romantic walk in the downpour.

Romantic. That was what she'd said.

He had given her his mac, and now he could feel the cold through to his skin, but he had to admit that this was romantic. He squeezed her hand, and when she looked across at him and smiled he sent a silent, thankful prayer to whomever it may concern.

"So, you got any energy left for me after your night out?"

Yvette smiled up at him. "Always, baby."

Errol bent to kiss her lips.

"You know…" Yvette curled her hand into the palm of his. "There are still things we haven't explored."

Errol raised an eyebrow. He knew that tone of voice. "Are there? Enlighten me."

"Rain…" She twirled a finger. "Remember that film *9 1/2 Weeks*?"

A flash of lightning was followed by rumbling thunder, it was time to get a move on. Grabbing Yvette's hand, Errol glanced to his right and they stepped into the road.

He hadn't heard the engine as a car headed straight for them, its headlights off. "Jesus!" he shouted, stepping back instinctively. Yvette, however, hadn't registered the danger and for a split second she stared at the approaching car with disbelief. Reflexes quick as a cat's sent Errol diving into her, knocking her out of the car's path. But there was no time to swing himself clear. He felt a sharp, explosive pain in his side as the vehicle struck and he was sent somersaulting onto the hood of a parked car. Blackness spilled like blood across his vision, and the sound of the car's engine roaring away receded into nothing.

Errol was unconscious before his body hit the ground.

He was sure he'd opened his eyes, but everything seemed

unreal. Everything was too bright, too misty, unstable…

I must be dead, he thought.

"Errol?"

He could hear a voice, a familiar voice, and he turned his head slightly to where he thought it was coming from.

"Errol?"

Now the cloudiness cleared enough for him to be able to make out a figure by his side.

It was Yvette. He wasn't dead after all.

"Eve."

She took his hand and placed a cool palm on his forehead. "Hi, lover…" She struggled to keep the emotion out of her voice. "How you feeling?"

Errol thought about the question. He really didn't know the answer. Not only that, but he wasn't sure who or where he was.

Everything faded out again.

The next time he opened his eyes he could focus. He could feel pain; it hurt to move even a fraction. He was in a white room with yellow curtains. A private room with no other bed. A television was bracketed to the wall ahead of him.

He turned his head to look at the figure sleeping in an easy chair by the side of his cot. Her head was almost touching her shoulder. He remembered why he was in here — the rain, their romantic walk, the car… and then the pain. He didn't know how badly he was hurt. All he knew for certain was that he was.

Yvette woke up and looked at him through red eyes. She pushed the concern from her face to show a smile of bravery. "Errol," she breathed out with relief.

"You been here all the time?" he croaked, surprised at how weak his voice sounded.

She poured him a glass of water and held it to his lips as he raised his aching head a little from the pillows. "Where else would I go when my man's in hospital?"

He found it hard to concentrate on remembering what he

needed to ask. Things were slipping out of his mind as quickly as they appeared. "Are you okay?"

"A little bruised, mostly on my backside. That was some tackle you dropped 'pon me."

Then memory came back more clearly, the scene flashing before his eyes: the car, speeding towards Yvette, and his instinctive reaction. "God, my head…"

"That'll be the concussion."

Errol closed his eyes and licked dry lips. "What's the damage?"

"You've got two fractured ribs, one broken… oh, and the head. Any pain?"

"All over." He opened his eyes again and regarded her with suspicion. "Why are you smiling?"

" 'Cause you're still here, talking to me." She leaned closer and kissed him full on the lips. "Scared the life out of me, the way you just went out again last time you woke up. Anyt'ing's better than the things that ran through my mind when I saw you lying there not moving."

"Come here…" He raised an arm to her, wanting to feel her as close as possible, then howled in pain as the pressure on his ribs reminded him why he was there.

Later the police came to question him about the incident. They had already spoken to Yvette and declared that they had very little to go on and knew nothing for sure. Although they both had their suspicions, they decided not to leap to conclusions and incriminate Anne-Marie.

This was to turn out to be the wrong decision.

On Saturday morning Yvette rose slowly. The space next to her was still empty, but Errol would be discharged tomorrow. She had already planned to stay at home with him for a few days until she was sure he was over the worst. Men! When they weren't well they were worse than babies.

As usual on a Saturday, Tyrone was out playing football. The house felt extremely quiet and empty.

Dressed in a shortie negligée she tied her hair up and

descended the staircase. She picked up the mail from the door mat and, placing the phone bill aside, began to sort through the cards and letters. Probably more well-wishers. They'd had more than enough get-well cards over the past couple of days. Errol was well loved, and missed at the studio. Marion had sent flowers and cards, and visited Errol every day. Chris had turned up with Dean and Colin, bringing with them enough alcohol to knock an elephant out. Errol had had to sit and watch them without touching a drop because of all the pills he had inside him.

One by one, Yvette opened the letters addressed to her. The last came in a lavender-coloured envelope and was a single folded sheet of notepaper. It was all typed, including the signature.

>   *Dear Yvette,*
>
>   *I thought it was time we had a little chat. Woman to woman, sister to sister. You don't know what you're living with. Errol doesn't really want you. At the moment you've got him hooked on your sex, but it won't last.*
>
>   *Errol is in fact in love with me. The only thing stopping us being together is you. I think he's scared of you but that's just my opinion.*
>   *You're not the kind of woman for him. He needs a woman with education, a woman who knows how to take care of her man, a woman with no ties, not a single mother looking for a meal ticket. Believe me he's going to realise.*
>
>   *Whatever it is he thinks he's getting from you is only because you've brainwashed him. He must be restless by now. I know him so well. He's not the settling down type. He needs a free spirit like me.*
>
>   *I'm only telling you this to save you the pain of an awful break-up when the time comes. I urge you to let him go now, if necessary throw him out, he'll always have somewhere to go.*

Let real love blossom.

Your sister in spirit,
Anne-Marie

Yvette had to read the letter again and again before it really sunk in. A shiver went down her back and she began to tremble, and she screwed the letter up in her clenched fist. Tears had already to begun to trek down her cheek. Her man was in hospital. He could have been killed by that bitch, and yet she still wouldn't leave them alone. She had to be the devil.

Breathing deeply, Yvette swept the hated tears away from her face, she had let Anne-Marie get away with enough. Yvette was not going to allow it again. Errol was hers, and she was going to fight for him.

She stood up and walked deliberately to the telephone. Errol kept a small book of contact numbers on the table there — it didn't take her long to find Anne-Marie's. Several other numbers were scribbled or Tipp-exed out, but not hers. Yvette, however, did not have time to think about this. She picked up the phone and dialled.

It rang four times before it was answered. "Hello?"

"You bitch! Where the fuck do you get off sending me a letter like that? My man is in hospital." Yvette sniffed back tears. "I think I told you before: stay out of my face, out of my life, and out of my — you hear me? — *my* family."

"Yvette, what is this?"

"Woman, you're asking for a good slapping. You show your face anywhere near me again and you're going to get it. I have a long memory."

"Errol's in hospital! Where?" Anne-Marie sounded convincing, as if she didn't know. Errol had said she was a good actor.

"Everyone in the country knows. I ain't playing with you. Why don't you just kill yourself and get it over with quickly, 'cause, believe me, it'll be a lot less painful than me getting my hands on you!"

190

Yvette slammed down the phone.

Miles away, Anne-Marie replaced the receiver and picked it up again. Her finger pressed the numbers 1471.

Ex-directory! I don't think so.

She was still in bed, alone as usual, but now she rose, her brain whirling. Over the past couple of days Anne-Marie had stayed out of circulation. Something strange had happened to her. It was as though a piece of her recent memory had been removed, wiped clean. She had done something she couldn't remember... and now Yvette had told her that Errol was in hospital...

She picked up the stack of newspapers that had been delivered over the past three or four days (she had lost count), carried them into the living room and switched the television on before sitting down.

She scanned every column. Nothing.

The next paper, however, screamed at her: ERROL WRIGHT IN HIT-AND-RUN MADNESS. There was a picture of an ambulance, Errol being lifted on a stretcher. Yvette in the background, a blanket around her.

Quickly Anne-Marie turned to the next day's paper. This time there was more information. The accident had happened at around midnight. The car was described only as a small black hatchback, no make, no registration number as yet. The police were appealing for witnesses...

Anne-Marie walked on shaky legs to the window and looked down to the street below. Her black Fiesta was parked at the kerb, just as it had been for four days, or so she thought...

191

TWENTY

If there was one thing Yvette hated, it was waiting — for anything: a man, a bus, food, time to pass... A few minutes ago the tannoy had announced a twenty-minute delay before the next train to Ladbroke Grove. Along with at least a hundred other commuters, she had mumbled disgruntedly. It was cold, and she waited impatiently, looking at her watch every other minute. She was going to be late for the start of the course.

The platform gave her the creeps. It looked like the set of a horror movie with its dark-green ironwork and dull orange light. She shivered and pulled her leather coat tighter round her body, almost expecting to see Dracula come through the tunnel, looking for his next victim. If only she had company. She could have done with Karen on this trip. That woman could chat. If it wasn't dissing men it was cussing kids, bitching about women with perfect figures or recounting her latest exploits with her boss, whom she loathed with a vengeance. They had had their laughs.

It was about time they had a holiday. A girly holiday. So what if they were both in their thirties with children? They also had men who could take care of the kids.

This trip was going to keep her away from home for two nights and three days. It was a new course in health and beauty, which Conrad had booked her into so she could ease herself back into work after Errol's accident. She had wanted to travel home in the evenings and then back to Ladbroke Grove in the mornings, but Errol wasn't having it. To him, it was bad enough that she was going at all. So he'd booked her into a hotel instead. So, the next three days was a break: a break from work, from her son, even from Errol.

Their life together still seemed like a dream. It was wonderful having him in her bed every night and every morning... but sometimes — only sometimes — she missed having her own space to think, to listen to her music at full blast, to watch what she wanted to watch on television, or to have perfect silence.

Of course this weekend wasn't going to give her all that, but at least she would have her own room for three days.

One person she was definitely glad to get away from was Anne-Marie Simms. Just thinking about that woman made Yvette clench her fists. The nerve of her! It was months now since her one-night stand with Errol, and she still couldn't grasp the idea that he was never going to belong to her.

The phone calls had started again — somehow she had got their new number — and more and more times Yvette had caught Errol taking his mail out with him in the mornings, or taking it into his study to open in private.

At last the display was showing that her train was approaching. The whole platform came alive — feet shuffled, cases and bags were hoisted off the ground, belongings secured — and Yvette walked a little further down, hoping to get a carriage that wasn't so packed. She wanted to sit down, even if it was just for a few stops.

She could see the lights of the train as it rolled down the tunnel into the station. "Thank goodness," she breathed. Why in the world had she chosen to wear these boots? They were half a size too small… but they looked good.

Suddenly a shove from behind threw Yvette off balance; her arms windmilled and she dropped her holdall, but she couldn't stop the momentum. She was heading for the tracks, and the train was still coming towards her.

Then she felt the grip of a hand on her arm, dragging her back to the platform, and safety.

"Easy! Are you okay? You could have been killed."

Her heart was beating furiously, but she nodded and straightened her coat. "Some bugger pushed me!" She craned her neck to look around.

Walking away from the platform was a woman, a scarf tied over her hair. Yvette didn't have time to see any more, before she was bustled onto the train. Her life saver made sure she got on safely this time.

Yvette felt tears of frustrated anger beginning to erupt. Anne-Marie. She's following me. Trying to kill me!

Three days later Errol, out of his bandages now, was sitting in traffic. He knew he was running late. Yvette was due back in London shortly, and he was stuck. He'd tried the back streets and they had led him right back into the jam.

He arrived at the tube station five minutes after the train had arrived, rushed frantically to where she'd said she would wait, and sighed with relief as he saw her pacing.

She smiled and walked towards him. "Boy, I knew you'd be on time. Never let me down yet," she said, kissing him.

He took her bag from her hand and drew her into his arms. "You look good enough to eat. I missed you."

"I can tell. So, how are you? Any pain?"

"Only an ache I'm sure you can cure," he teased.

"Ooh. We'd best get outta here then." She discreetly grabbed his hardening member as she stared into his eyes.

"Let's do that."

In the car she relaxed. One hand on his leg, she inhaled his familiar scent. She had missed him with a passion, never realising until they were apart how much she had got used to him being by her side in bed, or being there to give her a cuddle, a back rub, or to chat into the early hours.

After a few minutes of driving Errol pulled the car into a cul-de-sac of disused garages and industrial units.

Before Yvette could open her mouth to say anything he was on top of her, hands scrabbling for her underwear, lips all over her face, sucking her lips into his mouth, biting his way through her dress. She gasped for breath. Slipping her shoes off, she raised her legs to the dashboard, allowing him easier access. Together they worked his trousers down to his knees, her drawers hanging off one ankle by now, and he plunged himself deep inside her. Yvette's bare feet were on the windscreen, her head at an awkward angle as she pushed her buttocks towards him, feeling him hit her g-spot time and time again. "Oh God, yes!" she screamed. Errol's perspiration was dribbling down his cheek. She licked the salty liquid from his face. His breathing became faster, his thrusts deeper, as she felt his penis engorge and shoot into her. They came together in a simultaneous blast of passion that took them both by surprise.

"Oh, boy, did I miss you!" he breathed, collapsing on to her heaving chest.

After a few minutes of recovery he stepped out of the car to straighten his clothes.

He had to stop by the studio. On the way, he switched the car's humidifier on, which also produced an air freshener, and by the time they arrived he was calm and collected again.

"You want to wait here or are you coming up?"

"I might as well stretch my legs."

She waited on set while he ran to the dressing room. She walked across the deserted stage. So, this was where it all happened... She looked up at the audience seating area, now dark and empty. How did it feel to be so famous? She strolled over to the sofa and sat opposite Errol's armchair.

"Welcome to Barker's Hour..." she giggled, then stopped suddenly.

Were those footsteps she'd heard?

The studio was quiet. Too quiet.

"Errol?" She stood up, barely raising her voice.

Get out, a little voice in her head told her.

Again she heard a noise, and this time she spun towards its source. It had been a rustle from behind the set.

"Errol?" This time her voice was a little louder, with just a hint of nervousness in it. She walked up to the brightly painted backdrop. Made of wood, it was at least fifteen foot high. A loud creaking sound suddenly filled the air. She looked up and realised too late that a large weight, the shape of a bolster, had come loose and was whizzing towards her. It brushed her shoulder and sent her reeling as it crashed to the floor, but she was still on her feet.

The weight, however, was still rolling. It hit the edge of a huge flat, the size of a small house, and there was a loud creak as a section of scenery teetered, then started to fall towards her. She turned and ran, but not fast enough, and pain exploded as she was suddenly flat on her stomach, the weight of the flat on her back and legs. Groaning, she struggled to wriggle out from under the wooden wall.

People must have heard the deafening crash, because she heard running footsteps and raised voices approaching. She touched a finger to her head and it came away with blood on it. A lump was already rising. Her shoulder throbbed painfully.

"What happened?"

"Are you okay?"

"What were you doing here?"

Hands were reaching for her and pulling her free while other faceless bodies lifted the set.

"I'm fine," Yvette croaked, looking around for Errol.

"Anything broken?" A tall woman with wild brown hair was bending down to feel her legs.

"I'm fine," Yvette insisted. "Has anyone seen Errol?"

"Errol Wright? You're here with him?"

"Yes." Yvette tried to stand and a big man dressed completely in black rushed to her aid, lifting her as though she was as light as a feather.

"Hold on, I'll get someone to page him for you," the woman said. "Anton, can you do that, please? I'll get... Sorry, what's your name?" she asked Yvette, who told her. "I'll get Yvette to his dressing room."

She was made comfortable in his dressing room while she explained what had happened.

"It wouldn't just fall," the woman, who had introduced herself as Jayne, said. "Those weights are always secured. Okay, that particular piece of the set was new, but I'm sure it's had all the safety checks. Someone had to have undone the bolts and used force to shift it."

Yvette felt as though she was being accused of meddling. But she didn't say another word. She wanted Errol, and she wanted to get home as quickly as possible. She'd had enough brushes with death for one week.

Errol was by her side ten minutes later. They only had to look at each other to know what had happened.

Jayne hovered by the door. "I'll need Yvette to fill out an accident report."

"Okay, okay, get one to me later."

Jayne knew when she wasn't wanted.

Christmas came round with startling suddenness. Only a few weeks ago Yvette had thought she and Errol were finished. Now they had the house she wanted. There had been no hold ups with chains or the mortgage, and the place was theirs. Errol had bought a Christmas tree which touched the ceiling, decorated by the men of the house in silver, with the tiniest of twinkling lights. Presents lay in abundance at its base. They had bought each other at least four each.

Tyrone was the first person down the stairs that morning. He might have been closer to a teenager than a six year old, but Christmas still meant little more than presents to him — especially when his mum's boyfriend was a celebrity, a black man of means.

Errol and Yvette followed, after giving each other their first Christmas present, which didn't involve spending money. They ate a cooked breakfast Jamaican style, compliments of Mrs Donaldson, who had no one else to take care of at Christmas time.

Once they were washed and dressed, Errol announced, "Wait — there's a present missing..."

Tyrone looked at his mother, who shrugged and smiled back at him.

"Damn!" Errol slapped his head and looked at him. "I left one of your presents in the car! You wanna come and get it with me?"

"Safe!" Tyrone knew Errol had something up his sleeve.

Yvette watched them leave the house, Tyrone in the lead. Errol was dressed casually in dark blue trousers and a satin high-neck waistcoat, over which he'd thrown his leather jacket. Tyrone was in a Fila track suit and brand new trainers that were one of his presents.

"So, what'd you get me?"

"Have patience."

"You might as well tell me. I'm gonna see it anyway."

"Not so fast. We've got to drive a little way to pick it up."

Tyrone looked up at him, studying his face with a mixture of curiosity and impatience. "You do know the shops are closed today innit?"

Errol just smiled. "We are not going to a shop."

They got into the car and Errol headed for Marion's house. It was while they were driving that he noticed the boy scrutinising the windscreen. He looked at the glass. A pair of smudged but still clear footprints had materialised on the steamed-up glass.

"Why… ?" Tyrone began, but was instantly silenced as Errol switched on the fan.

"Don't ask," he was warned.

Tyrone studied the roads they were driving down. They turned into Marion's street, and he knew that this was obviously the hiding place for his present. If he'd searched for it at home, he wouldn't have found it.

Paul answered the door. Tyrone was standing behind Errol, his hands shoved into his pockets.

"What's up, Ty?" Paul greeted the boy with a slap on the shoulder. "I don't know where this one is stretching to — soon taller than me!"

"All right, Paul?" He shuffled into the flat behind Errol.

Errol made his way into the living room. "So where is it? You two haven't gone and sold it, have you?"

They all looked at Tyrone, who frowned back at them. Something weird was going on here.

Marion sat with Diallo, her son, on her lap. She nodded towards the Christmas tree. "It's right where it belongs."

Errol shoved Tyrone forward. "Go get your present, son."

Tyrone took his hands out of his pockets, a smile breaking on his worried face. "Which one is it?"

"You'll know when you see it." Errol was grinning wider than Tyrone now. Marion and Paul were just looking amused at the whole fiasco.

Why the hell was his present here? Did Errol have to get Marion to buy it for him? Why the big runaround?

Tyrone saw why soon enough. Lying by the Christmas tree in a huge basket, previously hidden by the armchair, was a grey puppy. A great dane.

Tyrone looked at Errol enquiringly. "Mine?"

"Yeah, it's — or I should say, *he's* yours."

Tyrone wrapped his hands around the sleeping dog, who yelped and woke up to look into his new master's face. A few months previously, Tyrone had complained that his mum wouldn't let him have a dog where they'd lived because it was too small.

Errol hadn't forgotten.

Tyrone loved it instantly.

As they left with their new family member, Errol turned to Marion. "Don't forget Yvette's present."

"As if I would…" She smiled sweetly.

"Just leave it on the doorstep and I'll get her to go out and pick it up before we sit down to dinner."

"Don't worry, I've got it under control." They kissed cheeks and Errol took his family home.

Tyrone sat in the back with his new pet. "I can't wait to take him out. He can go out now, can't he?"

"Yeah, he's had his jabs. We'll take him out tomorrow, so long as it's not too cold."

That evening Marion and Paul arrived with more gifts. As agreed, Marion left the present from Errol on the doorstep.

Yvette looked radiant, in a gown made of sequins and beads which fit her every curve, her chest pushed up high, her hair wrapped into a French plait. "You got me a surprise present, didn't you?" After dinner Errol told Yvette that there was one more present but she had to go outside to get it. Thinking it had to be a car, she squealed excitedly.

Errol looked surprised when she came back. The box was a lot bigger than the one he'd given Marion.

Errol had a funny feeling in the pit of his stomach as he watched Yvette tear the gold paper off. Inside the box was something smaller, wrapped in red tissue paper. Yvette reached in like an excited child and pulled it out. Then, surprising them all, she grimaced, gasped and dropped it.

Yvette shrieked. Her hand was covered in blood — blood that had dripped from a still warm dead rat, its head now protruding from the tissue paper at her feet.

The next morning Errol took Tyrone and the puppy to the Common while Yvette slept at home. She'd had a pretty rough night; their Christmas day had been ruined. Errol had stayed up with her through the night, talking constantly about anything else except what had happened. In the morning Tyrone made them breakfast in bed, then they had left her in peace.

Tyrone needed to train his new puppy — great danes grew fast and need plenty of discipline and exercise. Besides, Errol could do with a little himself after the amount he had eaten over the last few days. They had decided to call the dog Charles — Sir Charles to be exact, because he looked so distinguished.

Errol parked at the edge of the common. Tyrone, holding Charles's lead tightly, jogged out onto the grass.

Anne-Marie waited in her hired car until they were far enough away not to notice her, then she followed at a distance. The young boy obviously respected and loved Errol. He followed his instructions with a patience and admiration rarely seen in boys that age. And Errol looked well; the accident hadn't crippled him — indeed, there were no visible signs that it had even happened.

She still couldn't recall whether she had been involved or not, and the news hadn't reported any updates. So, for the time being at least, she was safe.

They were oblivious to her as they trained their new pet.

The puppy was just as excited as Tyrone, and jumped, ran and yapped as they threw a frisbee between them. Occasionally the dog would catch it and dash off with it in his mouth.

Unable to take this show of family solidarity any longer, Anne-Marie returned to the road. She looked at Errol's Saab. It looked so flash, so expensive, so perfect, so Errol Wright. She remembered the small knife she kept on her key chain and, looking around her, she pulled her keyring from her pocket, released the knife, and very quickly stabbed two of his tyres. Let him try to get home in that.

She almost laughed, but she was crying. No matter what she did, he still didn't want her.

So now she wanted him to hurt like she did.

It was hours before Errol arrived back home. He'd had to call out the RAC, and then they'd had to call out a specialist company for the tyres. On a bank holiday that was no easy feat. Errol had paid, grudgingly, and by the time they pulled up outside the house he was not in a good mood.

Tyrone took Charles straight upstairs while Errol went into the kitchen to make himself some hot chocolate. He was surprised to find Yvette in her dressing gown at the kitchen table. She had her head down and was sobbing.

He pulled a chair up. "Eve, honey, what's up?"

In her fist she held a crumpled note. Errol teased it from her hand and unfolded it:

> *Did you have a good nap, Yvette? I hope so, because you're going to need your strength. By the way, blood red's the perfect colour for you. Someday soon you're going to be covered in the real thing. That's a promise.*

It was unsigned.

TWENTY-ONE

New Year's Eve, and outside a cold wind blew.

More snow, Yvette predicted as she sprayed Eternity into her cleavage. So far the night was clear, but there had been frequent, heavy falls over the past two days. What a night to be going to a party! She'd have been happy curled up in front of the fire with her men by her side.

A moment ago a car had sounded its horn outside her house. The limousine Errol had arranged for her had arrived. She was to meet up with him at the party, held at a country mansion in Essex.

He'd told her about the do two weeks ago, and she'd had a frantic fortnight trying to find a dress that would be appropriate. It had been the hardest shopping trip ever.

She threw on her cashmere coat, a present from Errol, and left the house. The car was parked at the kerb, a silver grey model with tinted windows. So often she had seen this type of limo passing her on the streets of the West End and wondered which celebrity sat behind that darkened glass. Now she would be the one whom people would be wondering about. The thought made her smile indulgently.

She opened the back door and climbed into the warm, sumptuous tinted glass interior. She had no idea where she was going, but the chauffeur had his instructions.

She settled back and enjoyed the luxury of the leather seats, helping herself to a drink from the bar.

Half an hour later, she was bored and tipsy. She tapped on the dividing glass to attract the chauffeur's attention.

Nothing.

"Hey!" She tapped harder. "Driver!"

Still nothing.

The car accelerated as it joined a motorway.

"How much further…? Hello…?"

The first little alarm bell went off inside her, like a quiet bleeper. "Driver!" she shouted, then opened an assault on the dividing window again. The panic bleeper was turning up its power now. Her breathing speeded up, her stomach muscles tightened.

Kidnapped. No, this can't be happening, she told herself. I've just got a deaf driver. She collapsed back against the seat. That's it. I'm the prisoner of a deaf driver.

Kidnapped, indeed! Who did she think she was? So long as he got her where he was supposed to, why panic?

But as she sat back and tried to make out some detail beyond the tinted windows, a slow but sure feeling of claustrophobia crept over her. She struggled to suppress it, but it escalated until she couldn't bear another minute.

Just as she was about to try breaking the glass with the heel of her shoe, the car came to a stop. She heard the locks click open and slid her foot back into her shoe, using her fingers to get her heel in. Now she prepared to give the chauffeur a piece of her mind. There was no way he was getting away with this behaviour, deaf or not. He hadn't checked on her once during the journey. Whatever happened to common courtesy?

She grabbed her bag, jumped out and stormed round to the driver's door.

That proved to be a big mistake. The car took off immediately, the rear door jolting shut.

"Hey, where the hell are you going?" she screamed.

The car didn't even slow down.

Yvette looked around her. It was pitch dark, she was standing on a snow-covered dirt road, with woods on one side and a wide open field on the other, and it was freezing. She wore sandals on her stockinged feet, and nothing but a light wrap over her evening dress. She'd left her cashmere coat in the car. No headgear, no scarf...

Last night's snow still lay in clumps everywhere. And wasn't that snow she felt touch the tip of her nose?

What was this? Some kind of sick joke? Who would do this to her?

The answer came to her, crystal clear.

Anne-Marie.

Yvette screamed, but there was no one to hear it.

The jazz music in the background was mellow, and complemented perfectly the mix of people in the room. Everyone here had something to do with the media. Errol was deep in conversation with a script-writer when suddenly he felt eyes watching him. He glanced up from his conversation and saw Anne-Marie beckon to him.

He excused himself from the group, his face set rigid, his jawline punctuated by drawn-in cheeks, and walked purposefully towards her.

"What the *hell* are you doing here?" he hissed.

"I was invited." Anne-Marie smiled. "Errol, darling. Am I late? I had *such* a job deciding what to wear…" Her voice had deliberately risen, and a few of the closer guests and waiters had turned to look.

Errol, confused and furious, clenched his teeth. "Where's Yvette?"

"How should I know? I'm here to be with you, not her."

Errol caught a glimpse of Marion Stewart entering the room and made a huge effort to smile nonchalantly.

Marion dropped her eyes and turned away.

Damn it, Errol thought. She thinks there's something going on. How many of the others think the same thing?

Another hour of mingling and networking passed before Errol suddenly realised that Yvette had still not arrived. It was almost midnight. He knew she was never on time, but he had sent a driver for her. There is no way the car would have been late, not this late. To make matters worse Anne-Marie was following him around like a lap-dog, and he was having great trouble controlling his temper.

Again he excused himself and went to find a phone.

Marion watched him leave the room and, telling Paul she was going to the ladies', followed him out. In the huge foyer she spotted him and gently called out his name.

Taking a deep breath, he put on a smile. "Yvette hasn't arrived. I'm getting worried. A car was bringing her."

Marion touched his arm. "I'm sure she's okay. Have you called the car company?"

Errol silently fumed. "I left the number at home. I was just about to call there, see if Yvette's still waiting." He paused, as if deciding whether he should reveal his suspicions to his friend. "Marion, I'm convinced Anne-Marie is behind this, but I can't prove anything, not here..."

"I doubt it somehow. But I'll go talk to her — you make the call. Yvette's probably sitting at home waiting for it. Come and find me when you finish."

"Thanks, Marion."

She smiled reassuringly and made her way back to where she had last seen Anne-Marie.

The phone rang seven times before the answering machine picked up.

"Eve, it's me. If you're there, please pick up..." He waited a few seconds, then left the number of the house. "Call me as soon as possible. I just hope you're on the way... Anyway, I'll see you soon."

He hung up and pressed his back into the nearest wall.

He knew she'd had doubts about fitting in at one of these functions. She'd told him this morning she would have preferred to stay in tonight...

Maybe she had decided to go clubbing with her friends instead...

But no. This was their first New Year's Eve as a couple — she wouldn't do that.

So where was she?

Yvette was shivering with the cold. Yet somehow, as she walked, she could feel herself getting colder. It was snowing quite heavily now, the fresh fall covering the previous day's slush and whiting out everything she saw. Her feet and fingers were numb, and as she took each faltering step she had to keep blinking to stop the liquid in her eyes from freezing over and blinding her.

She had been trying to follow the dirt road that her

kidnapper had brought her along, but some time ago she had lost it under the new snow, and was now walking through a field. The ground here was soft, and she sunk into it up to her calves with each step, having to stop and rub her legs every few feet with fingers she couldn't feel, to try and keep the blood flowing. She exhaled with her mouth open, to let the warmer air touch her face briefly before it was whisked away. She was almost panting now anyway; whenever she tried to breathe more deeply she couldn't seem to get enough air into her lungs.

She was passing out of the field now, into some woods. She couldn't feel her feet at all but she continued to move, looking straight ahead and trying not to panic. Despite the cold her fingers felt hot — burning cold, if there was such a thing.

At least the snow gave her enough light to find her way through the woods. Her wrap covered the bottom half of her face and her hands were balled under each armpit as she emerged the other side into another field.

After a few shaky paces, her legs refused to move any further and she found herself on her hands and knees in the snow. She willed herself to stand, to get back on her feet before it was too late, but she sank to her elbows, her hands clawing at the sodden turf. Suddenly her elbows gave out too, and she found herself face-first in the snow.

She thought of Tyrone: Tyrone as a toddler, his smell, sitting in front of the TV with his Nintendo, his smile and his laugh. She thought of how he would feel if she never came back.

Against the judgement of her heart's slow beat she somehow hauled herself back up on her knees. But it was too hard. She felt pain, ferocious pain, as she tried to move a body she couldn't really feel.

And then, quite suddenly, it didn't matter. It seemed so crystal clear to her: she didn't have to go on. She could give it up, throw in the towel. She had had a good and full life, she'd cared for those whom she'd loved, she had no regrets. She had been very happy — and she had brought Errol and

Tyrone together…

Mum and Dad — they would be heartbroken. The thought cut through everything. She felt tears try to come, but nothing happened.

Her clothes were now soaked, and it felt as though the material was freezing to her skin in the chill wind, becoming one. She was becoming a part of the ice and snow, a part of the frozen landscape.

To be at one with nature, she thought.

Someone, take care of Tyrone, she prayed, and Mum and Dad.

Errol, I love you.

Just before she closed her eyes she thought she saw clouds coming towards her, heard the tinkle of bells. Clouds and bells. She was going to heaven.

She smiled before she fell unconscious.

For the second time in as many months Errol walked down a hospital corridor. But this time there was no pain, just a deep-seated numbness. He didn't hurry. He took steps that reminded the nurse accompanying him of a pall bearer.

He had arrived home from the party just before two a.m., and had called out for Yvette, hoping she had stayed at home for some reason. After a search of the bedroom he'd gone to the living room and found his answerphone blinking.

Two messages: one was his own, which he fast-forwarded immediately; the second was from a hospital, who asked him to call and ask for a Dr Turner as soon as possible.

He knew it was Yvette even as he dialled the number. He almost sensed that she was hurting somewhere.

Another certainty was that it was down to Anne-Marie.

As soon as he had confirmed it with the hospital he'd called Yvette's brother and let him know what had happened, promising to call again straight after he'd seen her. He'd been told that Yvette was in intensive care, suffering from hypothermia. She had been found unconscious in a field by a farmer who'd been rounding up his sheep from the bad weather. Errol's name and contact number had been in her purse.

From the description of her circumstances Errol pieced together what must have occured that night. The way his heart was beating erratically he knew that, if Anne-Marie were to appear right before him at that moment, he would quite happily throttle her, smiling as the life was squeezed away.

Errol hesitated in the doorway to the intensive care unit. There she was.

She had the room to herself. There was a chair by her bed, and Errol slumped down into it, weary with guilt and anger. The nurse left them alone as he took Yvette's hand and bent his head to kiss it.

"Yvette... honey?" He tried to raise some kind of reaction from her but she lay still, eyes closed, unconscious. The doctor had said she was stable, but she might lapse in and out of consciousness for a while before coming round completely. Even then she would be drowsy for a couple of days.

"You don't know how sorry I am that I let this happen." Errol raised her warm hand to his cheek. "It's all my fault — and I promise I'll make it up to you. I've learnt a valuable lesson..."

He swallowed hard and shut his eyes wearily. "You can't trust anyone, sometimes not even yourself. If anything good has come out of this, it's that you are going to be my wife — sooner than later — 'cause tonight I have realised that, if I lost you, I couldn't go on. Of course I'd have to, for Tyrone's and Aaron's sake, but it would be the most difficult task I would have ever undertaken."

Watching her face, he was sure he saw her eyelids flicker — or was that wishful thinking?

An hour later he was being woken up from a deep sleep.

"Mr Wright, Mr Wright..."

The voice was coming from somewhere above him. At first he thought it must be a tannoy, then he recognised his own name and opened his eyes.

He'd only left the room to get coffee and sunk into a chair while he waited for the queue to go down. He must have drifted off, his fatigued mind recognising an escape route.

"Ms Barker is now conscious, Mr Wright. Her temperature's back to normal."

Errol jumped up, and a smile emerged through his exhaustion.

The sister followed him back to the room. "She's still very drowsy and a little confused... Don't expect too much."

"She's going to be okay then?"

"As far as we can make out, Yvette never actually stopped breathing the whole time. There is no apparent brain damage."

The heart monitors were bleeping steadily as he entered the room. Her eyes were still closed, but her chest was moving up and down regularly.

Errol experienced a fresh surge of fury, tempered only by the sentiment of pity. His voice was a hoarse whisper. "Eve? Eve, what happened? What happened to you?"

Yvette's eyes opened.

It was past midday by the time Errol left the hospital and made the diversion towards Streatham and Anne-Marie's block of flats.

Outside, he sat in the car for a few minutes looking up at her window. How many times had she done exactly the same thing to him — sat outside his home and watched him going about his business? Crept about in the night, posted letters through his door, left him unwanted gifts... Instead of abating, his anger grew. Yvette could have died last night.

From the hospital he had called the limousine company

hired by the station. Their car had arrived a few minutes late and there had been no one in. Anne-Marie must have hired another car, picked Yvette up and kidnapped her, leaving her in the middle of nowhere to freeze to death.

He stepped from the car, his jaw rigid, cheekbones standing out clearly. He rang the intercom to her flat and waited.

About thirty seconds later it was answered. "Yes?"

"It's me."

"Me who?" came the reply.

"You know who it is," he hissed loudly.

"What do you want?"

"I want to talk to you."

"Oh, so *now* you want to talk?"

"Open the fucking door."

There was a buzz as the door was released. He swung it open and took the stairs to her second-floor flat, where she stood smiling in the front doorway. She was wearing work-out gear: a cropped top and leggings.

"I wasn't expecting company — especially not yours. But you're welcome."

She stepped into the flat, eyeing his attire as she let him pass. "Where did you sleep last night? I can see you haven't been home—"

"You make me sick!" He spun round, his eyes flashing, fists clenched at his sides. "Why Yvette? Why couldn't you leave her alone?"

"What are you talking about?"

"Don't play the innocent with me." He couldn't even look at her for fear of losing control. "She could have *died* last night, being left out there..." His voice broke in anger on the last word.

"Left where? I have no idea what you're talking about, Errol." She walked away from him and into her kitchen. "Can I get you something to drink?"

Errol ignored the question. "Why couldn't you just go and get yourself some help when I asked you to? You don't know what you're doing to us!" His voice was almost a sob as he thought of the usually strong Yvette lying in a hospital bed.

"I haven't touched Yvette. If you remember, the last time I saw her she tried to attack me…"

"Are you telling me you didn't kidnap her last night and take her place at the ball?"

Now Anne-Marie laughed, throwing her head back theatrically. "*Kidnap*? I turned up at the party because I was invited… and to be with you." She walked round the counter, a glass of wine in her hand. "I couldn't care less if she was there or not… although I wouldn't have had you all to myself if she had been."

She stopped in front of him, allowing her hand to creep up his shirt to his shoulder. "Don't you think I've shaped up pretty well?"

She kissed him on his lips and he pulled away, a revulsion so violent rising from the pit of his stomach that he couldn't stand to be close to her. Before he could stop himself, he swung his arm and knocked the glass out of her hand. It rose in the air, spilling wine before shattering on the edge of the counter and falling in splinters to the floor.

Anne-Marie's brown eyes become black with anger. "There was no need for that! What — don't I kiss as good as Yvette?"

"Don't even utter her name!"

"Errol, look at me…" She raised her crop-top over her head and quickly unfastened her sports bra, exposing her firm round breasts. "I'm no different to other women. I have needs…"

Despite himself he felt his penis jump and lengthen. He turned his back. "Cover yourself up. I didn't come here for that."

"Why? Having trouble getting it up?"

"You're not well, Anne-Marie. Don't come near us again. I won't be responsible for my actions if you come anywhere near my family." And with that he spun round and headed out of the flat, slamming the door behind him.

TWENTY-TWO

The drive from London to Devon had taken them five hours, but as they finally neared the beach cottage Yvette smiled. At last she could hear the sound of the sea, and a salty, fresh smell filled the car.

She put a hand on Errol's leg and breathed in. "I'm feeling more relaxed already."

Errol looked over at her and forced a smile to his lips. He had been far away in his own thoughts. On one side of them was the ocean, white-tipped waves lapping up to the beach then rippling away to nothing. On the other side were hillsides and fields, and every now and then a guest house or cottage.

The orangey twilight shone warmly through the glass of the windscreen, and Yvette closed her eyes and sank lower into her seat. "Yeah, man…"

Errol knew he'd made the right decision to get her away from everything that had been going on since he'd made the mistake of getting involved with Anne-Marie Simms. She had been out of hospital a week now, and ever since he had kept her cocooned at home — on her own during the daytime, but in the evenings Tyrone and Errol hadn't let her lift a finger. They would do the cooking, cleaning, ironing, running baths, giving massages, fetching her drinks…

He still blamed himself, but felt he couldn't apologise enough verbally, so he had made up for it by showering her with affection, by surprising her with little love notes left in places around the house where he knew she'd find them. A single lily had arrived every other day.

Yvette was strong, and felt she was well on the way to recovery, but she had enjoyed being pampered by her men. She'd kept herself busy around the house during the daytime, indulging herself occasionally by dropping in at the gym for a full body massage — well, that was her excuse, but really she was checking on her business. Conrad was running things well, but she knew her clients liked the personal touch, and she didn't want to lose them.

But what she really wanted more than anything else was revenge. She tried to tell herself that Anne-Marie wasn't important, that Errol loved her and was here by her side. But that woman had made it personal; it wasn't about keeping her man any more, it was about showing Anne-Marie she didn't need a man to keep her under wraps and protect her. She could take care of herself, and she wanted to demonstrate this to Anne-Marie. In short, she wanted her right where she could lay some licks 'pon her body for messing with her life.

Every day she regretted not having given her a few blows on the couple of occasions she had been face to face with her. Now the woman who had the means and the motivation to have killed her several times over was still out there somewhere, free, living her life while others had had theirs turned upside-down.

The car turned onto a narrow dirt road and ascended a hedged path up the hillside. Yvette opened her eyes and could see the cottage they would be staying in. It was like something out of a fairy tale: stone-clad walls, two chimneys — which meant open fireplaces, log fires... She looked up to see French windows leading to a balcony.

She hopped from the car as soon as it pulled up at the back of the house, and with the excitement of a child she rushed round to the front. She gasped at the breathtaking view. The sun had reached the horizon, and the sea was ablaze with oranges and reds. A pathway led from the front garden down to their own private section of beach.

Errol's mouth was against her neck as his arms circled her from behind. "Hey, you," he whispered.

She leaned back into his body as he pulled her close. "How did you find out about this place?"

"I have my sources. Now, are you going to help me unpack all that food? And then, if you feel up to it, we can go for a walk along the coastline."

"Feel up to it? Boy, you couldn't stop me!" She turned

and clung to him as she looked out at the sea. "It's perfect…" She looked up into his smiling eyes. "I love you."

"And I love you — more than life itself."

They kissed deeply before walking back to the house, arms around each other. The inside was as she'd imagined. Even the dining room had a log fire. The bedrooms had four-poster beds, with white cotton and lace bedding and curtains, and en suite bathrooms.

After unpacking and taking a walk by the sea, which now looked like Tango, complete with bubbles, they settled down on the sofa in front of the log fire in the living room. Their glasses held pink champagne; the rest of the bottle cooled in a bucket of ice by their side. The room was filled with the gentle glow from the hearth, and a soft soul CD played on the portable machine Errol had brought with them.

"Could this possibly get any better?" Yvette sighed.

Errol smiled. "I'm sure it can."

"That's impossible."

"Nothing's impossible when I'm around."

He proposed to her that night. The setting was their private beach, the only witnesses the moonlight and the stars. Dinner was served by a lone, uniformed waiter; he didn't bat an eyelid as he brought the food and wine across the pebble and sand beach.

Yvette's ring was served on a silver tray in a polished oyster shell. As he took it and slipped it on her finger, Errol recited a poem he had composed from his heart. It was a night Yvette knew she would never forget.

"You were right," she whispered as she accepted the proposal with a deep, deep kiss.

"I was?"

"It did get better."

When they arrived back to face the new year in London,

they both wanted the romance to carry on. Announcing their engagement was top on Errol's list, and he set about making arrangements for a party immediately. Helen took care of sending the invitations and arranging the catering; Yvette just had to supply her with a list of guests.

Marion's gift was an enormous crystal chandelier, which she had delivered and installed before the engagement party. Yvette looked upon Marion as a new friend. Errol loved her, and so it followed that she should too.

The message in the accompanying card made her smile:

> *Someone had to tie him down. Glad it's you. Enjoy*
> *every minute it lasts. Look after him for me, Marion.*

Errol turned his car into the driveway, and was about to press the remote control for the garage door when he saw Tyrone coming up the road, not alone. The boy was arm-in-arm with a young lady. Could this be the Charlene that called him every evening — the calls he had to take in his bedroom? The boy was only twelve going on thirteen, what did he know about dating?

Charlene looked a like a woman dressed as a thirteen year old schoolgirl. Her hair hung in two short bunches and she had a side-parted fringe. Errol had to admit even at his age that his eyes were drawn to her bosom — the girl must have been chased around the playground by every adolescent in the school.

His school bag slung over his shoulder, Tyrone must have seen Errol's car because he and his girlfriend stopped a little way up the road and talked.

Errol, curious, left the car on the driveway and got out to wait for Tyrone, who kissed the girl's cheek and called out as they parted that he would see her tomorrow.

"All right, son?"

"All right," he answered.

"Was that your girlfriend?"

Tyrone looked at him. "Dat's a bit personal, innit?"

"Sorry…" Errol remembered back to his schooldays: you don't tell your parents that kind of thing. "So tell me, how was school today?"

Tyrone shrugged and hitched his bag back on his shoulder. "It's all right."

Errol made a mental note: never ask the boy questions which can be answered with "It's all right". Their conversations these days were definitely getting shorter. It seemed that since Tyrone had moved up a year at school he had left behind half his vocabulary. Errol intended to give the kid a little more attention. Tyrone was definitely not going to be another statistic…

Errol pulled his door keys out of his pocket. "So, you cooking dinner tonight?"

Tyrone gave him the exact same look his mother had often used on him. He called it the are-you-crazy? look. Then the boy smiled as he saw the amusement in Errol's eyes.

"Only ribbing you, Ty. But you know it won't be long before I have you in that kitchen."

Errol swung the door open, and immediately they both knew something was wrong.

"Charles!" Tyrone called. Dropping his bag in the hallway, he went into the living room and called again. "Charles! Here, boy!"

As he looked back at Errol there was concern in his eyes.

"Maybe Mum took him out with her." Errol knew this was most unlikely; Tyrone knew it too, and climbed the stairs in leaps, calling his pet.

Errol walked through to the back of the house and the kitchen. As he pushed open the door a smell hit him with some force. A rotten smell — and another: dog's mess. He scanned the floor, then rushed over to where the dog was lying by the back door.

"Tyrone! Tyrone, call the vet!" At first Errol had thought he was dead, but on closer inspection he noticed the dog's eyes were only half-closed. In a feeble display of loyalty, the animal tried to wag its tail and get up. It barely managed to move at all.

Tyrone skidded to a halt behind him. Errol turned and reassured him with a smile and a nod. "He's gonna be okay. You go and call the vet. You know where the number is?"

Tyrone barely nodded; there was shock and hurt in his eyes as he stared at the weak animal. "What's wrong with him, Errol?" His dog, the strong beast that had chased him around the park since Christmas, the pet that always welcomed him at the door... He felt tears in his eyes and turned away quickly to make the call from the living room.

A few minutes later he had taken Errol's place by the dog's side as they waited for the vet. He was talking to the animal and Errol was relieved to see Charles's reaction to his voice. Every now and then a whimper would accompany Tyrone's voice. The vet was prompt, and collected Charles plus samples of faeces and vomit from the floor. He said he would call and let them know as soon as he had any news, but from the evidence it looked like some kind of poisoning.

Poisoning! The words hit Errol like a blow to the stomach. Where would the dog have found anything poisonous?

The answer was obvious: he was fed it.

Errol finally went to the police. The situation had become too serious to ignore. He now knew he couldn't just sit by in the hope that Anne-Marie would just go away. She had tried to kill the dog, and, more seriously, himself and Yvette. At the police station Errol was taken into an interview room by a young officer who opened a pad and began to make notes.

"Okay, Mr Wright, what is your complaint, and who is it against?"

"Her name is Anne-Marie Simms, and she's been harassing me for several months now," he answered.

The PC's pen hovered over the pad. "Forgive me, but... would this happen to be a lovers' tiff?"

Errol was taken aback by the inference. "Not exactly, no."

"Then what, exactly?"

Errol leant forward to tell his story. "I met this woman sometime last year, in the Autumn. A few weeks after we met... well, I slept with her. It happened once only. We both understood that it wasn't to happen again. You see, I have a girlfriend; she's now my fiancé. Now... this woman... well, she calls me, sends me letters, gifts..."

"Hardly a reason to complain, sir. I mean, we can hardly arrest someone for being in love, can we? What evidence do you have that this woman means you harm?"

Errol was surprised by the officer's attitude, but continued calmly. "If you'll let me finish... Recently she has become irrational. She's tried to harm my girlfriend. She's had us both in hospital — she tried to run us down in her car. She's slashed my tyres, and tried to poison our pet."

"Are you sure it was she who did this?"

"Yes! Yes, of course..."

"Any witnesses?"

"No. None that I know of."

The officer put his pen down. "There's not a lot we can do without evidence, sir."

"I just want her to stop. She's harassing me and my family. There's no telling what she might do next."

"We can't arrest someone for what they *might* do—"

"I don't necessarily want her arrested — just cautioned. Someone official to talk to her. I want it to stop."

"We could talk to her, but it might make things public — and I'm sure you don't want that, being a celebrity an' all..."

Errol met the policeman's eyes. He had recognised him.

"It might even aggravate the situation," he continued. "Why don't you apply to the courts for a restraining order?"

"Can I do that without evidence?"

"Unfortunately not, catch her at it..."

Errol left the police station with a new purpose. He had to catch her in the act — but how, when he never knew what her next move might be?

TWENTY-THREE

Errol sat in first class, opposite Marion Stewart. A pair of reading glasses were perched on the end of her petite nose, and a magazine was spread on the table between them. The train was bound for Manchester, and a recording of a celebrity quiz show.

They chatted amiably in between periods of quiet reading. Marion's series was over, and so she was constantly in touch with her agent to get small jobs like this one to do. She was thinking of going back into journalism.

Suddenly she looked up from her magazine. "I saw the show you did with that drug addict."

Errol laughed, then looked rather embarrassed. "I can laugh about it now, but I hate it when disorganised things like that happen — it doesn't do the show any good. They didn't tell me the guy had gone cold turkey only the day before."

"Believe me, it didn't do your ratings any harm."

"Sad world, isn't it?"

Marion leaned towards him and lowered her voice. "Are we allowed to talk about Anne-Marie Simms?"

Errol raised his eyebrows. "Who?"

"That bad, eh?'

Errol suddenly seemed exhausted; he gazed out the window at the passing fields. "Can we *not* do this?"

Marion reached over and placed a hand on his knee. "All right. But if you ever want to talk — or even if you don't, but have to — make sure it's me you bell, okay?"

He nodded, and gazed out of the window again. "Yvette's actually coping better than I am."

"Is that so?"

"I'm a total wreck and she's like a solid rock."

They were interrupted by the show's director who had lurched into their carriage to explain the finer points of the quiz game to them.

So, Anne-Marie was definitely out of bounds, and Marion would have to fight the urge to find out more about what she was up to — her journalistic instinct, she told herself.

The hotel had a leisure complex attached, and Errol had decided to make the most of it. With a towel thrown over one shoulder he entered the swimming area and suddenly stopped, watching the lone swimmer. The woman was doing laps so smoothly and quietly that he hadn't heard a sound, and had expected the pool to be deserted. She was athletic, dark-skinned, and for a crazy moment Errol thought it was Anne-Marie. He almost began back-pedalling to the changing rooms, but as she pulled herself to the edge of the pool for a breather he could see it wasn't. She was pretty, even dripping with water, slender, not as muscular as Yvette, with long arms and even longer legs. She had jet black hair which was tied with a band; she pushed a few stray strands off her face and briefly glanced up at him before turning and dolphin-diving back under the water.

Her stroke was effortless, strong and rhythmic. It would be a shame to disturb her, Errol thought, so he lay his towel on a bench, climbed into the opposite end of the pool and started a quiet routine, washing away the stresses and tensions of the day. It was the first time he had loosened up in ages, the business of the past few months having hung heavily on his conscience.

He did five widths before coming up for air. He shook water from his head, and when he looked up he saw the woman sitting on the side, staring at him.

Used to being recognised, Errol swam over, ready for the usual "Don't I know you from somewhere?"

"Only five laps!" she laughed, her voice a musically lilting West Indian. "Cho', a fit young man like you mus' can do bettah!"

Errol stopped just in front of her, sculling the water with

his arms to stay afloat. "I'm only just warming up," he quickly pointed out, irritated at this slip of a woman belittling him.

She was grinning mischievously. Pulling her ponytail forward she squeezed water from the end of it. "Maybe…"

"That sounds like a challenge to me."

"Men! Cyan' tek criticism without seein' it as a challenge! You in good shape, though. I'll tek you on."

Now it was Errol's turn to laugh. "You serious?"

"Are you?"

She was too up front to resist. "You're on. Fifty laps?"

She slid her brown body into the water and came up beside him. "Your call, mister."

"After three?"

She nodded.

"One… two… three!"

They took off together but, even though he'd had the advantage of being the caller, the woman soon started inching ahead. He'd underestimated her.

He caught up on the second lap and stayed with her for ten, when again she pulled ahead. After thirty he was feeling the strain in his shoulders. But his competitor was apparently feeling no such fatigue, and made the fifty laps well before him.

She climbed out and waited for him to finish.

Breathless, Errol dragged himself up beside her and they sat on the edge, dangling their legs in the water. "You're good," he said. Up close she was even better — he could see every muscle that had prompted her to win.

"I know it," she laughed. This lady was not modest. "I'm Jazz…" She held out her hand. "I t'ink I ought to know who I jus' beat."

"Errol," he replied, shaking it. She hadn't recognised him.

"You know, you're not bad — jus' not as good as me. You got to learn to move with the water, not against it."

"I was doing the best I could."

"Never min', darling, better luck nex' time." She patted

his back and they both laughed.

She was funny. It felt good to laugh for a change. Real good. Real necessary.

"So, do you come here often?" he asked.

She shook her head, her hair dripping little crystals of water. "Dis pool, a couple a times a week. I work part-time for a print comp'ny up the road. You?"

"I'm a visitor. Staying in the hotel. I needed a relaxing work-out... and that was nothing like a relaxing work out."

They laughed again. "You need a challenge every once in awhile. Get your blood boiling, y'know."

"Yeah, but I've had my share of blood boiling recently. So, how come you're so good at this?"

"I used to swim fe me school back home. It's one t'ing I hold on to from me was a yout'."

"It shows."

"An' what do you do?"

"I..." he stopped himself. He'd made the mistake of getting too friendly with strange women before. Never again. Besides, this was nice — just chatting without talk of his career and being a celebrity. "I'm a mechanic," he lied.

"Mmm. So dat's where you get dose muscles." She ran a hand over his shoulder. It wasn't a caress, more like testing a piece of furniture for firmness. "You're strong, but a real clumsy swimmer... On the other han', you do look good in swimming trunks."

Errol blushed and automatically moved his hands to hide the bulge in his trunks.

Jazz suppressed a giggle. "You hungry? I was gonna pop in to my favourite Chinese restaurant on the way home."

Errol hesitated. But what was he worried about? Tomorrow night he would be on his way back home to Yvette. And this Jazz woman hadn't even recognised him. "Chinese? Sure. I'll join you."

They met in the lobby of the restaurant. She wore jogging bottoms, a V-necked body suit and squash trainers. She'd brushed her hair back and clipped it at the nape of her neck. Over dinner they chatted about their past and ambitions. Usually he would be the questioner, inquisitive about what made someone tick, but he found Jazz so easy to talk to that by the time they'd finished eating he had told her much more than he'd expected. However, he had managed to skirt around his television role, making up the story of his life as he went along. She was a freelance graphic designer. Her name was Jacintha, but everyone she knew called her Jazz and she had adopted it.

Two hours had passed so comfortably that they were both surprised when the waiter, after hovering for fifteen minutes, told them that the restaurant was closing. It was eleven thirty. They paid the bill — going Dutch, she insisted.

"Can I give you a lift home?" Errol asked, before remembering he had no car but could always call on the stand-by driver.

"No, I 'ave me own car."

"I'll walk you."

They walked to the car park. "That was a most enjoyable evening," Errol said.

"The food or the comp'ny?" she asked, watching his face.

"Both."

"You know, Errol, you're all right. Guys like you are usually married and will still try somet'ing."

"Don't think I haven't thought about it… and as for getting married, I *have* found the right woman. We just haven't got around to it… yet."

"This is me," she said, stopping by a red Metro.

"Thank you… for your company tonight."

"My pleasure." She kissed his cheek. "Maybe we'll meet again."

Errol watched her get into her car, and was about to reach for one of his cards when he remembered they had his profession printed on them. Instantly she would know he had lied. She could also turn out to be another adoring fan, or a maniac.

So he stood helplessly, and waved as she drove out of his

life.

He thought about Jazz as he made his way back to his room. He had the curious feeling that he knew her from somewhere. In fact, she reminded him of Marion. Lying on his bed that night, he felt extremely proud of himself. In the old days he would have charmed his way into Jazz's bed. Now he had Yvette, all that was behind him, and he had no regrets.

He turned over and picked up the phone, dialled home, and grinned as Yvette answered on the second ring.

"Hey, you..."

The next morning Errol was up early to start recording. He had to share a dressing room, but it wasn't the first time. The other guy was Roy, a comedian, also up from London. "Another hole in the wall," he sniffed as they were pointed in the direction of their room.

It was a narrow, windowless cubbyhole with a long counter bolted to the wall. A mirror ran above the counter, surrounded by bare bulbs, half of which had blown. There was a small pile of envelopes on the side. Errol ignored them, but his roommate scooped them up. "Looks like people know you're here — they're all for you."

Errol's brow creased. He took the letters Roy handed him but didn't look at them. His eyes were riveted to the far end of the dressing table, where a single red rose stood in a clear vase. A small card was taped to the side of it.

Roy followed his gaze. "I guess that must be yours too."

Errol couldn't believe it. This had Anne-Marie stamped all over it. But how could she have known he was here? Another sweet-smelling, blood-red rose.

He didn't even read the card. He wouldn't give her the satisfaction. He snatched it off the counter and dashed the whole thing in the bin.

"Hey, don't you want to find out who it's from?"

"I have a pretty good idea."

"But all the same..."

Roy retrieved the rose. He took the card out of the envelope and handed to Errol, who sighed and accepted it. As he read it a strange smile curled his lips upwards.

"Errol. Can't get you out of my mind, Yvette."

She'd had it sent to him.

Errol laughed with relief, took the rose from Roy's hand and placed it back on the counter. "It's from my girl. She's missing me."

During a break Errol finally caught up with Marion. "Hi there, got time for a coffee?"

Marion grinned. "For you, I can probably spare a few seconds."

Errol laughed, and she was glad to see it. This was the real Errol shining through again.

Over coffee he told her about the rose. "Freaked me out at first, but…"

"You thought it was from her?"

"Yes. Silly, huh? I'm getting so paranoid."

"Considering what she's done I wouldn't say so. Look, I'd better get back on set, I have to redo my make-up."

Smiling to himself, Errol trotted back to his dressing room, a spring in his step. But the smile froze on his lips when he glanced at the long mirror, and his heart thundered in his chest.

Scrawled across the glass in red lipstick was a message:

MISS ME YET? I'M CLOSER THAN YOU THINK, ERROL. WE'LL BE TOGETHER SOON.

Before leaving Manchester Errol called the police station where he had reported Anne-Marie. He needed to find out if they had talked to her, maybe even arrested her.

"Mr Wright… Yes, we did talk to Miss, er… Simms."

"And?"

"She admits sending you letters and calling you, but says

that's all she did. She claims she's in love with you, sir, and wouldn't want to hurt either you or your family."

"She's lying!" Errol barked. "I have no proof, but she is."

"I don't blame you for being upset, Mr Wright," the officer said. "If what you say is true, someone has made an attempt on your life. But we can't arrest her for sending you letters or flowers. We did give her a warning, though. A pretty strong one. But without evidence connecting her to the other incidents, there's not much else we can do."

"Well, your warning didn't work." Errol was trying hard to keep his temper under control. "I'm up in Manchester, and she's been here — in my dressing room, writing on my mirror in lipstick."

The officer's voice became a little more alert. "Did you see her, sir?"

"No, but… how many stalkers do I know?"

"Listen, sir, as soon as you have some proof, something we can use, we'll be happy to help you."

"Sure," Errol replied, and hung up. At least she wasn't in London causing Yvette any grief.

It was a consolation that did little to help the way Errol felt. He would have to be on his guard.

Two days later Anne-Marie was still on Marion's mind. She reached forward and pressed the intercom on her desk. Her assistant answered.

"Mike, can you come in here with a pad, please?"

The door opened seconds later.

"Find out all you can about Anne-Marie Simms? She's a psychologist and author of a book called *Internal Bleeding*. We should have her on file somewhere — I was going to use her for a show before the cuts. Use research if you have to."

A few hours later there was a knock on her office door, and a file was dropped on her desk. She dreaded what she might discover, but nevertheless leant forward and read.

TWENTY-FOUR

Anne-Marie stepped from her car and took a deep breath before looking up and down the residential street. So far so good. It was three thirty. Any minute now he would be coming to the gates.

The school was comprised of four single-storey buildings, and because Anne-Marie wasn't sure which one Aaron would emerge from she tried to keep a vigil on them all. Anyway, there was only one exit to the road.

Two hours ago she had called the boy's mother and pretended to be Errol's secretary. From what Errol had told her about Tanya, she'd known she wouldn't question a change of plans if it saved her a journey. She had told Tanya that, instead of picking Aaron up from her home, Errol would be collecting him from school.

As the children started to flood out of the buildings, Anne-Marie smiled at the waiting mothers and nannies — some with other children, toddlers, babies in prams... Of course Aaron would be no problem. He knew Anne-Marie, and she was certain Errol wouldn't have concerned his child with the recent goings on. He would go with her.

She recognised him waiting just inside the gates, and approached slowly. "Hello, Aaron. Remember me?" She smiled her most friendly smile; it wasn't hard — she genuinely liked the little boy.

At first, she could see, he had trouble placing her face.

"Anne-Marie," she reminded him. "I'm a friend of your dad's."

"Oh yeah!" He smiled back, revealing a cute dimple.

"He's asked me to come and pick you up and keep you occupied for a few hours."

Aaron cocked his head one side, and for a second he looked just like his father.

She took his arm and began leading him towards her car. "Would you like that? Just the two of us..."

227

Aaron grinned, and in no time they were driving towards town and the Trocadero, where she hoped to exhaust him and, of course, give him a treat.

Errol knocked impatiently on the front door again. This time a light came on and Tanya opened the door, holding it to her body, just her head appearing in the gap. "Did you forget something?"

"Sorry?"

"Look, I'm busy — what do you want?"

Slightly confused, though quite accustomed to Tanya's abrupt manner, Errol controlled his voice. "I'm here to collect my son. Remember — Friday night?"

Now it was Tanya's turn to be confused. "But didn't you pick him up from school? I thought that was the arrangement."

Errol placed a hand on the door. "What arrangement? You mean he's not here?"

Panic took over in an instant. "Oh my God!" Tanya's hand flew to her throat. "I... I got a call... from a woman who works for you — an assistant... no, secretary. She said you were picking Aaron up from school as you wanted to surprise him. I just thought... I mean, how could I know—"

Errol had stopped listening. "You stupid, selfish cow! You know I would never let someone else call about my child!"

He whirled back down the path towards his car.

"How was I supposed to know? Errol! Errol, wait!"

But he was already back in his car and heading towards Anne-Marie's flat, holding his mobile in his left hand and dialling 999. He was thinking about what she had done to their dog. It didn't bear thinking about what she might do with his child.

Finally put through to the police, he blurted out a few details of the kidnapping and where he thought she may have taken his son. Too many questions started firing back at him... and Errol was hardly thinking straight as it was.

He switched off, cutting off the officer mid-sentence, and dashed the phone on the seat beside him. He put his foot down, threading dangerously through the traffic in his haste and panic. When his son's welfare was at stake, his own safety was a lower priority.

Screeching to a halt outside the private flats where Anne-Marie lived, he jumped from the car and tapped out her number on the intercom pad. It rang eight times, Errol agitatedly hopping from one foot to the other, before he punched the number again. It rang once more before the door was opened by someone leaving the flats.

Errol didn't wait for the lift to take him up to the second floor; he dived up the stairs and was soon hammering on her front door. Still no answer, and now he began to get very frightened. There was no noise from inside the flat — no television, no radio, no voices.

A middle-aged white woman came out of the flat opposite as Errol began to call through the letterbox. "She's not there. I think she's gone away for a few days — she had suitcases with her this morning."

Not even thanking the woman, Errol dashed back down the corridor and headed for the stairs. Now he knew this was premeditated — if she had packed she could be anywhere. Her way of getting back at him, once again.

Back in the car his mobile was ringing. "Yes!" he answered.

It was Tanya. "Errol, what's going on? Have you found him?"

"No I haven't. Look, have you called the police yet?"

"No. I thought you—"

"Well call them. I'll let you know if I hear anything."

He speed-dialled Marion's number. She might have some idea where Anne-Marie could have gone.

"Marion, it's me."

"Errol! How are you?"

"Look, Marion, I think Anne-Marie's got Aaron. She's taken him from his school," he said breathlessly.

"*What*? How?"

He explained all he knew so far. "I thought you might have some idea where she could have gone."

The line went quiet. Then, "Her mother's house. She still has it; it was up for sale, but—"

"Do you know where it is? An address?"

"Meet me outside my house."

She hadn't realised how much fun a seven year old could be. Aaron was a happy child, and Anne-Marie found she could easily make him laugh. And what a laugh! What a smile — just like his father's. They had gone to the Trocadero, played on the virtual reality machines, and she'd watched him laugh with delight on the mini rides. He'd beaten her easily on the video games, even though she was trying her hardest.

The train ride back was bliss. They hugged, Aaron sitting on her lap with one tiny hand hooked around her neck. She breathed in the little boy's scent and felt tears in her eyes. She had no idea what she was going to do with him. *Could* she take him away — just leave the country? She hadn't thought that far ahead; she'd just wanted to scare Errol a little. But how could she take him back safely and avoid capture?

She closed her eyes. She needed to think.

It was eight o'clock when Anne-Marie finally turned into the road where she'd grown up. She held Aaron's hand. He was dragging his feet — he had fallen asleep on the train — and she realised how tired she felt too.

Mum's house would be cold — she'd forgotten to put the heating on — but there would be food. Earlier she had cooked for them both, knowing the boy would be hungry.

She had made up a bed on the sofa too. She would decide what to do with him tomorrow.

"Anne-Marie, I'm hungry."

"Not long now. We're nearly there. I've cooked you some chicken. You like chicken, don't you?"

"Yes," he nodded.

Such a well-behaved boy. She would miss him — almost as much as she missed his father.

She had just put the key in the front door when she was grabbed from behind and Aaron was whisked away from her side. She uttered a yelp and turned to face Errol Wright. Marion held Aaron against her shoulder.

"What did I tell you? What did I tell you?" Errol yelled.

Anne-Marie gulped air. She had never seen him look so mad. Even before, when he had threatened her. There was a wild look about him, all the coolness gone; there was also fear in her eyes. Fear of being out of control.

She looked from Marion to Aaron, and back to Errol. She didn't dare open her mouth, afraid of the reaction it could provoke.

"*Why*? Why *us*? You've brought an innocent child into this madness. You must have some sense of right and wrong…"

"I didn't want to hurt him…"

She was right. Her voice got the reaction she had feared. Errol grabbed her by the throat and shoved her up against the wall.

She struggled, trying to free herself.

"Errol, no — let's get out of here. Let the police deal with her," Marion coaxed.

For a second it was as though he hadn't heard her. Then Marion grabbed his arm and pulled him away from Anne-Marie. Gasping, she slid to the ground.

"I'm warning you, Anne-Marie — stay away from my family or I'll kill you!"

He started to walk away, then turned and pointed his finger like a gun. "That's not a threat, this time it's a promise!"

Yvette heard the front door open and close, the beep of the alarm being disarmed and set again. She shook her head, her expression sombre.

Her dream home was becoming a prison. Every time

they opened a door or a window they had to remember to disable and reset the alarm. Convenient control boxes had been installed in of most of the rooms; the perimeters of the house had been heightened by railings and barbed wire. There was no way in or out of the back garden any more, apart from the back door.

"Hi." Errol entered the living room and dropped into the seat beside her.

A faint look of amusement touched her eyes. It was hard these days. "What, no kiss?"

Errol leaned towards her wearily — almost grudgingly, she thought. She turned to meet his lips and received a quick peck before he slumped again into the seat.

Yvette used the remote control to lower the volume on the stereo and lifted her eyebrows slightly. "Headache?"

"I don't know. Not enough sleep, I think."

He stood abruptly, staring straight ahead, his eyes hooded with memories. "I think I'll just take a bath and get an early night," he said, walking towards the door.

"Want me to come with you?"

There was the tiniest pause. And did she see an expression of strain crossing his face? "No. I just need to relax, Eve. Come up when you're ready."

She stood at the doorway as he took the stairs. "Can I get you anything?"

"I'll be fine. Let me fall asleep before you come though, yeah? And remember to set the alarms."

She watched him drag himself upstairs, his head hung low. This was not the Errol Wright she knew — the world knew. His bounce and vitality had gone.

She looked at the clock — it was barely six. Before all this, Errol would work until about eight at night, then go on to visit friends, stop for a drink, meet business contacts or play sport. He had been an active man. Now he would rush home, having called her several times during the day, and was fast becoming the most knowledgeable man in London on security systems.

Even when Tyrone left the house he had to have his

mobile phone on him, had to call in regularly to let them know where he was. The order hadn't come from Yvette, but from Errol, who was becoming obsessive about knowing where his family was going to be at any given time.

Yvette, who had found the situation quite amusing at first, was now beginning to resent it. Tyrone was only twelve, and he was being made to carry a mobile! Anne-Marie had a lot to answer for.

And yet, she was nowhere to be found. She had vanished, ever since Errol and Marion had rescued Aaron from her clutches. Errol had hired a detective — he wasn't after her arrest, he just wanted to know where she was and what her movements were. He wasn't going to be taken by surprise again.

But now Yvette was afraid it was getting out of hand. He'd even made her install security cameras inside and outside the gym. So if Anne-Marie turned up there they would have it on tape.

Back at work Errol assumed his TV persona. Nothing touched him in front of the camera. Errol skipped easily down the step and faced his audience. "Thank you..." he said, but they continued to clap so he gestured for quiet. "Thank you... thank you to our guests — Lennox Lewis and Rianna Scipio!" In the midst of further applause he bowed. "Thank you — and goodnight," he said, then straightened up.

And then he saw her. She was standing at her seat, applauding with the other viewers. Watching him. Him, and nobody else.

His heart pounded, he felt light-headed, and then something inside him snapped. He dashed towards the auditorium.

"Errol, what's going on? Errol, your mike!" the floor manager called after him, but his words fell on deaf ears. Errol was still moving. He unclipped the microphone from his waistcoat and scanned the crowd as they shuffled into the aisles. They were turning into a sea of bobbing heads.

"You're in for a surprise, Anne-Marie," he muttered under his breath. "Excuse me!"

He squeezed past two women who, realising it was him, tried to get his attention, one grabbing his sleeve. But he pulled away and slipped his way through the smiling faces, the people chatting about the show and what they would be doing next.

The lobby was packed. "Excuse me, please! Excuse me — I'm in a hurry…"

Faces turned towards him, startled at first, then annoyed, then softening in recognition.

"Great show, Errol. I wonder—"

"Thank you!" He was already past them.

He craned his neck as he reached the stairs to the front door, and saw her again — the back of her head, heading down.

"Coming through!" He barged past a group of teenage girls.

She was wearing a red sweater, a long brown skirt. She'd stopped to read a poster.

Got you, Anne-Marie. I've got you now…

He marched right up to her and grabbed her arm.

"You don't give up, do you!"

He spun her round to face him, and found himself looking into the startled brown eyes of a complete stranger. "Hey! What do you think you're doing? What is this — some kind of joke?"

The woman pulled her arm free and backed up a step.

"I… I'm sorry." Errol's hand flew to his head. "I'm sorry — I thought you were someone else."

The woman shot him a look to kill and hurried towards the exit, looking back every now and again to make sure he wasn't following her.

Errol turned to face hundreds of eyes, some of them shocked — obviously those who had witnessed his pursuit. The chatter that had filled the lobby died down as he approached, then started again as soon as he had passed.

234

Embarrassed, he made his way back to the set and the dumbfounded faces of his colleagues.

Errol passed the phone to his other ear. "*How* much? Well you might as well get him a new one. I'll put a check in the post for two hundred — get him a decent one with ten gears. Can I speak to him?"

Yvette walked into the room and curled up on the sofa with a magazine, donning her headphones, which she had to wear so the television noise wouldn't interfere with his surveillance. Errol had arrived home agitated, unable to sit still for more than a minute. Every noise would have him out of his seat, checking all the systems. He patrolled the house, not even trusting the lights that indicated everything was secure.

And to make matters worse he had taken to phoning Tanya every night.

Yvette lowered her magazine and gave him worried looks every few minutes. When he finished his call he got up to check the locks on the windows for the thirteenth time.

"Can I get you something to drink?" she asked, putting her magazine aside. "Herbal tea, brandy…"

He barely glanced at her as he pulled the curtain aside. "Brandy sounds good. Ice, please."

"Are you expecting anyone?"

He looked up as though she had asked a stupid question. "No. Why?"

Yvette shrugged. "I dunno. Could be the fact that every couple of minutes you look out the window."

"Well… I thought I heard something," he replied.

"Like what? I've been sitting right here and I heard nothing."

His eyes were full of scorn. "That brandy sounds real good, Eve," he said pointedly.

She breathed out heavily and forced down a temper that had been threatening to explode. Her lips puckered, but she said nothing. She would get his brandy, with ice — he sure as hell needed it. Then she would go upstairs, change into her work-out gear, turn Biggie Smalls up to the fullest, and have a long, invigorating step work-out. Goldie had certainly trained her well enough.

Errol turned back to the window as she left the room.

There was that black car again. In the last eight minutes it had gone past slowly three times. He pressed his face against the window pane, his eyes following the vehicle until it disappeared from view.

"It's going to come back, I know it..." he whispered.

Sure enough, the car reappeared a minute and a half later.

Yvette was coming back from the kitchen when Errol dashed past her and bolted out of the front door.

"What... Where are you going now?" she called after him as he hurtled down the front steps.

"She's here! She's still out there!" She heard him yell back.

Yvette left the drinks on the hall table and took off after him. He was pounding along the pavement by the time she got to the front door. There was no one else around apart from a solitary black car, its brake lights on, double parked a little way up the road.

Yvette watched with horror as Errol caught up with it and proceeded to hammer on the driver's window. She ran to see what was going on.

The minicab driver looked up from his A–Z, startled, then vexed. "What the...?"

Errol shuffled backwards as the man got out and loomed large. He looked about seven foot tall.

Yvette stepped in between them, grabbing Errol round the waist. "I'm sorry," she said, now backing off as well. "We thought you were someone else..."

Much to her relief, the cab driver squeezed himself back into the car and sped off.

As he drove away he glanced at the two figures in his mirror. "Couldn't find the bloody address anyway," he muttered. "People can't get addresses right and nutters runnin' loose attacking innocents on the street…"

He decided to go straight home to his bed and his wife.

They lay in bed that night, their arms around each other. Yvette could hear his heart beating steadily in his chest.

"I've been so wrapped up in protecting you, I forgot that part of that protection should be shown to you physically."

Yvette sighed. "You've been here, Errol. That's more than a lot of women get."

"I may have been here, but my mind hasn't. My mind has been hunting for that bitch. I just didn't want her to harm you or my boys."

Yvette leant up on one elbow. "Errol, what happened was not your fault. The woman isn't well. Anyway, she's gone now. Maybe she's finally looking for help."

"If it wasn't for me she would never have been anywhere near us in the first place."

Yvette had had enough of this self-pitying guilt. She wanted her man back — the man she had fallen in love with. "Why don't you get away from here for a while?"

"Not all of us?"

"No, you. Remember you told me about that opportunity to record in LA?"

"Montell Williams's show?"

"Yeah. Go for it. You'd only be gone a month. The yanks would love you; it'd build up your confidence again."

"I couldn't leave you, Eve — she's still out there somewhere…"

"Errol, I'm a woman. I'm big and bad enough to take care of myself. Tyrone's here, Karen's down the road, and anyone else — including you — will be a phone call away."

"If you're sure… ?"

She squeezed him. "Baby, I know how hard this is for you but it's been harder on me watching you go through it."

"You want me to go, don't you?"

She laughed. "Yes, I do. For both our sakes."

TWENTY-FIVE

Yvette grabbed a tea towel and rushed to answer the phone.

"Yo, baby!"

She smiled. His voice sounded so good. He'd only left the country this morning but she missed him already.

"Hi, honey," she purred.

"You know where I'd like to be right now?"

"No… Tell me." She grinned.

"I don't have to tell you — you know."

She knew all right; only this morning he had been there, making love to every inch of her body. Her grin widened as she remembered the orgasm. "So, are you there yet?"

"Yes I am."

"And what's it like?"

"Babe, I only just arrived. Give me a chance to look around, get to know some people… How's things at home?"

"I'm on my own. Tyrone begged to stay at Anthony's."

"And you let him go?"

"Errol," she warned. "I'm a big girl now."

"I tell that boy to look after you while I'm away and what does he do? The first day, and he leaves you alone."

"Look, I'm glad of the break. I'm a lady of leisure for the weekend. Everyone I need is at the other end of the phone."

"If you're sure… Talking of numbers, I've got one you can reach me on."

Yvette took it down. "I miss you already," she said.

"You too. Make sure you lock up — and switch the alarm on before you go to bed, okay?"

"Of course. Will you call me tomorrow?"

"Yep. I gotta go. Love you."

"Love you more."

And he was gone.

She put the alarm on, double locked the door, and on her way up the stairs flipped off the hall light. She felt suddenly quite exhausted. It had been a long day, and it would be an even longer night without her men around.

She crossed the thick carpet to her bathroom and began to fill the tub, knowing she'd probably fall asleep in the soothing water. Thoughts of the past weeks tried to crowd her head, but she didn't want to think about it. The worst was over. The police would find Anne-Marie and put her away. She was a seriously sick woman.

Back in the bedroom she dropped a Johnny Gill cassette into the stereo and undressed lazily in front of the mirror, tossing her clothes across the foot of the bed. Her eyes fell to her breasts, then continued down to her flat stomach and pubic hair, her taught thighs and the curve of her calves. "I am woman," she mimicked, laughing, then turned to get a view of her backside. Wicked body. Never needed silicone or plastic surgery. "Errol, you are one lucky bastard…"

She turned off the water, tied her braids into a loose bun on top of her head, and stepped in. Sighing, she sank slowly into the perfumed water, feeling it lap soothingly over her skin. She closed her eyes, stretched her legs out, and let herself drift off to the sound of Johnny telling her nobody can love her like he could.

After a few minutes she opened her eyes, and was sure she'd been woken by a noise downstairs. She tensed, straining to hear above the sound of the music.

Nothing.

Shit, she was getting jumpy. The house was locked and double-locked and alarmed: a fly couldn't get in here.

She closed her eyes again and thought of Errol in the water with her, and suddenly felt extremely turned on. She thought of the vibrator in the other room. What good was that when she didn't have the energy to use it?

The water was starting to cool. Not wanting to end up cold and wrinkly she washed quickly and stepped out.

Skin smoothed and scented with cocoa butter, she returned to the bedroom naked and slipped into the long silk nightdress Errol had bought her on their first night here.

Ready for bed, she thought a drop of brandy was just what she needed to aid restful sleep. She didn't drink often

— but a comforting glass of brandy just before bed isn't really drinking, she told herself.

She checked the alarm again as she walked past the front door. All the little lights were lit on: armed and dangerous. She poured herself a drink in the dining room, then switched lights off on her ascent.

With only her bedside lamp on she slipped between the cotton sheets and sipped her brandy, the liquid burning its way to her stomach. Still a little too awake to go straight off, she picked up a book from her bedside table.

Minutes later the book slipped from her hand. Yvette didn't even wake up as it thudded on to the floor.

"Yvette…"

She turned over and pulled the covers over her head.

"Yvette… Can you hear me?"

That was her name. Someone was calling her…

No… must be dreaming. The house is empty.

Sleep…

"Yvette!" Sharper this time. A woman's voice.

Yvette bolted upright, her eyes wide open. "Oh shit," she hissed. Anne-Marie Simms had managed to get into the house, past the alarm system! Impossible…

No, it wasn't. Yvette remembered the rush they'd been in that morning, the frantic last-minute packing… They had forgotten to set the alarm… She must have gotten in then.

Which meant that she'd been here all evening.

She started to tremble and her stomach tightened. Where the hell was the woman?

"Answer me, Yvette. You know I know where you are. I've come to claim my home, my rightful place."

The voice was coming from downstairs, and didn't seem to be getting any closer. She probably wanted Yvette to come to her.

Then it all made sense. The keys had been in her coat, New Year's Eve… the cashmere coat she'd left in the limousine.

"Here I come, ready or not. Do I sense fear, Yvette? Are you all alone without your Mr Wright?"

So, she wanted to play games. Silly, childish games.

No. That was wrong: what Anne-Marie wanted was a murderous game. Cat and mouse. She wanted her rival out of the way for good.

The house was suddenly totally silent, the voice gone. Yvette didn't realise she'd been holding her breath until she let it out. She could hear her own heart, feel sweat beginning to bead on her forehead. Somewhere in her house was a mentally disturbed woman, bent on her annihilation.

She moved slowly off the bed and slid her feet into her slippers.

What the hell do I do now?

She reached for the phone. The police — she had to get the police.

Her eyes were trained on the doorway as she dialled 999.

"Emergency — which service do you—"

The line went dead.

"Hello? Hello!" Yvette stabbed at the buttons with a shaking finger. Nothing. She'd cut the fucking line!

Okay. Deep breaths, Yvette. She's only a woman. A sick woman, but still human. I can take her.

She tried hard to remember all she had learned in self-defence classes. But those had been months ago, nearly a year. She really should have paid more attention.

She looked towards the bedroom window. She was three storeys up. Too high to jump.

She froze, listening. Still nothing. What in hell was she doing down there?

Looking around frantically for something to defend herself with, she threw up her hands in despair. She was in the bedroom. A coat hanger, a toilet-brush handle from the bathroom — what choice did she have?

She dashed to the bathroom and unscrewed the wooden handle from the brush. Then she moved slowly towards the open door. Staring down the landing, allowing her eyes to adjust to the dark, she could see nothing — no shadows, nothing out of place. Her heart felt as though it was in her neck, which felt like sandpaper. She swallowed and heard a dry click in her throat.

She edged along the wall. "Where are you, Anne-Marie? I know its you," she called, risking revealing her position in an attempt to locate that of her rival.

Her slippered feet were soundless on the carpet as she took the top step. Why didn't I just lock myself in the bedroom and wait this out? she suddenly thought. But that would have been stupid. She would have been trapped, a sitting duck. She found herself thinking of all the horror films she had seen. The victims all went looking for danger, didn't they? You never saw them sitting around waiting for the killer to come and get them. No, they heard a noise and went to check out what it was.

And didn't they always get killed, Yvette?

Come to think of it, they did.

She could probably kill Anne-Marie with her bare hands. Poke her eyes out, reach down her gullet and yank out her tongue...

She saw the movement before she heard the menacing snarl. A pair of hands was reaching for her, floating in the darkness up the stairs towards her. She dropped the brush handle and threw her arms up to defend herself, but lost her balance and fell on to her back, a stair digging uncomfortably into the middle of her back. She heard the brush-handle knock inoffensively against the banisters.

Then she dared to look up, and in an instant she knew the truth.

This woman wasn't Anne-Marie. Yvette's brain registered Marion's features, but she had trouble equating the fact that she was being attacked by her. For this reason she didn't fight back — that is, not until Marion lunged at her face with her nails outstretched.

Yvette caught her wrists when those claws were just inches away from her face, the fingers clenching and unclenching. Mustering up the kind of strength that is brought on only by fear, she wrenched her assailant to one side and managed to roll on top of her. With the momentum of their movement she brought her knee up and caught Marion just below the ribs, winding her. Now Yvette registered that she was dressed entirely in black: black roll-neck top, black leggings and trainers. Like a shadow.

"Marion, what the hell are you doing?" she screamed.

"Surprised? Ha! You mean you didn't know?" she rasped. "You *really* didn't know?"

Yvette just stared and shook her head, her grip loosening on Marion's wrists. "It was *you*! You've been trying to kill me? All this time it's been you—"

Marion ceased to struggle. "Not all the time. Anne-Marie was my inspiration." She was breathing heavily. "You took him away from me." Her hand was slowly slipping down to her waist band. "Once he had you, he... I hardly saw him. I *loved* him, Yvette — for so long." She held Yvette's attention with her eyes as she spoke. "It was always me he came to when he was down... Until you came along..."

Her arm suddenly flew up. Yvette saw the the knife just in time. She screamed and side-stepped the thrust.

Marion was trying to stand up. Ignoring the knife, Yvette reacted quickly. She grabbed Marion's hair, lifted her, and threw her headlong down the stairs.

Yvette didn't run. She kept her back pressed flat against the wall as she watched Marion tumble to the bottom and land in a heap, groaning. "I don't know what bit you, Marion," she whispered, "but I hope that bump on the head just cured it."

Then she moved. She hurdled over the banister, losing a slipper on the way. The front door was not an option: by the time she had the locks, bolts and chain off, Marion would be on top of her. She headed instead for the back of the house. Turning the corner in the hallway, her thigh smashed into the telephone table, knocking the vase of flowers to the floor. Pain shot up her leg, but she was oblivious to it. Before slamming the kitchen door shut and jamming a chair under its handle, she turned to see Marion's head coming around the bottom of the stairs and the glint of the long silver blade.

243

She's crazy! Crazy and armed. And all this time she was supposed to be a friend—

Move — fast! her inner voice was telling her, and instantly she obeyed. One foot bare, she headed for the back door and outside, knowing that as soon as the door was opened it would trigger an alarm at the police station — if the line hadn't been sabotaged, that is.

She was outside before she realised that the garden was now totally sealed off. She was still trapped.

"Now what?"

She ran towards the trees at the end of the garden. Maybe she could hide, dodge her attacker until the police got there. There was no moon; maybe Marion wouldn't be able to see, or she'd fall into the pond, break her neck and drown.

Where are the bloody police?

If she could just keep out of her way long enough...

She hadn't seen Marion coming out of the house, although she'd heard the chair collapse as she'd forced the kitchen door open. She looked back at the door now, straining her ears, pushing all her senses to the limit like a hunted animal.

She heard a movement — somewhere on the path. Lowering herself to the cold ground, shivering, trying to muffle her breathing, she prayed.

She was controlling the urge to jump out and rush her. Take the consequences.

Wake up, Eve. She's got a knife.

"Yvette?"

She couldn't tell how close the voice was and she couldn't see her. Afraid to move in case she drew attention to herself, Yvette swore silently as she thought of the lost chance she'd had to arm herself in the kitchen.

"Yvette... come now. We're grown ups; can't we talk?"

She sounded very reasonable. It was a negotiating voice, the kind that says, "You do me a favour and I'll do one for you."

Then she laughed. "I can't believe you didn't know it was me! I didn't mean to hurt Errol, you know. The car should have hit you, he just got in the way. Such a hero!"

She laughed again. "Anne-Marie — the perfect cover. Her mistake was just wanting Errol; hardly thought about you at all... But I did."

Yvette heard a rustle of leaves to her right and lifted her head a little, straining to see in the dark.

"Yvette..."

The voice was closer this time.

Where were the goddamn police? It seemed like an age since the alarm should have gone off. Probably dozing over their cups of cocoa...

A second too late Yvette realised that Marion had found her hiding place. She was grabbed by the hair and dragged to her feet, the knife inches from her face. Instead of fighting back Yvette focused on the blade.

"How about I scalp you, Yvette? How would that be?" Marion giggled like a child. "Show you how sharp my blade is. I sharpened it myself."

"Marion. please... maybe we *can* talk about this..." Yvette's eyes switched back and forth between the knife and Marion's face. "You want Errol? Okay — well, he could still choose you... if he knew how you felt."

"He slept with Anne-Marie," Marion sobbed. "He could have had me, and he chose her and then you. Every time I saw you together he did nothing but drool; if he had a tail he would have been wagging it... No, I'll *never* have him, not with you around!" she shrieked, and she sliced through Yvette's extensions in one swoop.

But it meant that Yvette was free, and she got hurriedly to her feet and yelled in the darkness, her shortened braids bouncing on her head: "Bitch! Why can't you just leave me alone?"

"You've got my man! I want him back — and if that means getting rid of you—"

"You know the police are on their way?"

"Yeah?" Marion said with mock surprise. "Can't hear the sirens..."

Yvette's breathing was heavy but she tried to stay as

quiet as she could, backing away in the dark. This game was living torture. She still felt that if she talked to Marion, tried to reason with her, she might snap out of it, realise what she was about to do. "Listen, Marion — I've got a son, so have you. What about him? What is he going to feel like when he finds out what you did? And Paul... finding out you did it for another man. He's already put up with a lot from you — could you really hurt him again? Do you want to make your son motherless? Come on, girl, give it up..."

"He won't be. Yours will, though — such a shame." Marion leered, her eyes sweeping the dark garden. "But you're right — we don't have much time..."

Yvette was moving away from the voice. Marion wasn't coming straight for her; her voice seemed to be weaving from left to right as though she were leaping from side to side. This was the moment. Yvette turned to run back to the house and stepped on something that flipped up and slammed into the side of her ankle. She skipped her next step, feeling pain shoot up to her knee, before reaching down for the object.

It was Tyrone's tennis racket. She gripped its handle and felt its weight. This was like landing on a safety-net after free falling. Finally she had a weapon.

The kitchen door was a few feet behind Yvette when Marion loomed out of the inky darkness into view. She knew that if she turned to open it Marion would have her.

"Hi, Yvette. We meet again!" Marion was grinning, slicing the air with the knife. Suddenly she yelled and rushed at Yvette, lunging with the blade, her face twisted into a grimace of murderous intent.

"No!" Yvette hollered, and her left hand joined her right on the handle of the tennis racquet.

To her, it seemed like slow motion. In the split second that followed it was as though all the survival techniques she'd been taught at the gym combined with an animal instinct she didn't even know she had. She bent her knees, planted her back foot firmly on the path, and, starting low, she swung the racquet up... and through.

EPILOGUE

EXCLUSIVE:
'I'M NOT MAD' SAYS MAZ

MARION STEWART GIVES HER OWN ACCOUNT

Marion Stewart, disgraced ex-presenter of TV chat-show Mantalk, last night accused Errol Wright, presenter of rival show Do the Wright Thing, of wanting people to think she was mad.

Speaking for the first time about her current troubles, she said it suited Mr Wright and his 'comrades' to get her out of the way — because they don't want anyone to know the truth about their illicit affair.

Ms Stewart was sectioned after attacking Errol Wright's fiancé Yvette Barker with a butcher's knife. She is on police bail while she is treated in a psychiatric hospital in Kent.

At an impromptu press conference outside the central criminal court, Ms Stewart also claimed that her common-law husband was in league with the Wright clan in a conspiracy against her.

Last week's attack was the culmination of a campaign of harassment that has allegedly lasted months. It was originally thought that Anne-Marie Simms, a former colleague of Mr Wright's, was the perpetrator. Ms Simms admitted in court that she had sent him love letters and persistently telephoned him.

Marion Stewart, however, turned into a copycat stalker.

The trial continues tomorrow.

*   *   *

They held hands in the back of the limousine, while around them the streets of Hammersmith buzzed. Yvette kissed Errol's cheek, then removed a long white silk glove and rubbed the lipstick off with manicured hands. She'd always wanted to wear silk gloves to a function.

"Hey, lover, stop shaking. You're starting to scare me."

"I'm not shaking, am I?"

"Baby, you've got no competition."

He wished he had Yvette's confidence. The Black British Entertainment Awards was being held tonight at the Palais. In the chat-show-host category Errol knew he really didn't have any competition, but that didn't ease his nerves.

A month ago they had found a new home in Finchley, North London; The contracts were going through at the moment. Tyrone would have to go to another school — which he wasn't too happy about — but it would be too much of a trek back to South London.

Yvette was on the lookout for new premises. Commuting to and from Woolwich to the gym was becoming a drag. She didn't need to work, but there was no way she was giving up her independence and the business she had sweated to build. No, she was going to build it bigger.

The new premises would include, a pool, saunas, jacuzzis and toning tables.

Errol was thinking about Marion. She would have been his main rival tonight, if...

She had sustained injuries to her jaw and a fractured skull from her fall. He hadn't been allowed to visit. It was recommended that, until the treatment was seen to be working, he stay away from her completely. Paul kept him up to date on developments.

Errol wondered time and time again why he had missed the signs. Marion had seemed such a sweet, loving person...

The Bentley pulled up outside the venue and Errol waited while the chauffeur walked round to his side and opened the door on to the red carpet. The streets were packed with fans, curious to see their idol. The queue for tickets stretched out of sight round a corner of the building.

The cameras flashed as Errol, dressed in a tuxedo, turned and put out a hand to help Yvette out of the deep leather seat. Her exceptionally long, curvy legs attracted the attention of the photographers, who surged towards her. She was sheathed in a clinging black silk creation, off the shoulder, that exposed a cleavage many women would give a year's salary to have. She had relaxed hair now, with the help of a weave, shoulder length. Bernard Evans, celebrity stylist to the stars, had spent hours on her this afternoon.

She was truly striking — and she was Errol Wright's fiancé. The thought gave her a powerful high as they walked arm-in-arm, smiling and waving, through the glass doors and into the theatre.

"The nominations for the best talk-show host are…"
Brenda Emmanus opened the gold envelope in her hand and read out the list. When Errol's name was mentioned the cheer that rang through the hall was louder than the applause the other nominees received.

Junior Simpson then opened another envelope. "And the winner is…" There was a drum roll. Errol was squeezing Yvette's hand so hard she would have screamed, were she not holding her breath.

"… Errol Wright — for *Do the Wright Thing*!"
The audience shrieked its approval. He was releasing her hand and standing up. The theme tune to his show blasted out and she saw the cameras spin towards him as he kissed her on the cheek and trotted towards the stage.

"Thank you," he said, accepting the trophy, and when the cheers had died down he began his speech.

"I would like to thank my producer, John Everett, for his support and encouragement over the past two years. Also the production crew, forgive me for making your lives so miserable…" This brought some laughs and wolf-whistles. "A special thanks to my fiancé, Yvette Barker, who has stood by me through the good times and the bad. Love you, baby."

Now the audience was in rapture. It took Errol a minute

to calm them down enough for his conclusion to be heard: "And finally to my viewers, especially those of you who came to the studio week after week. The show wouldn't have been the same without y'all."

He held the trophy in the air as he walked triumphantly back to his table.

A handful of celebrities were waiting outside for their cars to be brought round. The majority of the public audience had headed home hours before, but some die-hards still hung around for autographs or photos of the stars.

Errol and Yvette clung together, the trophy grasped firmly in her gloved hand. She still thought she was dreaming.

"Can I have your autograph please, Mr Wright?"

The girl had obviously been waiting for him to come out. She stood there, about five foot seven, wavy brown hair cut level with her jawline, her creamy skin blushing as he met her eyes. She held out a pocket book.

Errol knew a few people who had a problem with signing autographs, thought it was an invasion of their privacy or something. But he always enjoyed it. It put him in touch with his public, and if it made others happy...

He pulled a photograph of himself from his inside pocket. "Of course. What's your name?" he asked, producing a marker pen with a flourish.

Her eyes twinkled. "Angie. I'm a big fan of yours. I wouldn't watch *Do the Wright Thing* if it wasn't for you."

BESTSELLING FICTION

❏ Sistas On A Vibe	Ijeoma Inyama	£6.99
❏ Bursting The Cherry	Phyllis Blunt	£6.99
❏ Single Black Female	Yvette Richards	£5.99
❏ When A Man Loves A Woman	Patrick Augustus	£5.99
❏ Wicked In Bed	Sheri Campbell	£5.99
❏ Rude Gal	Sheri Campbell	£5.99
❏ Yardie	Victor Headley	£4.99
❏ Excess	Victor Headley	£4.99
❏ Yush!	Victor Headley	£5.99
❏ Fetish	Victor Headley	£5.99
❏ Here Comes the Bride	Victor Headley	£5.99
❏ In Search of Satisfaction	J. California Cooper	£7.99
❏ Flex	Marcia Williams	£6.99
❏ Baby Mother	Andrea Taylor	£6.99
❏ Uptown Heads	R.K. Byers	£5.99
❏ Jamaica Inc.	Tony Sewell	£5.99
❏ Lick Shot	Peter Kalu	£5.99
❏ Professor X	Peter Kalu	£5.99
❏ Obeah	Colin Moone	£5.99
❏ Cop Killer	Donald Gorgon	£4.99
❏ The Harder They Come	Michael Thelwell	£7.99
❏ Baby Father	Patrick Augustus	£6.99
❏ Baby Father 2	Patrick Augustus	£6.99
❏ OPP	Naomi King	£6.99

I enclose a cheque/postal order (Made payable to *'The X Press'*) for £ _____
(add 50p P&P per book for orders under £10. All other orders P&P free.)

NAME _____

ADDRESS _____

_____

 Cut out or photocopy and send to: X PRESS, 6 Hoxton Square, London N1 6NU
Alternatively, call the X PRESS hotline: 0171 729 1199 and place your order.

X Press Black Classics

The masterpieces of black fiction writing await your discovery

❏ The Blacker the Berry   Wallace Thurman   £6.99
 *'Born **too** black, Emma Lou suffers her own community's intra-racial venom.'*

❏ The Autobiography of an Ex-Colored Man   James Weldon Johnson   £5.99
 'One of the most thought-provoking novels ever published.'

❏ The Conjure Man Dies   Rudolph Fisher   £5.99
 'The world's FIRST black detective thriller!'

❏ The Walls of Jericho   Rudolph Fisher   £5.99
 *'When a buppie moves into a white neighbourhood, all hell breaks loose. **Hilarious!**'*

❏ Joy and Pain   Rudolph Fisher   £6.99
 'Jazz age Harlem stories by a master of black humour writing.'

❏ Iola   Frances E.W. Harper   £6.99
 'A woman's long search for her mother from whom she was separated on the slave block.'

❏ The House Behind the Cedars   Charles W. Chesnutt   £5.99
 'Can true love transcend racial barriers?'

❏ A Love Supreme   Pauline E. Hopkins   £5.99
 'One of the greatest love stories ever told.'

❏ One Blood   Pauline E. Hopkins   £6.99
 'Raiders of lost African treasures discover their roots and culture.'

❏ The President's Daughter   William Wells Brown   £5.99
 'The true story of the daughter of the United States president, sold into slavery.'

❏ The Soul of a Woman   Zora Neale Hurston, etc.........£6.99
 'Stories by the great black women writers'

I enclose a cheque/postal order (Made payable to '*The X Press*') for

£ _____

(add 50p P&P per book for orders under £10. All other orders P&P free.)

NAME _____

ADDRESS _____

_____

**Cut out or photocopy and send to: X PRESS, 6 Hoxton Square, London N1
6NU. Alternatively, call the X PRESS hotline: 0171 729 1199 and place your order.**